I0563445

Into the Foxhole

By

Nicoline Evans

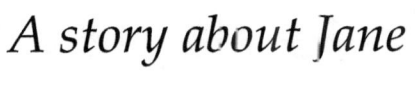

A story about Jane

Author: Nicoline Evans – www.nicolineevans.com

Editor: Emily Kline – www.ekediting.com

Cover Design: Nicoline Evans

A special shout-out to my beta readers and a big thank you to everyone who has offered me support (in all ways, shapes, and sizes) during this entire process.

To those who save themselves

Saving Jane: A Guide

The Fox's Journey to Recovery

THE MIND GUIDE

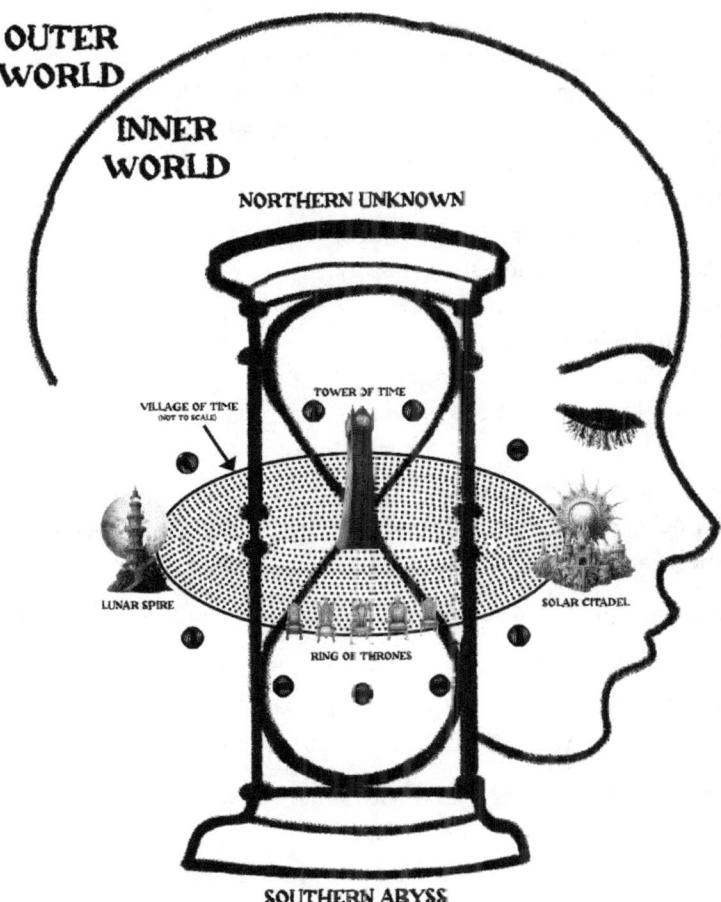

OUTER WORLD

INNER WORLD

NORTHERN UNKNOWN

TOWER OF TIME

VILLAGE OF TIME
(NOT TO SCALE)

LUNAR SPIRE

SOLAR CITADEL

RING OF THRONES

SOUTHERN ABYSS

= POCKETS OF THE MIND

Character Guide

JANE

The Faces:
Day – Jane as she presents herself to the world
Night – Jane when she is alone
Time – Jane within her relationship with time
Awareness – Jane as she learns self-awareness
Worthiness/Fox –Jane as she navigates her self-worth
Trust – Jane as she learns to trust herself
Control – Jane when she is in control
Chaos – Jane when she is not control
Happiness – Jane when she is happy
Sadness – Jane when she is sad
Fear – Jane when she is fearful
Anger – Jane when she is angry
Anxiety – Jane when she is anxious

Jane within the Pockets:
Each pocket manifests as fantastical representations of specific emotions and mindsets that Jane has experienced.

Within each pocket are many memories associated with its specific emotion or mindset.

There are many "Janes" within each pocket, but for the sake of clarity in this book, we will only follow one Jane per pocket.

Jane within the Pockets = Jane within her memories

Malsana – the monster embodying Jane's mental health struggles

NOT JANE

Solís – the boy within the sun
Luna – the girl within the moon
Father Time – the god of time

VILLAGE OF TIME
BIRD'S EYE VIEW

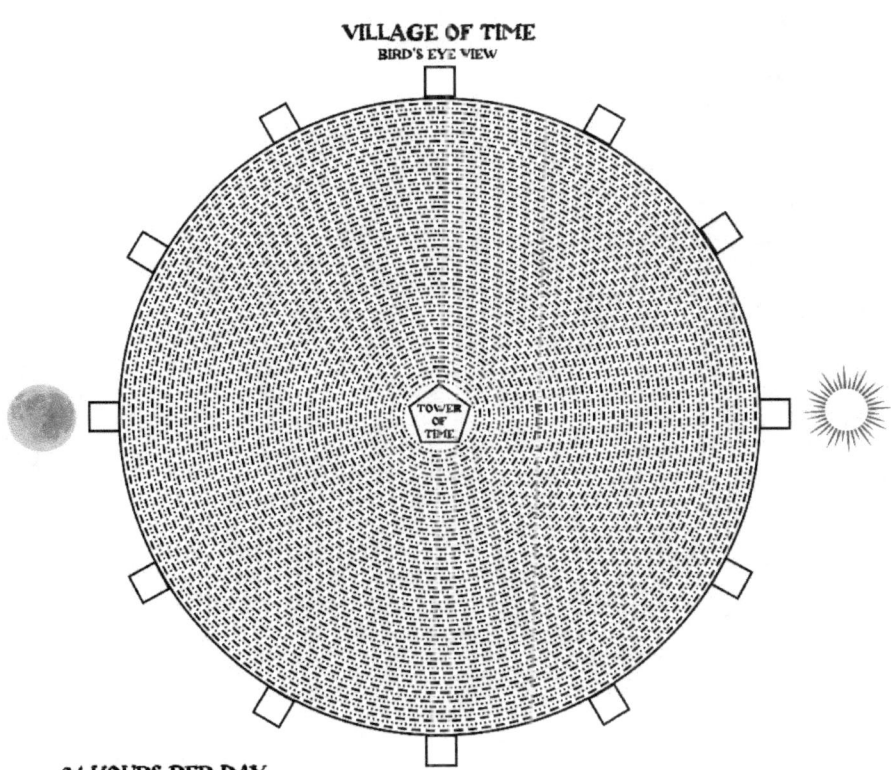

TOWER OF TIME

24 HOURS PER DAY

CIRCLETTES (HOURS)
12 HUTS
EACH HUT GLOWS TWICE PER DAY

JIFFIES (MINUTES)
30 ROWS
EACH ROW GLOWS TWICE PER HOUR

BITLINGS (SECONDS)
30 ROWS
EACH ROW GLOWS TWICE PER MINUTE

☐ = CIRCLETTE (EACH HUT = 1 HOUR)

– – – – – – = JIFFIES (EACH ROW = 1 MINUTE)

·················· = BITLINGS (EACH ROW = 1 SECOND)

A note from the Fox

Welcome to the mind of Jane Doe.

I am she, and she is me.

Within her mind, I am the Face of Worthiness, but for the sake of clarity, you can call me Fox. We begin this tale at a point in Jane's life when I had forgotten who I was.

I can't promise much, but I can promise that I will be a friend.

Together, we will journey through the mind of someone you will never meet. A girl ravaged by sickness, not of the body but of the mind. An illness that turns food, a vital life source, into a secret enemy. Torn apart from the inside, desperate to appear whole while withering away—this is a tale of suffering and sorrow, a glimpse into the psyche of an unraveled girl.

Why, you might wonder, would I ever burden you with such a story?

Compassion, empathy, relatability—perhaps her story isn't too different from yours. Or maybe you know someone like her, someone suffering who needs to feel heard.

We each carry a story inside of us.

Perhaps her story will help you realize your own.

Though we each evolve within drastically different stories, how we become our uniquely developed selves is quite the same.

Time delivers experiences, which we process and collect. Together, the never-ending puzzle pieces tell a singular, ever-evolving story—her story, their story, your story.

Let me explain how it works:

There are three worlds—the shared outer world, our private inner worlds, and the pockets formed by our unique experiences.

Within each of our inner worlds is a sand clock—it hides undetected in our minds and regulates the timing of our lives. We keep our secrets, dreams, demons, and greatest joys around

1

this sand clock. This is where our identities reside. Each emotion, mindset, and personality trait exists in assigned pockets of the mind, ruled by the Faces we wear when we give them life.

The unique moments we collect, and how we process them, shapes who we become. Most moments dissipate with time, others make their lasting mark before fading, and some linger forever, molding us into the people we become. Benevolent or nefarious, we cannot always choose which experiences will greet us in life, but we can choose how they settle in our minds—awareness bridges the gap between ruin and growth.

Ha!

Easier said than done.

I am she, and she is me—I live in the foxhole of her mind—and we struggled for years before learning how to choose love over ruin.

How do I factor into the equation? I will show you, but first, you must see what we survived: the takeover of a healthy mind, the charade of control, the sickness altering every crevice of our identity, the attempt to hide while remaining in plain sight.

Follow me. I will guide you through time, through the mind. When the journey feels grim, stay with me, for light awaits on the other side of the storm.

Do not fear the darkness.

Sometimes, the monsters arrive disguised as friends.

Sometimes, you lose before you win.

At the end is where this story begins.

I am she,

and she is me.

Welcome to Jane's mind.

The Day of Discovery

When: The 24th Cycle
Where: Jane's mind—The Graveyard, Southern Abyss
Who: The Gravedigger

Memories fell from the sky.

One by one, day after day, I gathered all that I wished to forget.

Shovel to dirt, I buried them deep.

I hid parts of myself with those memories—it was the only way to ensure their eternal sleep.

"Not again," I griped as burnt feathers and porcelain exploded into the sky. Daylight's gleam reflected off the falling pieces, glaring so brightly I was grateful not to have eyes.

Through the hollow voids where my eyes used to be, I saw the world in shades of shadows.

I looked down at my hands—decayed flesh over exposed bone.

I had little left to give.

A fast plummet, raining death over me, the carcass of day fell into my graveyard. Shards of porcelain and charred white feathers—I hobbled to the dirt patch where these pieces landed.

"You are killing me," I chastised the remains of this tormented creature.

I had seen her face many times in my garden of death. Beautiful, pristine, and covered in golden scars. Every time she fell from the sky, I wondered why. Why did the porcelain girl keep repeating the same mistakes? Why did she let the sun burn her over and over again? Her plot held the remnants of her many lives.

She always returned.

Someone, somewhere, rebuilt her every time she fell apart. I didn't know why they bothered, though. Her life always ended in the same fiery explosion, and I was always left to clean up the mess.

3

Dead flowers lined the plots where the past was buried.

Shovel to dirt, I dug up her grave. Withered feathers and soil-stained porcelain came into view. I added her newest pieces to the collection.

It wasn't enough.

If I wanted the porcelain girl to stay silent, to rest in peace, I had to give up a piece of myself, too. I tore a hunk of flesh from my forearm and tossed it into the open grave.

Together, forever, in death.

Agitated about disturbing my graveyard yet again for her and losing another part of my already decaying existence, I kicked the pile of dirt over her newest pieces, leaving the plot a mess.

She never learned.

I spat on the fresh soil, covering her latest demise, then turned my head toward the sky.

She would be back. She was the only one I couldn't smother completely.

I lived in the Southern Abyss; everything that existed here was not wanted above. My job as the gravedigger was simple: discard the unwanted mementos and, at all costs, do not let the dead rise.

Straightforward, but not as simple as it might seem.

Not everything buried here was dead. Most were from parts of the mind still very much alive—not underground, but existing above with pieces missing. Bits of them fell from the sky into my graveyard, sentenced to death.

These were the hardest graves to manage. The memories fought me. They haunted me and often reemerged unexpectedly, battling the constraints of their tethered coffins. These were not sentient beings; they were unintelligent fragments of the past, and they plagued me daily until I learned how to trick them. Burying bits of myself with each recollection conned them into a peaceful slumber. This simple act mollified

4

their hostility—buried side by side. I fooled them into thinking there was no one left to fight.

Every day, I pruned the rows of plots, carefully checking that those I had buried stayed in their graves. Neatly spaced lines of dirt-filled rectangles stretched across my yard, and I navigated them with methodic precision. This responsibility consumed me; it was all I lived for.

I walked past the gravestones, each marked with a drawing of what it entombed—a rustleweed, a golden thread, a black feather, a shard of glass, a black pearl, a fragment of porcelain. Countless mementos marking the graves of that which I wished to forget.

All was well.

All was still.

The dead did not challenge me today.

Tall and skeletal, my long legs ached as I limped back to my mausoleum. The sun high above was setting, and the moon was preparing to ascend into the Northern Unknown.

I sat on the front stoop, waiting for the sun to descend into my hemisphere. I hated him—Solís, the scorched boy who lived in the sun. He was coddled, privileged, and arrogant; he ruined my day every time he let that girl burn in his fire.

As the moon ascended, the sun dipped into my half of the mind. Little Lumineers of light bustled around his massive form, fussing over his wellness and pampering him.

"You did it again!" I shouted.

"Did what?" he asked, bored.

"You killed that porcelain girl."

Solís scoffed, his golden gaze impatient. "How many times do I have to explain this to you before it gets through that thick, decaying skull of yours? She chooses that fate time and time again. I try to warn her, try to guide her, but she always chisels cracks into her porcelain armor."

"Every time you kill her, you kill a little piece of me, too," I tried to explain.

"No," he countered. "You do that to yourself. No one told you to hoard mementos from the past."

"It is my duty to bury them. I am the gravedigger."

Solís laughed. "Is that who you think you are?"

"Of course, that's who I am."

"You're just as hopeless as Day."

"The porcelain girl?"

"Yes, she is the Face of Day."

"And what am I?"

"You're supposed to be the one who sees reason, but it seems you've lost your way."

"Everything fell out of the sky at once."

"Unlikely," Solís countered.

"That's how it felt! It started with a storm of black marbles," I paused, unable to recall the order in which the mementos arrived, "then everything else! My yard was littered with hurt and embarrassment and insecurities. What was I supposed to do?"

"You certainly weren't supposed to give those horrible mementos a home. No wonder the Face of Day keeps digging for the past within herself—it all lives here!"

"You're wrong. This is my job. This is why I'm here."

"I have a *real* job to do," he said as the Lumineers pushed him through the bottom of the Solar Citadel. Night was ending—the sun had finished a full rotation of the Southern Abyss. How had so much time passed?

The sun housing Solís disappeared, reappearing a few seconds later in the Northern Unknown. My hollow eye sockets adjusted, and through the shadows, I saw the silhouette of a winged woman dragging the sun through the sky.

That girl—the Face of Day—had been rebuilt yet again.

The moon entered the Southern Abyss through the Solar Citadel's basement at the same time the sun departed. Always crossing paths but never allowed to connect. The moon would orbit the Southern Abyss until it was time to rise in the north once more.

6

Alone on this side of the mind, I was the only one who knew the backside of day and night. I usually preferred the company of the moon, but lately, her wallowing had grown tiresome. Her contagious sorrow often infected me with a similar melancholy. Disinterested in hearing Luna sob for twelve hours, I retreated into my mausoleum. I lifted the large stone concealing my sarcophagus and crawled inside.

Time was irrelevant here—the dead had no need for clocks.

The sound of sobbing woke me hours later. I opened my hollow eye sockets to stark nothingness—my crypt was a black void.

"Be quiet!" I shouted.

The crying continued.

I pressed my bony fingers against the top slab of my stone coffin. Light infiltrated as it moved. Pushing harder, I used all my strength to widen the slit enough for my skeleton to slither through.

As I crawled out of the sliver, the melancholic whimpering grew louder. Painful, stiff steps carried me out of my mausoleum. Bone scraping bone, I hobbled to the source of sorrow.

Luna sat inside the moon, large silver eyes glimmering.

"What's wrong?" I demanded.

She sniffled, brushing her stringy black hair off her face. "I don't want to be here anymore."

"Neither do I, but you don't see me crying about it."

"You *have* to be here," she countered. "This is the only possible place for you to exist—you were created to serve this body. When this life ends, so does yours. I, on the other hand, was assigned to this vessel. When this mortal life ends, Solís and I will live on. We are eternal."

"You are from elsewhere?"

"I am, and I want to go home." Her eyes shimmered with frustration as she further explained. "While our presence here is important, we are not directly bound to this Host."

"You are not her?"

"I am not her. She is not me." Luna sighed. "I suppose you wouldn't understand."

"I have too much else to worry about. Look at this place—it's littered with unwanted memories."

Her moon-disced eyes examined my graveyard. "You really need to tidy up this mess."

"That stupid girl keeps getting burned by the sun, and every time she falls into my yard, I have to bury her. If I want her to rest peacefully and leave me alone for eternity, I must bury a piece of myself with her, too." I opened my skeletal arms wide, showing off my maimed carcass. "She's killing me."

"Maybe you ought to let her go."

"If I ignored all the garbage falling from above, I'd be living in a junkyard."

"Take the fallen pieces to the edge of the forest. Drop them into the abyss."

Her suggestion startled me. "Then they'd be gone forever."

"Isn't that the point of letting things go?"

"Yes, but by keeping them in my graveyard, I can dig them back up if they're ever needed again."

"Letting them go doesn't mean you'll forget. But having them here taking root versus releasing them is the difference between being held hostage and being set free."

I didn't want to believe her.

"You stopped crying," I noted.

Luna glanced down, surprised by this revelation, too.

When she looked up at me, her saucer eyes held deep kindness.

"Your sorrow surpasses mine."

"I'm not sad," I argued.

"Look at what you've become," she replied.

"I'm not sad," I repeated, my frustration rising.

"Maybe you're angry. Or maybe you're just lost."

"I am none of those things!" I shouted as the Moonchanics carried Luna higher into the sky.

8

"Think about what I said," she called down before disappearing into the Northern Unknown.

I thought about what she said, but ultimately decided that her selfish grief had tarnished her mind. She wanted to leave; she hated this place. Whereas I cherished my graveyard. I worked hard to make it nice.

I grabbed a pair of gardening shears and marched into the yard.

Any blossom threatening to exist among the deceased was scissored dead. I sliced and diced until all that remained were pointy stems outlining each rectangular plot. Though the flowers' roots remained, allowing them to keep growing, I never let the beauty of their blossoms see the light of day.

I couldn't see the colors anyway; my eyes were buried in these scattered graves.

The shadows guided me through the rows and rows of buried memories. Perfectly gloomy, my heart sang with accomplishment.

The dead would not rise today.

I rested next to the nearest gravestone marked by a single black feather.

I sang, "In this graveyard are the bones of hes and shes and these and those. Under dirt, the past remains; buried deep is where they'll stay. Moonlight marks another day the dead did not come out to play. These memories are mine to keep—forever safe in eternal sleep."

My song ended.

I stared at the drawing of the black feather I etched long ago.

"Together forever, I hate you so."

I thought of what Luna had said: *Let the past go.*

"I keep you here because I do not trust you," I explained to the buried feather. "I do not trust you at all."

My hollow sockets grew heavy; my body needed sleep. I tried to climb to my knees, but I was too weak. I toppled over, face-first into the dirt.

The wind swirled, causing the barren tree branches to creak. An eerie whistle followed.

In the brief moment between day and night, I was alone with the dead.

Always alone with the dead.

I lifted my dirt-covered face and screamed into the sky. Throat raw, flesh decayed, the whisper that left my body was ravaged. So broken, so weak, I hardly made a sound.

No one would hear my cries.

I wondered if anyone even knew I was down here.

My hollow sockets examined the world above—bustling, vibrant, and full of life. The view from below was enticing; the beauty of life taunted me. Neon creatures of time orbited the sand clock, hustling with purpose.

Everyone above had a reason to live.

All I had was death.

I buried the moments the world above no longer wanted.

A pitiful smile stretched across my face—half my teeth were buried in random graves; the other half were rotted in my mouth. Tears pooled in my hollow sockets.

I was one of the unwanted.

What did I care? This was all I had ever known. I brushed the soot off my face, emptied the water from my sockets, and stood. I didn't need the world above. They needed *me*.

"You're buried under so much of the unwanted past, you've forgotten what life was like before you collected trash."

"Shut up," I snapped at Solís, who now orbited the Southern Abyss.

"Chaos has consumed you, too."

"Go away."

"You are useless without eyes," he scoffed. "This mortal depends on your ability to see."

"How?"

"You wallow, you hide, and you blame when you ought to be listening, learning, and growing. Each memory in those

10

graves should have made you wiser and stronger. Instead, you let them weaken you."

"I challenge you to trade places with me. You would never survive the horror I endure."

"It's only a nightmare because you make it so."

"This is what I have been given!"

"You cannot keep them buried forever. Let them go."

I growled.

He said nothing more.

The Lumineers carried him onward, far and away.

All these warnings were a nuisance. The moon and sun could not understand the perilous dilemma I faced every day. One buried memory resurrecting could cause our entire existence to spiral.

I was important, my mission was imperative, even if no one else understood why I suffered for the greater good.

Solís said I could not remember how things were before, but this was all I knew. And if the past was any indicator of the future, this was how it would always be.

I fell asleep in the dirt next to the grave of my favorite memory—the unassuming black pearl that fell into my yard not too long ago. She arrived without fanfare and caused me minimal strife. This memory kept her anguish to herself, and for this, I adored her. When I dug her grave, I buried with her my heart.

Luna left me alone as she orbited the Southern Abyss.

I slept soundly without the know-it-all celestials telling me who I should and shouldn't be.

The hammering of a war drum startled me out of my empty dream.

Rhythmic thuds shook the terrain.

I dug my skeletal fingers into the soil, attempting to take root, but the beating was too strong. It rattled me to my core, preventing my attempts to secure solid ground.

I searched the area—there was no army, no war drum to be found.

11

"Who are you?" I shouted to no one.

The haunting rhythm continued. I scrambled to my knees, backing away in fear. Who beckoned me? Why were the beating drums of battle calling for me?

Out of the soil, red tendrils tore apart the grave, viciously ripping through the perfect plot I had made for the black pearl.

"Stay dead!" I demanded, tearing the last remaining piece of flesh off my left forearm and throwing it at the disturbed grave.

The tendrils snatched the rotted fragment of flesh and threw it back at me.

My sacrifice was not enough to lull the dead back to sleep.

I leaned in closer to discover that they weren't tendrils at all—they were veins.

Appalled, I began to dig, searching for the source of this madness. When my fingers touched a soft, swollen organ that pulsated harmoniously with the war drum, I was forced to pause. It was my heart—it was the source of this madness.

I tore through the soil until there was enough space to free my heart from its grave. I cradled it in my hands.

"Why?" I asked.

It could not respond.

Instead, my answer came on the wings of time.

An ethereal man arrived cloaked in the dust of wars past. His eyes were as hollow as mine and his beard longer than time itself.

"Who are you?" I asked.

"You know who I am."

I faltered—I did not recognize him.

"Your messiness has hindered the functionality of this sand clock," he said.

"Everything was tidy until a moment ago!"

He shook his head and continued, "Your purpose is to help, yet you've only caused more hurt. What led you astray?"

"I do not understand."

His sunken expression shifted with irritation. "How did you lose your eyes?" the ethereal man asked, outraged by the concept. "It's a travesty. You were born to see."

"I was born to dig," I countered. "I am the gravedigger."

"No, you are not," he corrected. Ancient struggles echoed in his anger.

"Who am I, then?"

He scoffed. "Blind, you are useless. Fix your vision if you wish to rediscover who you are."

"I can still see."

"Only in shadows. Your inability to see clearly has worsened the mind of this mortal. Beware—a storm is coming."

"A storm?"

"It will undo the damage you have done. How you choose to respond determines everything else."

"What do I need to do?"

"Be aware."

He lifted into the sky on a plume of dust.

"Don't go!" I begged.

He disappeared; only the stench of death lingered.

Thunder cracked, booming so loudly I feared the dead would rise. As I scrambled to press the dirt with my shovel, securing each tomb, lightning followed. The surge of light split into countless branches as it struck the soil. Each plot was hit with electricity—an uninvited resurrection of the dead.

"No, no, no."

I panicked.

My heart lashed on the ground where it lay, whipping the dirt with its red tendrilled veins. In the plots all around, the lost parts of me clawed their way to the surface, no longer content to stay buried.

"If you rise, so will the dead," I cautioned, but my discarded pieces did not heed my warning.

My left ear wiggled out of the rustleweed grave. As it reentered the world, familiar sounds emerged: the soft pitter-patter of rain as it hit the ground, branches rustling in the wind, my frantic footsteps.

My right ear arose from the grave of shattered glass. The full roar of thunder rattled my bones. I buckled over at the inundation of noise; my muffled world was now deafening. All these sounds were familiar—I had heard them once before.

The world filled with color.

A sensory overload—blues, reds, purples, greens. Colors I recognized but had not seen in years. My beloved shadows disappeared.

Everything I cherished looked different now.

I crawled to the grave where I had buried my eyes. There were so many black marbles—my eyes were somewhere among them. I clawed through the smooth glass balls, desperately seeking my eyes. Searching for white within the black, seeking my hunter-green irises among the darkness. I followed a trail of displaced marbles and found my eyes in a dirt pile near the golden thread grave.

"No," I objected, but it was too late.

My mouth was exhumed and the golden thread I had sewed my lips together with unstitched itself. The inner voice I had silenced years ago spoke loudly now.

"You are a disgrace," it declared.

"I was doing my best."

"You lost your way."

The storm worsened.

Overwhelmed, I grabbed my most important pieces—eyes, ears, mouth, heart—and secured them in my satchel. I wasn't ready for a full reunion yet.

A twister of black smoke and electricity formed. It ripped toward me, splitting my stone mausoleum in two.

Frantic, I snatched mementos from my favorite, most cherished graves—those that hurt the most to bury.

I wasn't ready to let go of the past.

Arms full, I carried them as I ran from the storm.

14

With my eyes locked away in my satchel, I was guided by shadows. Dark trees, mounds of terrain—I did not know where I was going, only that the persistent storm was following me there. Flashes of light swallowed the shadows, rendering me blind with every lightning strike.

I could not hear the thunder as clearly as I had a moment ago, but I felt its booming presence each time it roared.

I raced away from the graveyard, mementos from the past in my grip. Farther than I had ever run before, over and beyond the hills surrounding my yard of death.

Through the shadows, I felt the vitality of this new and foreign place. Life swarmed all around me.

The land was fruitful and alive—death did not live here.

Searching for a safe spot to hide from the storm, I darted between tall pines and over heaping boulders until I found a small opening in the trunk of a massive evergreen. I squeezed inside, astonished to find the space within was much larger. In fact, what should have been a condensed nook was a spacious cavern.

My bones rattled at the crack of thunder.

Lightning followed.

The sky was on fire, momentarily illuminating this curious place.

It wasn't a tree nook at all—it was a long corridor that stretched with no seeming end.

I was safe here. The storm could not reach me in this mystical space.

Darkness resumed.

I walked the lengthy corridor, arms growing tired from carrying the weighted past. Breath growing thin, I couldn't march onward without making a change. I wanted to keep going. I needed to discover what awaited me at this corridor's end. Though my heart wished to hold on longer, my mind knew it was time to let go. I let a few black marbles fall from my grip—the weight I carried grew lighter.

I let go of the black pearl next, recalling the resilient girl who faced the world alone.

Then the black feather—the persistent fight against destructiveness that plagued our sleepless nights. As the feather fell, my energy lifted, and I saw the value in what I once viewed as failure. It was much easier to carry my gratitude for Night's tenacity rather than my disappointment for how it all went wrong.

These memories were too heavy to carry—no wonder I was weakened beneath their weight. One by one, I released them, recalling their importance before letting them go.

The burned-out fuse, the sacrifice that defined our worth for years.

The rustleweed, when we chose ruin over love.

I still remembered the green- and red-eyed shadows of the Fringe; I remembered all the love lost to chaos. I retained the memory despite letting it go—it just felt different now. Less dire, less defining of who I was. Why hadn't I done this years ago?

I dropped the golden thread next—the reckless dream to disappear.

Then the shard of glass. The face of the boy soldier flashed before my eyes. His eyes were wet but filled with pride. I honored him by letting him go.

More black marbles fell to the ground—the battle that no one saw us fight.

Then the piece of porcelain, our endless plight to wear a brave face.

Released into the wild, liberated from my chains, the past was with me still but lighter in weight.

Set free with nothing left to carry, my heart was lifted.

I was them, and they were me—each piece of the past I clung to so desperately—we were intertwined harmoniously.

I now understood how they could live in me without digging roots into my soul.

All that I still carried were my missing pieces knotted in my satchel. I unlaced the bag as I reached the end of the corridor and made myself whole. Heart, ears, teeth, nose, and lips positioned in their rightful places, I began to remember who I was.

As my eyes settled into my hollow sockets, I could see clearly again.

I was the Face of Awareness.

Hands pressed against the cool dirt wall, I dropped to my knees. The song I often sang escaped my lips again, but the words were different now.

"In the graveyard, I see bones of hes and shes I knew before. I tried to keep them under dirt, but life to dust the moonlight births. They waltz before my very eyes—a curse I'm forced to realize. Ravished, empty, torn apart—I can't escape my buried heart."

It was time to face everything I had tried so desperately to avoid.

Alone in the darkness, alone with my thoughts, I was finally aware.

A note from the Fox

The day of discovery.

That is where our healing began.

On that day, I found a trail of mementos littered along the path of my foxhole, a trail of memories leading to the Face of Awareness.

In hindsight, I should have realized that all the mementos belonged to Jane, our Host, which meant they also belonged to me, but I wanted no part of them. I did not want to see my involvement or lack thereof.

To fully understand, let me take you back to where our downfall began, long before the day of discovery.

Many years prior, I had abandoned my post.

I had forsaken the Host.

Why did I run?

You'll find out soon enough.

I vanished from her life the day I chose this foxhole over my throne.

Hidden here, I was able to escape my duties.

Far from home, I enabled ruin over love.

I ran as fast as I could away from the sting of my own thoughts.

I wasn't worthy.

I wasn't enough.

The neon lights of my assigned pocket taunted me, never leaving, no matter the distance I gained. My own glowing flesh was a sickly reminder of the world to which I no longer felt attached. Beneath my glass flesh, I glowed a pinkish red—helium and neon bubbled, giving me vibrant color.

Problem was, I did not wish to be seen. I wanted to disappear.

I dug into the glassy flesh at the nape of my neck and tore out my fuse. Disconnected, the inner wires frayed and sparked. Black char dirtied the tiny tube.

I surrendered this part of myself to save those I loved the most; my thoughts would not contaminate Jane. Not if I was detached.

Or so I thought.

I tossed my burned-out fuse into the abyss.

The further I traveled from the city of lights within my assigned pocket, the less I looked like myself. Light red fur now covered my clear glass flesh and my body shrank in size.

I was changing.

I was adapting.

Dashing away from the light, shedding my shadow as I ran.

I had to change to be accepted.

I had to disappear to be seen.

I did as my thoughts commanded—I vanished, unaware that with each passing day, Jane wasted away without my love.

When all that remained was darkness, I stopped running.

Tall trees surrounded me—a sight never seen in the part of the mind I left behind. Evergreens covered in honey blossoms lined the remainder of my journey.

A lake appeared before me, its surface reflecting like a mirror. In it, I saw myself. Once a girl made of neon glass, now a tiny lonesome fox. The only thing that stayed the same was my moss-green eyes.

The longer I stared, the less I remembered my past.

I stared until the memories were so dim, they became mere wisps in my mind. Old ghosts too weak to scream, too tired to haunt me in my sleep.

The longer I stared, the worse off I left Jane.

I was failing her.

Listen … I know what you're thinking: How could I do such a thing? Honestly, I did not know, not then, anyway. It wasn't until the day of discovery that I remembered why I ran.

The first memento I encountered was the black marbles.

When I picked one up and touched its shiny surface, my consciousness was stripped.

I was sent into a living nightmare.

I was shown the monster who had poisoned my mind.

Memento #1

When: The 13th Cycle
Where: Jane's mind — Pocket of Fear
Who: Jane Doe through the Warden of Fear

Four black marbles rotated in my grip, methodically churning as I focused on the horizon. Hypersensitive to every sound, every shape, every movement, I marched toward the unknown.

The world was filled with demons — horrible creatures embodying fears. Each warden was assigned a monster, and we were tasked to keep our fears in line. Some wardens mollified their monsters by coddling them. This strategy always weakened the warden and, subsequently, turned them into Sleepers. Others, like myself, fought back. We were Walkers. We went through life refusing to submit to our fears. Our monsters stalked, haunted, and hunted us, creating a daily living nightmare.

Mine was out there, somewhere, though I hadn't seen her in a while.

The sun beamed bright, casting an orange glow on my day. It was among the few colors I knew — grays blanketed most everything else, and any other colors trying to peek through the shadows were dull and faded.

Rows of picket-fenced holding pens constrained the Sleepers, who ogled and fawned over their hideous pets, though I suppose they saw them differently than I. What appeared as monsters with slick scales, hairy antennae, and spider eyes to me likely appeared as kittens to them.

They were dozed. I was roused.

Sleepers were slaves to their fear.

I kept walking in search of reprieve, for a break from the chase.

I would not give in.

It was a never-ending walk to somewhere else, a place unknown. I'd wear the soles of my boots into nothing if it meant I'd get a break from the hunt.

I pulled my long, midnight-brown hair into a braid and fixated my grayish-green eyes on the sky.

Fluffy cumulus clouds drifted in front of the sun, blanketing my surroundings in a shadow. Heart thudding, I walked quicker, terrified of what the darkness might bring. If I kept moving, maybe my fear would not find me.

A warden across the street broke into a sprint. I looked over my shoulder to find a three-headed lion with a scorpion tail charging after her. A monster in full form meant bravery—like me, this warden refused to surrender.

Breath held, I watched her outrun her fear.

The marbles revolved faster between my fingers as I instinctively searched the area.

I was ready to run.

Tired but strong-willed, I was *always* ready to run.

Orange light resumed as the clouds moved, but my nerves did not settle. Daylight was just as dangerous as the dark. The marbles scraped against each other as they rotated in my grip.

There was only one road here, and it was lined with rows of perfect little homes filled with perfectly enslaved wardens. This town was a prison disguised as a utopia. One of those homes belonged to me, but it stayed vacant and dark—stagnant souls were too easy to locate, too easy to snatch and devour.

I was a Walker, a wanderer.

One day, I'd find a place where my monster could not find me.

The sidewalk stretched as far as I could see. The only ones who walked freely were wardens like me, people who refused to greet their monster as a friend. To settle was to surrender, and I never wanted to live in a cage.

I suspected there was no field of freedom beyond the quaint suburbia plagued by beasts of terror.

I worried I might walk forever and never find reprieve.

A winged banshee with ten rows of fangs screeched as it swooped down from the sky and snatched a warden who walked a few paces ahead of me. He had let his guard down—he was taken.

I watched as the banshee dragged his body into the sky, sucking on his soul and depleting him to the brink of death. Her silhouette was beautiful—long billowing hair and a perfectly sculpted body. Before killing him completely, she lowered and dropped him to the ground.

I paused to assess the situation—the man was ghostly pale, and his body looked deflated, as if the banshee had hollowed out his insides.

His monster hovered overhead.

A demon camouflaged within the image of an angel— her beauty was an illusion.

She flashed a mischievous grin at me before rocketing back into the sky.

I shoved my marbles into my pocket and ran to the man.

"Are you okay?" I asked, reassessing my surroundings every few seconds to make sure I wasn't making myself easy prey for my own monster.

"I love her," he revealed, voice frail and weak.

"She is a monster."

"How dare you!" he spat.

I took a step back. "She will kill you one day."

"Never," he argued. "She needs me."

He was right—without their assigned warden, the fear monsters starved. They could only feed on their assigned warden.

"It'll be an accident; one day, she will take it too far."

"I don't care. I'd rather die in her embrace than live without her touch."

He was as lost as the Sleepers.

"I'll leave you, then," I offered, stepping over his mangled body.

"Surrender! Set yourself free!" he called after me.

I ignored his manic advice. I had thought he was a Walker, but he was a Sleeper in disguise—he was devoid of life, he was soulless. He had let his monster win.

I looked around to assess who else might be wearing a brave façade.

It was impossible to tell.

The Walkers lived their lives in motion, never stopping, never pausing, for fear their monster might attack during a moment of rest. It was a battle of will, a motivation to survive—if we stopped, it was by force, by accident, or due to a physical inability to keep moving forward.

I would walk until I was forced to run, and if my legs gave out, I would crawl.

The sewer grate in the middle of the road shifted.

Metal scraped concrete.

The Walkers around me heard the noise, too, and the sidewalks turned into a running track. No one knew whose monster would emerge, and it wasn't worth sticking around to find out.

We sprinted as fast as we could. I passed a few individuals, outpacing the slowest around me, but it didn't matter how fast I ran—the monsters did not torment those at the back of the pack. They specifically targeted the warden to whom they belonged.

The sewer grate rocketed into the air and fell onto the road with a clanging thud. A looming creature emerged—I could feel its enormity without glancing back.

I ran faster.

As I darted down the sidewalk, everyone around me slowed. Many came to a stop and stared beyond me at the creature I was trying to outrun.

If it wasn't their monster, was it mine?

A ferocious, gurgling growl echoed through the perfect sky and the hair on the back of my neck rose. I glanced over my shoulder.

Menacing black marble eyes were fixated on me.

Malsana had found me.

She appeared as something new every time she emerged; her marble eyes were the only thing that stayed the same.

Larger than normal and more hideous, too, she had arrived in the form of a dragon.

The Sleepers in their picket-fenced pens looked up with empty stares, watching the showdown of me versus my fear.

I unsheathed the sword hanging from a scabbard across my back. With it firmly in my grip, I turned to face Malsana.

"I am not afraid of you!" I shouted.

You ought to be, she hissed. Only I could hear her speak.

"Come closer and I will gut you."

You can't kill me—I am a part of you.

"Your words won't work on me," I countered, my grayish-green gaze murderous, my energy focused.

One day, you'll be dozed, and we will become friends, Malsana sneered.

"Never!"

I charged sword first toward the belly of my beast. As my blade reached her slick, scaled gut, her horned wing swatted me into the sky. I flew, landing across the road on my back.

The hit knocked the wind out of me, and as I struggled to regain my breath, Malsana sauntered toward me. Unable to stand, I gripped my sword and played dead.

Malsana hovered over me, nostrils billowing with smoke.

I would not surrender; I would not be put to sleep.

Another step closer and Malsana's huge body straddled me. She leaned in, stepping on my long braid so I could not move my head, and prepared to consume my soul. Split tongue extended and dragging across my face, Malsana toyed with her dinner.

Motionless, I waited, feigning surrender.

Malsana's jaw opened, displaying countless rows of dagger teeth, and as she leaned in to feed, I lifted my sword from where it lay and plunged it into Malsana's eye socket. Black blood spurted out of the wound, splattering all over my face. I held my position, locking my monster in place with my sword. A few twists and jabs cut her marble eye free. The black glass sphere fell to the ground with a clink.

Malsana recoiled, howling in anguish.

"You will never win!" I screamed, wiping the monster's blood out of my eyes. Black smears stained my face as I watched Malsana fly away.

She would be back—she always came back stronger and more determined than before.

I plucked the black marble off the ground and wiped it on my pant leg, cleaning off the greasy blood, then placed it in my pocket with my other trophies. Each marble marked a victory and served as a reminder that I was strong enough to survive.

"Are you okay?" an unfamiliar voice asked.

I looked over my shoulder to see a woman jogging toward me. Like me, her hair was knotted into an assortment of warrior braids and she wore a tank top with combat suspenders attached to her cargo pants. Her arm muscles were bigger than mine, indicating she had fought her monster longer than I'd fought mine.

I quickly picked myself up.

"I'll be fine. I took her eye; she will need a few days to heal."

"You're covered in blood," she noted, grimacing at the sight of my face.

"It's war paint." I returned my sword to its scabbard. "Maybe it'll keep my monster away."

"Unlikely." She was right—there were no simple remedies to end the hunt. "What's your name?" she asked.

"Jane Doe," I replied.

"Yeah, me too."

"Really?" I examined her closer—her eyes were the same grayish-green color as mine, but her nose was longer, her eyes more circular, and her hair much lighter.

"Yes. What's your *other* name?"

"Jane is the only name I've known. What's *your* other name?"

"Guardiano della Crescita. Just call me Cressie. Our names hold meaning."

I hesitated. "They do?"

"Mine means *Guardian of Growth*. I have served my purpose here, and now I am searching for elsewhere."

"Elsewhere?" I asked, interest piqued.

"Yes. There is a world outside of this one. That's where I'm trying to go."

"There is a place where our monsters can't get us?"

She nodded. "They cannot leave the Pocket of Fear."

I was fascinated. "Is that where we are now?"

"Don't you know anything?" She clicked her tongue. "Yes, we live in the Pocket of Fear." She sized me up. "I suppose you haven't been here as long as I have."

"Let me go with you."

"You can walk with me, but you cannot leave with me. You're still needed here."

"If you can leave, why can't I?"

"My monster grows weaker with each passing year," Cressie explained.

I felt incompetent. "Why does mine only seem to grow stronger?"

"Yours appears to be an adult fear. Mine was juvenile."

"You know what your fear is?" I asked, astonished.

"It took a while, but as it grew weaker, it also grew more transparent. I am the warden of imaginary monsters."

Such a notion forced me to pause. "There is such a thing?"

"In the outside world, yes, but it appears my fear does not age well, so I have been set free."

"How do I find out what my fear is?" I asked.

"After seeing your monster, I suspect yours is much more severe."

"I need to get out of here."

"You need to stay and fight," she argued.

"We can't kill them, so what's the point?"

"We keep them submissive."

"For what purpose?"

"To protect the inner mind."

"Whose mind?" I asked.

"Our mind—the Host's mind."

I groaned, utterly confused. "I want to be free."

"I'll show you the way, but know, if you escape, your fear will run rampant without a warden. If we can't keep them tame, no one can."

"Mine doesn't seem very tame to me … "

"Here, in this pocket, yours is a ferocious nightmare, but outside the pocket, it's likely just a passing thought."

"How?"

"The beast exists within your control."

"And if I leave, the monster wins?"

She nodded. "The walk is long. Join me. You have plenty of time to decide between fighting and fleeing."

My stomach lurched. I wished to fight, but I was tired. I was tired of being the prey in this never-ending hunt.

Cressie walked quickly. Her strides held great purpose. I was in awe of her confidence; I'd never met someone who knew so much about this place.

"How long have you been here?" I asked.

"A year after the start—my monster and I were the first to arrive."

"Was it always this perfect little utopia?"

"No. In the beginning, it was a black hole of nothingness. We battled in a dark void—no solid ground, no light. Without sturdy footing, I struggled to survive. The Face of Fear respected my determination and altered the landscape. A single road and a tiny home appeared.

Other monsters soon arrived, which initiated the creation of new wardens. The humble landscape morphed into the sprawling suburbia we live in today. I heard the perfect appearance was to help maintain order, to give us something lovely in an otherwise horrifying world, but in my opinion, having a cozy home makes it easier to become complacent and succumb to the fears."

"Complacent surrender is much easier than a continuous fight."

"Agreed, yet the fight must be fought," Cressie advised.

I walked with this thought, knowing I wished to surrender without claiming defeat. I wanted to escape with my soul intact.

"How far away is the exit?"

"I'll know it when I see it," she responded.

We walked on.

The horizon never changed. The long street and sidewalks decorated with tiny, picturesque houses stretched as far as I could see. It was the only road; it was the only route to freedom.

"It has to end eventually, right?" I asked.

"I will find what I am looking for," Cressie replied.

We never found what we were looking for.

The perpetual afternoon sky darkened, setting my nerves aflame.

"Something is coming," I whispered.

"Something is always coming," Cressie countered with apathy. "I know it's not for me, though."

How many days had we been walking? Was it possible that Malsana had healed already? Was my monster already coming back for me?

I shoved my hand into my pocket instinctively to find courage. I took out three of Malsana's marbles and rotated them frantically in my hand.

Cressie gasped in horror.

"Get rid of those!" she demanded.

"Why? They are my trophies. They give me courage."

"They are dangerous."

"How?"

Before she could answer, thick gray clouds covered the sun, blanketing the world in darkness. A crack of thunder shook the ground, and in its echo, a monster growled. I couldn't see the source, the sky was too dark, but the sound of true terror approached.

The sky ripped open and black marbles rained down.

I shielded my head, watching in horror. My monstrous fear had returned with a vengeance.

The marbles fell like bullets—no one was safe. The Walkers ran, hoping to escape the onslaught of my fear, and the Sleepers took their pet fears indoors.

"Her arrival shouldn't affect the other wardens." Cressie clenched her fingers into fists to stop them from trembling—her wavering courage concerned me. "This only happens when a fear is about to take over."

"Take over?"

"Something happened on the outside that gave your fear strength."

"No," I groaned, reaching into my pocket and running my fingers through the black marbles of victories past.

"Only you can make this right."

"How? There is no monster to slay."

"If you get to know your fear better, you'll learn how to conquer it." Her expression tightened with remorse. "I cannot linger here."

"Where will you go?"

Cressie's grayish-green eyes glowed brightly as she realized something she did not say aloud.

She ran to the nearest sewer grate and wriggled her body through the large bars.

"Good luck," she shouted before letting go and falling beneath the grate.

I ran to the sewer and peered inside—there were no walls, no ground, just darkness. Cressie was gone.

Should I follow her?

No. I was the only one who could stop Malsana.

The black marble rain fell harder now.

Though I stood tall, my confidence wavered. How was I supposed to defeat an enemy I could not see?

The black marbles turned to sticky puddles of tar as they hit the ground. They oozed and steamed, emitting an offensive odor as they cracked open.

"Why are you so angry?" I shouted at the sky.

I am hungry! Malsana replied.

"I hope you starve!"

My reply was the wrong one; the marble rainstorm turned into a monsoon. Innocent bystanders collapsed to the ground, pelted unconscious due to my inability to wrangle my fear.

"You aren't supposed to hunt anyone but me," I argued.

These are desperate times.

I glared up at the dark clouds, unsure how to satisfy my monster's rage without surrendering my soul.

"I cannot give you all of me."

A taste would suffice.

The roofs of the nearby homes sagged beneath the weight of the black marble tar. Screams from the Sleeper wardens rang into the sky. Through a nearby window, I saw the wet liquid creeping through cracks in the roof, burning everything it touched—including the wardens. As the tar scorched their flesh, their screams of horror amplified.

I looked down at my own feet—steaming tar now covered my boots and trapped me in place. Every Walker within eyesight was trapped, too.

Malsana's laughter arrived as a rolling boom of thunder.

The marbles fell faster and the tar level rose. Though I wore knee-high boots, I was reminded that other Walkers did not when the tar reached our ankles. The haunting sound of brave Walkers crying for help shook me to my core.

This wasn't right, and it was all my fault.

They suffered because I could not wrangle my monster.

I trembled violently, both from fear and anger, unsure how I'd fix this mess while I was stuck in place.

"Show yourself!" I demanded of Malsana, furious that she had taken such an ambiguous form. "Fight me with honor!"

A giant crash came in reply—a house across the street buckled beneath the tar's weight, silencing the screams of those trapped inside.

I was running out of time and there was only one thing that would mollify Malsana.

"Fine! Just a taste," I conceded.

Immediately, the clouds lifted and the marble storm ceased. The ankle-deep black tar reshaped into marbles and rolled into the sewers, releasing the Walkers from their hold. The moment they were free, the Walkers dashed far out of sight, leaving me alone on the sidewalk.

Sleepers stared out at me through their windows.

The sun returned, the fuming sludge was gone, and the fallen house knitted itself back together—everything looked immaculate again.

My boots were ruined, but the terror had ceased.

I exhaled with relief.

Where was Malsana?

I removed my acid-burned boots, prepared to carry on barefoot, and reached over my shoulder to grip the hilt of my sword. Waiting and ready for whatever nightmare my monster had in store.

Nothing came.

My hand began to sweat—the suspense rattled me.

You promised me a taste.

"Where are you?"

Take your hand off your sword.

I did as Malsana instructed and a black puppy with black marble eyes trotted toward me.

"This disguise won't work on me."

It will ease the pain.

"I will gouge your eyes if you take more than a small taste."

I keep my promises, she hissed. *I am not to be feared.*

Her words sparked a thought—we ran in fear from our fears. What would happen if I stopped being afraid?

I looked at the adorable puppy. Its demon eyes were big and pleading. Down on one knee, I extended my arm, and the puppy licked my hand. It did not hurt at all.

"Is that it?" I asked, utterly confused. I felt no different, nor did I feel pain.

The puppy stopped licking my hand and stepped back.

I feel so much better.

"That wasn't so bad."

All these years, you fought me when it truly could have been this simple.

"I didn't want to become a Sleeper."

Only the weak go to sleep.

I wasn't weak—I was strong. Perhaps forging a friendship with my monster was the better strategy after all.

"Will you behave if I feed you in small rations?"

It is better than never eating at all.

Malsana was being too malleable; her submissiveness caused me unease.

"We will not rest," I warned her. "We will walk."

With no shoes? Malsana asked, her tone judgmental.

"I would rather walk barefoot than sit around idly with you."

Fine. I will walk beside you.

And so we did. We walked the endless sidewalk, losing track of time as we co-existed harmoniously.

"Are you hungry?" I asked, noticing that Malsana was walking slower than usual.

Very.

Pleased that she had not inquired herself, but waited for me to offer, I knelt beside her and offered her my hand.

I was in control.

Her puppy form licked my palm, closing her black marble eyes to savor every second of nourishment.

Again, I felt no pain.

I pulled my hand away, unsure how long I had let her linger.

"That's enough," I ordered, wiping her slobber off my hand and continuing my walk.

Where are we going? Malsana asked.

"Does it matter?"

What are you running from?

"Excuse me?"

There's nothing to outrun—I am with you now.

"That's not why we are walking."

Then why?

I huffed. "I will not be tricked into complacency."

I will not bite the hand that feeds.

My side glare was vicious; I did not trust her.

"If you don't want to walk with me, you can leave."

No, I will stay. I don't abandon my friends.

"You mean, you don't abandon your food source."

I thought we were friends.

She looked up at me with her demon puppy eyes.

My chest tightened.

Why did I feel guilty? Then I remembered my earlier thought: befriending my fear would end the relentless hunt. If I let her in and controlled her, I would be free from the chase. According to Cressie, the more I understood my monster, the more control I would gain.

"One day soon, perhaps."

Malsana skipped in puppy form, butt wiggling with excitement. It was hard not to trust such a loveable creature.

I let her snack on my soul once a day, careful not to let her linger too long. It was impossible to tell time here—the sun never moved in the sky—so I tried to count the seconds as she consumed me.

One, two, three …

I wondered if I'd catch up to Cressie. We were walking at a good pace. Perhaps I'd see her before she left this world for the next.

… four, five, six …

Was time different in the world beyond this one?

My thoughts tangled around a desire to learn the truth about our existence. There were so many questions, so many mysteries to solve.

… seven, eight, nine …

Malsana might know the answers.

I swatted the foggy web of thoughts until I saw the present clearly—Malsana had moved from my hand to my arm.

"What are you doing?" I yanked my arm away from her.

I thought you were being generous today.

"No! I just lost track of time."

My apologies, she offered, though she did not seem sincere.

I was angry, but I had no one to blame but myself. I was in control—I had slipped up and allowed her to take advantage.

"Tell me something," I demanded. "Is there a world beyond this one?"

Malsana's ears perked.

Who have you been talking to?

"Just answer the question."

Yes. Where we are now is a controlled environment.

"Controlled by who?"

The Face of Fear.

"Is that why everything looks the same no matter how far I walk?"

Precisely.

"Why?"

It's easier to monitor the progress and status of each warden when the scenery is bland. He needs to know who is awake and who is asleep.

"And what about the monsters? Does he monitor all of you?"

Yes, but he loves us more.

I was visibly antagonized.

Don't be upset, Malsana said, sensing my anger. *He is the Face of Fear, after all. It's only natural he is more inclined to favor us.*

"Is he your father?"

No. We are birthed on the outside, and if we are lucky, we find our way in.

"Then what is his purpose?"

He makes sure that once we're in, we never leave his cage.

But Cressie had said there was an exit; I was desperate to hang on to that hope.

"So, you've seen the world beyond?"

I've seen every layer: the outside world, the inside world, and this pocket we reside in now. The inside world is the most fragile—I was not there long. I saw the giant sand clock, and then the Face of Day wrangled me. I traveled from her to the Face of Night, and then to the Face of Fear, who tossed me in here.

"Do you want to leave, too?"

Malsana eyed me suspiciously. *You want to leave?*

"Don't you?"

It will never happen. There is a cage in the sky, and beyond its electrified chain links are our master's eyes. He watches everything we do. She paused in thought. *I don't want to leave. His love keeps us loyal. I would have dissipated in the outside world if I had not found my way here. Fears can't survive there without taking root in a fragile mind.*

I considered this. "Are we inside a mind now?"

Yes.

"Whose?"

Yours.

"Huh?"

It doesn't really matter whose mind we're in, just that we get to live. Without this space to exist, we'd be nothing. Malsana glanced up at me. *We aren't so different, you and I.*

"From what you've told me, I gather we are quite different. I protect the mind while you attempt to ruin it."

Even so, we are both prisoners in the same cage.

"I am good. You are evil."

You would not have been created if I hadn't arrived, and without you, I would starve.

"Perhaps I ought to stop feeding you, then."

You cannot kill me, but I can kill you. And with you gone, I will wreak havoc until I starve.

I groaned—our existence was too interconnected.

"I thought we were friends," I countered, using her own words against her.

Her puppy scowl flipped into a smile.

Co-existing is much easier when we are friends.

I agreed, so long as I was in control.

Our walk went on forever with never-changing views. Malsana trotted beside me in puppy form. When we caught up to some of the slower Walkers who had outrun the marble storm, they stared at me in disbelief—some wary, others impressed.

One Walker was in such shock he did not notice his fear biding its time in a cloud above.

"Is that one yours?" I asked, pointing at the cloud weighed down by a rabid koala bear. A red feather was braided into its mangy hair.

"Oh no," he gasped before turning to run, but the monstrous bear had already dropped. It catapulted through the sky and landed on the running man. He was pinned, squashed but alive, and the bear suckled on his weakened soul.

"That'll be a tough recovery." I grimaced. A kindness would be to die after an injury like that, but he would survive. The only true way to expire here was through the complete removal of a soul.

It was a cruel fate to endure.

Malsana kept bumping into my ankles as we walked.

"Why can't you mind your own space?"

I am hungry, Malsana griped.

I extended my hand to her without glancing down, and she licked at my soul like it was a bone covered in peanut butter.

One … two … three …

If a master oversaw our existence here, I wanted to meet him. Chin lifted, eyes narrowed, I examined the sky. Fluffy white clouds and orange skies concealed the cage containing us. Maybe the exit Cressie was searching for was a pathway to him, the Face of Fear. I needed to go there; I needed to better understand my purpose.

I lost track of time again.

Malsana was nibbling on my elbow.

"You are taking advantage of our agreement," I argued, yanking my arm free of her tiny, sharp teeth.

You are still you, she countered.

"What are you?" I demanded.

I am your downfall.

"I thought you were a fear."

I have become much more than that.

"Tell me what you are."

Malsana's puppy face smirked. *If I tell you, you might try to stick that sword of yours into my eye.*

"Tell me."

40

Fine. I am sickness in the mind.

"What does that mean?"

When I am given power, I make self-destruction feel like healing. If given free rein, our Host would think she is in control, but really, I would be.

"But you aren't in control," I confirmed.

Correct. I do not have access to our Host's mind.

I huffed. "Good."

A few miles more, my ankle began to itch. I stopped to scratch the growing rash. Back leaned against one of the picket fences, I lifted my pant leg and found a patch of swollen red bumps.

"What is this?" I asked, confused by the strange ailment.

Little bites.

"From what?"

Let me lick them. I will heal you.

The itch began to sting. Pain shot up my legs, searing my nerves.

"Make it stop," I shouted in agony. The pain intensified, and when I examined the rash again, I found raw sores on both ankles.

"Make it stop." I fell to my knees.

Malsana dragged her split tongue across my left ankle. Slime dripped down my foot.

"It hurts," I cried, feeling unworthy of my warden title. Weak, cowardly, insignificant—how could I save the Host from Malsana when I leaned on *her* to save me from a minuscule injury?

Malsana grumbled and groaned as her gooey saliva lathered my rash. I knew what she was doing—she was also eating more of my soul—but the sting returned to an itch, and slowly, the discomfort vanished.

It worked; she had healed me.

"Thank you," I expressed, mood sour.

Don't be so hard on yourself. Everyone needs help sometimes.

"I don't want to talk about it."

You should rest. Those were venom bites.

"Venom bites? What bit me?"

Heal first. We can pinpoint the cause later.

"I'm not sitting still," I argued, terrified that my monster was already taking too much of me. If I stopped moving, I'd become easier to subdue.

Malsana looked up at me with her marble eyes. I could not see the emotion they carried—they were black holes concealing a terrible unknown.

Though the pain was gone, the spot she had healed still ached. I stood, took one step, and toppled back to the ground.

I told you to rest, Malsana chastised.

Despite my efforts, I could not stand.

Weak and pathetic. Who was I becoming? Ever since befriending my fear, I felt like somebody else, someone I did not recognize.

"This has never happened before."

Good thing we made an alliance. Otherwise, you'd be easy pickings in your current state.

I was tempted to believe her—it made sense—but I also worried that my friendship with her was somehow causing this.

Can I have a little taste? she asked.

"No."

I was in control.

Malsana sulked a few feet away while I rested my injured ankles. I observed the Walkers as they hurried by—frantic and stressed as they desperately outpaced their fears.

Some successfully outran the monsters that chased them. Others were overtaken and sucked dry. I glanced to where Malsana lay, her furry body curled in on itself—I was grateful to be out of the chase.

Attention turned back to the ever-moving, adrenaline-fueled horror show before me, I succumbed to the nightmare. A one-hundred-legged centipede swallowed its warden whole, only to regurgitate his body before the soul fully perished. The monster scurried away, leaving its victim lifeless on the ground. The warden was rendered immobile for hours—I watched the entire healing process. Eventually, his soul remedied itself, resurrecting him from the brink of death. Once enough strength had returned, he stood and continued to walk, now with a slow and prominent limp.

I understood the emptiness in his eyes as he resumed his walk—Malsana nearly killed me on my first day here. Sometimes, I wish she had. It was a heartbreaking revival—a rebirth into the same nightmare that killed you. The terror was everlasting.

I never let it happen again.

The black marbles in my pocket were proof.

Breathing heavily, vision hazy, I felt the urge to sleep for the first time in my life.

"Am I dying?" I asked.

You are healing, Malsana replied.

Unable to fight the overpowering sensation, my eyes closed.

Fantastical images filled my head: I was flying in a place unknown, an ether where existence was suspended in an expansive nothingness. Wings of white extended from my back and pounded the hollow air. I lifted my hands and found they were not my own—they were made of porcelain.

Who was I? Who had I become?

My unconscious imagination was terrifying—I had never dreamed before.

I let the energy of this place consume me, allowing my mind to drift further from reality until this magical place felt real.

It was better here; my heart was happier here.

My tired bones lifted. My pain went away. I flew in circles around a giant suspended sandclock, observing the life bustling below. Grains of sand fell from the top orb into the bottom, one by one, counting time in a way I could not comprehend.

Content and comfortable, I wanted to live in this dream forever.

You can, Malsana whispered. She was nowhere to be seen, but her voice rang like bells inside my head.

"This isn't real," I replied, flipping in the ether before soaring forward.

It is very real—I have been here once.

I looked at the giant sandclock, amazed I hadn't pieced this puzzle together sooner.

"Is this the inner world?"

Malsana purred. *Isn't it lovely?*

It *was* lovely.

A faint glow outlined everything, highlighting the beauty, enhancing the mystique. Orbed pockets floated near the sandclock, each a different vibrant color. I propelled my weightless body there.

Magenta, gold, opal, turquoise, charcoal—my mind absorbed colors I'd never seen within the Pocket of Fear. I wanted to stay here forever. I never wanted to return to the orange-tinted monochrome nightmare that was my reality.

I weaved between the pockets, observing each one as I flew past. Some were glowing orbs, pristine and neatly kempt. Others were strangely shaped, disarrayed formations. I tried to peer into each pocket, but could not see past the outer shells.

"Why can't I see inside?"

Because you are in my recollection, and I never saw the inside of those pockets.

To my left, I located the Pocket of Fear. Orange and gray swirled beneath a spherical, steel cage. I soared closer, peering inside. Monsters of all kinds battled at the gate, fighting each other, fighting their cage, desperate to escape. Seeing it from the outside, I now understood the extent of my prison.

"I don't want to go back there."

I will go with you.

Her nefarious offer reminded me of my purpose—I was tasked to protect this inside world from *her*.

I shook my head, freeing myself from the dream.

Malsana was curled up on my lap.

"What are you doing? Get off me!"

You are still healing, she reminded me.

My left ankle wound had spread up my leg.

"No." I pushed the little monster off my lap and clutched my shin. Pain seared my nerves as my fingertips touched the raw, peeling flesh. Each loose flake revealed rotting muscle beneath.

You are sick, Malsana revealed.

"I was fine before I let you in!"

Sometimes, you have to break before you mend.

"Are you doing this to me?"

You are paranoid. Return to dreamland and I will heal you. When you wake up, you'll be stronger than ever.

"No!"

The weight of the marbles in my pocket hung heavier than ever, and I recalled Cressie's warning. Without hesitation, I grabbed a handful and tossed them. They rolled along the pavement, over the sidewalk curb, and into the sewer grate.

What are you doing? Malsana asked.

"Getting rid of you!"

She laughed. *It's too late for that.*

The pull of sleep took control again. As the sky darkened, the face of a man I had never seen before appeared in the clouds.

Black rain poured down, each droplet turning into a black marble as it hit the ground.

"What is happening?" I asked, unable to fight off my drowsiness.

The face in the cloud grew larger, enhancing each detail of the man's manic expression. I fought to keep my eyes open; I needed to know what was happening. A cackling laugh echoed, followed by swirling black smoke that shadowed the land.

"Among the monsters, who here is free?" the man's voice projected with god-like force.

Many of the fears attached to Sleepers stepped forward, but the face in the sky showed no emotion, no interest.

Malsana trotted away from me, puppy tail wagging and marble eyes turned toward the sky. With a shake, she transformed into an ogre—a towering monster with daggered, venom-tipped teeth. Her black marble eyes remained the same. Skin a sickly shade of gray, hair thin and shedding, she reached her massive hand toward the face in the cloud.

A grisly groan emanated from her gut as she volunteered herself.

Red light pulsated, filtering the pocket with chaotic madness.

I fought the urge to close my eyes.

The face in the clouds twisted with delight—he chose Malsana.

As my will to fight weakened and the pull of sleep prospered, my lashes fluttered.

I had lost the fight.

I had let my monster take control, and now, I was unable to stop it from joining forces with an outside terror.

My eyes trembled shut.

I was a slave to my fear.

A note from the Fox

The man in the sky was Chaos.

He was now Malsana's wrangler.

Like a well-crafted war plan, Chaos strategically dropped bits of Malsana into the various pockets of Jane's mind. His goal was to take over, and he would do so with Malsana's help.

After fleeing the Pocket of Fear, the nefarious duo visited the Pocket of Trust—a wise first stop, as an infected mindset resulted in a weakened resolve.

They needed Jane vulnerable and insecure. They needed her to lose faith in herself. They had to break her from the inside.

On the day of discovery, I did not understand the significance of the black pearl memento when I came across it in my foxhole. I did not recognize it as the first step of many in Jane's rapid decline.

I only recognized the sad story of betrayal between friends, with no comprehension that this betrayal happened within Jane.

A calculated infiltration.

This is where faith was lost.

Memento #2

When: The 13th Cycle
Where: Jane's mind — Pocket of Trust
Who: Jane Doe through the Little Clam

A friend to all who were a friend to me, my love, trust, and loyalty guided my existence.

Happy in every waking moment, content with the dreams that visited me at night, I knew no way of life other than the one provided by this joyous ocean.

The dolphins sang my name in greeting each dawn as they swam their morning laps. The whales offered me transportation whenever I wanted to leave my coral garden. The sharks told me tales of terror and adventure, captivating my imagination with every story they shared. And the oysters told me how to best care for my pearl.

I was a little clam, lucky enough to be blessed with a lustrous white gem of my own.

It was my figurative heart; it was my identity.

Without my pearl, I would be lost.

Day in and day out, I polished and cared for my pearly heart while making friends with the vibrant marine life within the sea.

Shells wide open, I sang a jubilant melody to all who cared to listen. My gratitude rang near and far, spreading joy into the world I so loved.

On a morning like any other, as the dolphins raced by singing my name, a small black octopus swam toward me.

"Hey, there," I greeted from my coral garden. "I haven't met you before."

"I am new here," she said, her shiny black marble eyes gleaming.

"Welcome! I am Jane. What's your name?"

"Malsana."

"Nice to meet you, Malsana. Would you like to spend time with me in my garden?"

"I would love that!"

Malsana lowered and nestled her long tentacles into a large bed of pink kelp. As she settled, I resumed my morning song.

She listened with her eyes closed, enjoying each note I sang.

When I finished, I found her staring at me.

"Can you sing?" I asked.

She shook her head. "I am not as blessed as you."

"You can learn," I insisted. "I'll teach you."

"Can you teach me how to find a pearl like yours, too?"

I suddenly felt self-conscious; my shells slowly shut.

"I was born with this pearl."

"I wasn't born with anything nice. No pearl, no singing voice. I have nothing."

"Don't be so hard on yourself! Surely there is something special and unique about you. We just need to discover what it is!"

"Will you help me?"

"Of course. It will be a wondrous adventure."

Malsana visited me every day for a week.

We tried new hobbies, attempting to locate her special talents, but she remained fixated on my pearl.

"It's so beautiful," she cooed after a long afternoon of aquatic gymnastics.

"Thank you. I would be lost without it."

"Can I hold it for a moment?" she asked.

I hesitated. "It has never left the safety of my shells before."

"You can trust me," she promised.

Two of her tentacles stretched toward me.

"Maybe tomorrow," I diverted, not yet ready to share my pearl.

Malsana's tentacles dropped in disappointment.

A surge of guilt consumed me.

"I'm sorry," I offered. "I've never been asked to share my pearl before."

"I just wanted to hold it." Malsana pumped her tentacles, lifting higher into the water. "I'm going home."

"Will I see you tomorrow?" I asked, nervous that I had ruined our friendship.

She darted away without answering.

I was left in a state of confusion—what had I done wrong?

Malsana did not return the following day.

The dolphins sang my name, the sharks shared quick tales, but my marble-eyed octopus friend was nowhere in sight. At twilight, as the setting sun cast shadows beneath the sea, I asked a passing whale to search the area.

Malsana was nowhere to be found.

I returned to my coral garden, more confused than before.

Cursed with anxious questions, I polished my pearl incessantly, trying to wipe away my crippling doubts. Should I have shared my pearl? Was I being a bad friend? My insides churned. Malsana only wanted to touch it. Would one little touch have been so bad? No, it was mine—I did not have to share. My gut screamed that I was not in the wrong, yet my thoughts kept insinuating that I was to blame.

A full week forsaken by my newest friend—what had I done wrong?

"I miss your songs," a dolphin shouted as it swam overhead.

The comment shook me to my core. I had not sung in days; my voice was gone.

I tried to find the courage to sing, but the stress of Malsana's absence left me weak. From morning light to evening dark, I did not make a sound. When the nighttime shadows blanketed my garden, I held tight to my pearl and surrendered to sleep.

My dreams were laced with imagined stress between all my friends and me—one by one, I lost them. The dolphins no longer sang my name, the sharks shared tales where I was the villain, and the whales ignored me as they crossed over my garden.

Darkness blanketed me.

The lack of friendship left me cold.

I was alone.

Sunlight crept through the small crack between my shells, forcing me awake. Afraid to open, terrified that my dreams might come true, I kept my shells clamped shut.

"Hey, Jane," a familiar, slithery voice greeted.

Malsana.

"Where have you been?" I asked, shells firmly closed.

"I was hurt. I needed time."

"I didn't mean to hurt your feelings," I offered, peeking through my shells.

Malsana's tentacles swayed in the current, occasionally whipping through the water to keep her in place.

"I know," she said. "We all make mistakes."

Her reappearance did not remedy my shame. I still felt guilty.

"Thanks for coming back," I said, my confidence meek.

"That's what friends are for."

Upside down and turned around, my mind spun in circles. Nothing made sense like it used to, and I clung to any fragment of logic within the confusion.

Malsana hummed a pretty tune.

Music.

Music still made sense to me.

I opened my shells and joined her song. Together, for the first time, we harmonized, and our blissful chorus settled my nerves.

This felt right.

"You've been practicing," I said after we finished our song.

"I was hoping to impress you."

"You did!"

Malsana twirled, tentacles spinning through the water.

I added, "We should sing together more often."

"I would like that!"

Malsana stopped pirouetting, and her covetous eyes locked on my pearl again.

Unease clenched my gut.

"Sorry," she stammered, sensing my discomfort. "It's just so pretty."

The guilt I had lived with for days returned, and though it battled every fiber of my intuition, I chose to ignore the ringing alarms in my mind.

"Would you like to hold it?" I offered.

"Really?" Her shiny black eyes beamed with excitement.

"As long as you promise to be careful."

"Of course!"

I opened my shells wider and she reached two of her tentacles inside. Suction cups at the tips latched to my pearl, and in a blink, she snatched it from the safety of my shells. Malsana's other tentacles wrapped around the pearly white gem, moving it fluidly from arm to arm. For a moment, it disappeared within her underbelly and my nerves rattled. Ink expelled from Malsana's siphons. Black stains covered my pearl when it reemerged from the dizzying array of moving tentacles.

"Be careful!" I shouted.

"Sorry! I'm just so excited."

"Give it back."

Malsana slouched as she delivered the pearl back to me. The moment it touched my tongue, my shells clamped shut.

"It's filthy," I chastised.

"I didn't leak ink on purpose," she replied, her brash tone matching mine. She showed no remorse, and her confident dismissal of my frustration forced me to pause and wonder if I was being too harsh. I did not wish to embarrass her.

I sighed. "It's okay. I can clean it."

"Excellent," she replied. "I'll be back tomorrow!"

Something deep inside me stirred; I didn't want her to come back.

I spent the night polishing my pearl and cursing to myself. Some of the stains wouldn't fully fade. My pearl was tarnished, sullied, and I was to blame. I had been more worried about keeping a friend than honoring my intuition. I could not make that mistake again—I needed to trust myself.

Malsana returned during my morning song the following day, somersaulting and whirling to the melody as she approached.

As I finished the final note, Malsana wrapped her tentacles around me and buried me in a hug. I squirmed, uncomfortable by her closeness—though I had many friends, none ever invaded my personal space uninvited.

"I'm sorry," she said.

Her apology shook me from my discomfort.

"For what?"

She let me go. "For getting ink on your pearl. I felt terrible."

"You didn't seem very apologetic yesterday."

"I was alone with my thoughts all night, and I felt awful. I hope you will trust me again."

"With my pearl?"

She nodded.

"I'd rather not."

My words were blunt.

Her reaction was harsh.

"You are a terrible friend," she spat.

"Why?"

"You were born blessed, and you won't even share a sliver of that privilege with your friends."

"I am kind, I am compassionate, I am patient. What more can I give?"

"You could stop being so stingy and share with the rest of us."

"I only have one pearl. It is my heart—I cannot give it away."

"But you could let me borrow it once in a while."

"Borrow?"

"Just for the night."

"But I need it," I argued.

"I have nightmares when I sleep alone."

"I don't see how my pearl would help with that."

"With your pearl, I wouldn't be alone."

I sat with this idea. She wasn't wrong. I cherished the comfort of my pearl's company. It was why I felt so reluctant to share.

Malsana sensed my contemplation.

She added, "I understand your hesitancy. Let me prove that you can trust me. I will hold your pearl here, in front of you, and I will not leak ink again."

I groaned—she was persistent. In order to make her stop badgering me, it seemed my only option was to oblige her request.

Before my shells were fully open, her tentacle swiped through and snatched my pearl. Secure in her suctioned grip, Malsana cradled my pearly heart, fixated on its comforting beauty. She kept it far from her siphons this time, honoring her promise.

After a few moments, she gave my pearl back without me having to ask. With a gentle release onto my tongue, she returned my pearl in the same condition as when it left.

"See," she said. "You can trust me."

"Maybe I can," I replied, attempting to silence the strange pull of unease in my gut.

I wanted to be her friend; I wanted to trust her.

Day in and day out, Malsana continued earning my trust. She visited every morning, held my pearl with care a few times each afternoon, and departed in the evening, content with the little I gave her. Throughout, we had great conversations about life below the sea, and she told me wild fantasy stories of worlds beyond this one. With time, I realized it wasn't all about my pearl—we had formed a true friendship.

My unease subsided as my trust flourished. I had nothing to fear, no reason to worry; the paranoia I once felt had been a waste of precious energy.

Just like I did with all my other marine friends, I began enjoying our friendship without doubt.

I lost track of the days.

When Malsana asked again to borrow my pearl for a night, the nerves lining my tiny body tightened. The discomfort I had forgotten returned.

"For a whole night?" I asked in response.

"Can we just try? I've shown that you can trust me," she pled.

She was right. For days or weeks—maybe even months—she had proven I had no reason to doubt her intentions.

"I suppose it can't hurt to try," I answered.

I opened my shells and let Malsana take my pearl.

She held it close.

"I will take good care of it," she promised.

"I trust you. Come back early with it, please. This will be the first night I've ever spent without it."

"Of course! I'll return at dawn."

Her black marble eyes blazed—I'd never before seen darkness burn.

She swam away, my pearl in tow, and I was left alone.

She did not return at dawn.

She did not return by dusk.

I spent the entire day pacing my coral garden, unable to think about anything else and terrified that I had misplaced my trust. Night arrived with no sight of Malsana.

I cried myself to sleep.

This became my routine—wait all day for Malsana to return, then sob myself into exhaustion when she did not come back.

Days passed in a blur.

I lost count.

It took a while to admit that I had been betrayed by someone I once called a friend, but when I finally did, the revelation sent me into a spiraling depression.

She wasn't coming back.

Along with my pearl, she had also stolen my ability to put faith in others and have trust in myself. My pearl was all I had; it was my heart. Without it, I was an empty shell.

My will to live stripped, my desire to fight numbed—she took a piece of me that I could never replace. The trust she betrayed created a void I could never fill.

I sealed my shells shut, prepared to never open again.

"Why?" I asked myself over and over again until the unanswerable question drove me mad.

I stopped listening to the dolphins' morning greetings. I ignored the sharks' tales, and I stopped asking for rides from the whales.

I wanted to be alone.

Darkness blanketed time.

I could not tell how many days passed—had I lost a few weeks or a few months? The all-consuming black veil was my new favorite sight.

Life became so stagnant, so empty, I sometimes wondered if I was still alive. My pounding thoughts and the pulsating heartbeat of the ocean created a deafening quiet.

I thought again of all I had lost, then recalled the strength it took to survive.

The memory of my lost pearl came into my mind and I felt a sudden surge of worth.

"I am me with you. I am me without you. I am all I need," I whispered to myself.

I repeated this mantra of worth over and over until the words were engrained into the underside of my shell so that even in darkness, I would remember to trust myself.

"I am me with you. I am me without you. I am all I need."

The darkness threatened to seep into my shell and consume me when I realized this darkness was my own creation. It came from me; I was its master.

I could lift myself and swim higher. I could relocate and find sunlight.

Only I could save me from myself.

My whisper turned into a shout as I repeated, "I am me with you. I am me without you. I am all I need."

I held tight to these words until the day a riptide tore me away. Caught in a dizzying tumble, I ricocheted to the other side of the sea.

Nothing made sense here.

Nothing felt right.

Somehow, in this new place, I felt emptier than before.

The small motto of trust and worth I had etched into the underside of my shell remained, but I no longer understood the meaning.

"I am me with you. I am me without you. I am all I need." I read the line aloud, but it stirred no emotion, no comfort.

They were just words.

I examined my new surroundings—my beautiful coral garden had been replaced by tall piles of rubble and bones.

A junkyard fit for a queen, I propelled myself to the top of the tallest trash pile and took my throne. I hummed a sad song, a simple melody dripping with sorrow.

I no longer trusted those around me.

I no longer trusted myself.

A note from the Fox

Those words of worth lost their meaning the day I ran away.

I had sprinkled a handful of worthiness into the Pocket of Trust before leaving, but it wasn't enough. It did not last.

Why, you might ask, did I leave?

Malsana came to me next.

After her escape from the Pocket of Fear and a quick visit to the Pocket of Trust, she visited me. Escorted by the Face of Chaos — you'll meet him soon — they arrived in the dark of night, invisible to all except me. Disguised as friends, they offered me kindness. They presented me with a token of comradery — a black marble.

I accepted.

They told me to swallow it.

Unaware of the repercussions, I obeyed.

I had caved to the monster's challenge.

I swallowed the black marble and everything changed. No more food, no more sustenance — all I craved were her black marble lies.

My thoughts became toxic, so I ran, abandoning my pocket and forsaking Jane.

I lived like this for years, oblivious to the cause of my deterioration.

But enough about me — I am not the only part of Jane's mind that was infected.

Slowly, one by one, Chaos snuck Malsana into the delicate pockets of the other Faces. They infected integral facets of Jane's identity, slowly stripping her sense of self.

The Face of Night did his best to wrangle the sickness before it touched the others, but he was no match for the potent monster.

These are all facts I have since come to realize.

Malsana's release from the Pocket of Fear was the beginning of Jane's spiral, and I regret to inform you that it only gets worse from here.

Have faith, though—there is beauty in the breakdown.
Wisdom blossoms in the aftermath of treacherous storms.

On the day of discovery, I knew not what Night fought, only that one of his black feathers was part of the garbage trail left in my foxhole.

As I lifted the long black feather, I saw his struggle.
Snout tickled by its vane, darkness consumed me.

Memento #3

When: The 13th - 16th Cycle
Where: Jane's mind—Lunar Spire, Northern Unknown
Who: The Face of Night

"You are perfect," I said to the girl inside the moon.

"In your grip, I can be nothing else," she replied.

"My love keeps you safe."

Luna wept silently. "Your love makes me no one at all."

I scoffed as I carried the massive moon across the sky, outraged by her ingratitude.

Without me, she'd never leave the Lunar Spire.

Without me, she'd have no one.

I was the Face of Night—my entire existence revolved around her, yet she spoke to me like I was her captor. Her misunderstanding was maddening.

Black feathered wings spread wide, I fulfilled my duty—absorbing the nighttime fears running rampant in the darkness and swallowing them whole to prevent tangible damage to the mind we called home.

I safely delivered Luna to the Solar Citadel where she could sink into the Southern Abyss and prepare for tomorrow's night. As I prepared to touch the portal that would return me to the Lunar Spire, a voice halted me.

"Night, wait."

I turned. The Face of Day stood on the opposite side of the tower, wings pearly white and spread wide. Her porcelain-coated flesh made her fragile, and though some of her movements were rigid and restricted, her facial expressions and joints moved fluidly.

"Yes?" I asked. We were equals in power—she carried the sun, I carried the moon—but our differences knew no bounds.

"I think you missed a nighttime fear."

"How dare you—" I began, but then she extended her hand, which gripped a sealed pouch. An unknown entity wriggled ferociously within.

"It fell from the sky," she explained, her forest-green eyes shimmering with concern. "I caught it before it landed in the village and infected the creatures of time."

"Did you touch it?" I asked, horrified.

"Only for a second."

I snatched the bag from her grip, reached my talon fingers into its depth, and seized the squirming fear. I tore it out of the bag and held it at eye level.

A worm with black marble eyes.

"Sickness in the mind," I concluded.

"Sickness?"

"It could manifest in countless ways: depression and anxiety disorders, eating disorders, substance abuse issues, addiction, schizophrenia, severe phobias, disassociation spells, psychosis, dysphoria, psychopathy—the list goes on." I swallowed the worm whole, choking it down as it passed through my shadowy figure. I examined Day. "I have to cleanse you."

"What do you mean?"

"You touched it—you are infected."

She scowled as I grabbed her perfect porcelain face and pulled her close. I kissed her fiercely, consuming every tiny trace of contamination.

When I let go, she stumbled backward, dizzy from the extraction.

"Was there a lot?" she asked.

"Enough to destroy you."

She nodded, tucking her luminescent white hair behind her ear. "Thanks. Just don't let it happen again."

"I'm sorry," I offered, but she waved her hand at me, shooing away my apology.

"Just do better."

She regained her composure and walked to the tiny illusionary sun that waited for her to carry it across the sky. As they ascended, the sun grew larger with each passing minute.

I was alone again.

The writhing sickness ricocheted inside my stomach—this was not my usual method of subduing the nighttime fears. Normally, they passed through me as I soared through the night, disintegrating into wisps of air that I delivered to the Face of Fear. But this one was different. It wasn't just a fear, but also a sickness. I had to physically digest it before it could be delivered—I was in for an agonizing day.

I pressed my hand against the moon etched into the golden wall, and the portal returned me to the Lunar Spire.

I was home.

Daylight meant freedom.

I had twelve hours to do as I pleased, but the sickening fear that had seen the light of day still rendered me immobile—the pain from its slow digestion was too intense. I wanted to use my free time to explore, to venture into the pockets beyond and acquire more perfect treasures for my collection. But I couldn't. I had to vanquish this fear before it grew too big; I had to make it go away.

I hobbled to my chest of treasures—my collection of perfect items I had found while exploring the various pockets around the sandclock. I wasn't supposed to take souvenirs—I wasn't supposed to leave the inner world at all—but I struggled to resist temptation. They were harmless, my treasures, and I kept them safe.

Seeing them now, my excruciating pain subsided. They gleamed in the sunlight, filling me with joy. Their perfection, their precision, their flawless existence set me at ease.

I lifted my favorite keepsake with a gentle touch—a dried sunflower blossom from the Pocket of Joy. It died before I took it home, but I had preserved its beauty with an embalming amber. Strange how something without life soothed me, but I found comfort in knowing it could never change. It would forever stay as it was: perfect.

I glanced past the crystalized flower resting in my hands to the assortment of treasures below. A teardrop in a vial from the Pocket of Sorrow. Untouched, I had caught it as it fell from the sky and bottled it before it ever hit the ground. I was the sole owner of this specific second of sorrow.

Red sand from the Pocket of Anger, corked in a stone phial to prevent the magmatic grains from destroying my home. Danger securely contained was not only perfection, but also exhilarating. I controlled its power.

Next to the red sand sat an empty and unhatched egg from the Pocket of Fear. Whatever monster had laid this atrocity gave birth to death, and I found its uncracked delivery intrinsically impressive.

The pain from the marble-eyed worm twisting through my insides returned to the forefront of my attention.

I placed my mummified sunflower back into the chest and collapsed to the ground as my body battled the sickness. How had I let this happen? How had I been so careless?

I was built to be a magnet for our Host's fears, but this one had managed to avert my pull.

How?

Why?

Our world was relatively new, and our Host was still young—I sensed something was changing, something bigger than we had ever faced before.

The day passed, and by the time Luna reemerged from the Southern Abyss, I had completely digested the sickness. I reached into my stomach to retrieve the fear, intrigued to see what form it had taken. Talons navigating the pit of my gut, I located the materialized fear—two black marbles. Yanked from my gut, I held them firmly in my grip.

I would deliver them to the Face of Fear when I flew over his throne later that night.

Luna arrived as a tiny version of herself, small enough to hold in my hands. I cradled my beloved moon and lifted into the sky. As we ascended, she grew bigger, and I carried the massive, glowing orb across the northern sky.

The usual fears came and went: being alone, the dark, imaginary monsters. Simple, manageable fears. Though this night felt normal, I remained on alert. My ears were perked for odd noises and I focused on locating anything abnormal. Something ominous lurked in the unknown that I could not ignore. I could not yet define the change, but I was prepared to battle it when it came.

Below me, the other Faces sat on their thrones, overseeing their floating pocket-worlds that existed harmoniously.

The first Faces to appear in the mind of this Host after Day, Time, and myself were Fear, Joy, Sorrow, Anger, and Trust. They were tiny at first. Their pockets were vibrant, but infantile. For a while, I often felt quite alone with just the Face of Time and the Face of Day, but as time passed, the other Faces grew, and new ones emerged.

The Face of Worthiness arrived during our eighth year. Her brilliant glow illuminated the darkness of the Northern Unknown. Confident and poised, she was a strong force of assuredness. I appreciated her arrival and solid presence. Her steadfast composure kept our Host's value high.

I'm not sure which year the Face of Awareness arrived, but she lived in the Southern Abyss where she caught discarded mementos and processed them before letting them go. Though I couldn't see her from this side of the sand clock, her presence here proved critical as our Host grew and began collecting more experiences in the outside world. Some memories were irrelevant to the Host's overall existence and were forgotten quickly, but the hurtful, confusing, and embarrassing memories required a wise eye for further development.

Mementos within the inner world dropped into the memory receptacle at the Tower of Time, where the Face of Time transferred them into the receptacle's outbox, which dropped them into the Southern Abyss. Mementos from the pockets were discarded in various ways, but they all found their way into Time's delivery box, where he transferred them down to Awareness.

But these were mementos—not fears.

My question remained unanswered.

Where were these new evasive fears coming from?

They must have snuck in from the outside world and averted my capture because, surely, none of the Faces within the inner world would summon such terrors from the Pocket of Fear, would they?

I watched them all. The Faces of Fear, Joy, Sorrow, Anger, Trust, and Worthiness fluctuated in size and power, often dancing with one another to keep each other in check. Joy and Sorrow led this pack, taking turns overseeing our Host's overall health.

Anger was often quiet—he never made much noise and seemed happy to disappear amid the bustling Faces.

Fear was also quiet, but he always paid attention. His presence loomed, his focus calculated, and the wheels in his brain always spinning. When needed, he spoke loudly, and now I wondered if he could be trusted.

I studied Fear—the only Face with direct access to the fears inside his pocket—and wondered if he'd commit such a crime.

The thrones of the four original Faces sat along the edge of the circular village, and his was positioned closest to the Lunar Spire. Wiry lashes outlined the Face of Fear's foggy eyes, and a crown of horns grew circularly from his skull. His shadow stood behind him as a guard and held the only item the Face of Fear cherished: an evergreen branch with a purple honey blossom. He couldn't touch it himself, the living flower would perish, so his shadow held it for him.

"I have a new fear for you," I shouted down.

The Face of Fear's olive-green eyes lifted slowly. He outstretched his hand and I dropped the marbles. Like a moth to the flame, they plummeted into his frozen grip.

This completed my task. He would imprison this black marble monster in his pocket, and I could finish out the night feeling lighter than before.

Luna wept the entire trip.

As we finished our journey, I placed her down gently, desensitized to her ceaseless melancholy.

"I hope you are happier tomorrow," I offered as I dropped her into the Solar Citadel.

"This is my burden—one day, I will be free," she confessed as she disappeared.

I released a heavy sigh. The girl inside the moon was beautiful, untouchable, pristine; I was unsure how a perfect being could be so sad.

I turned to the Face of Day, who waited patiently for the sun to arrive. She wore a blushing glow, one I was used to seeing, as she often spent her nights in the various pockets, falling in love with the creatures who lived there.

"Where did you go last night?" I inquired.

"Into the Pocket of Sorrow. It has evolved into the loveliest world."

"Your love for pitiful creatures will always baffle me."

Day shrugged. "We have different perceptions of beauty."

My thoughts returned to her fragile perfection and how I almost ruined her.

"How do you feel?" I asked, afraid that an integral part of the Host's identity might be tainted because of me.

"I feel great. I think you caught them all last night," she said with a wink.

"Our world is perfect, and I intend to keep it that way."

"Nothing is perfect," she corrected me.

"You are. Luna is. But I sense something is changing."

"Change can be good."

"Not if it ruins perfection."

"I think she is growing," Day revealed. "Our Host—Jane—I think she is experiencing new things. I feel new pockets forming."

"Don't use her name," I barked.

"Why not?"

"It's better that she feels far away."

Day huffed.

I added, "Do you think new Faces will arrive?"

"With new pockets comes new Faces."

"That fear you caught," I said with a shiver, recalling its strength. "It was unlike any of the others. It was potent, powerful, and poisonous."

"We have to let her grow," Day advised. "And I will fight to wear a smile as she does so."

"If you smile, so will she," I muttered, recalling our core purpose.

"And if you are brave, bravery will see her through."

"I just want to save her before she breaks."

Day shook her head and gently cradled the tiny sun. "Some of the most beautiful things in life are broken."

"Have you gone mad?"

She continued, "Their beauty resides in their fight to survive."

"You've lost your mind," I confirmed. "I'll stop this unwanted evolution for the both of us."

"Be careful, or you might be the reason she breaks."

I ignored her warning.

On an ordinary day nearing the end of our thirteenth year, I noticed that the Face of Worthiness was not on her throne.

I soared to the Ring of Thrones.

"Where did she go?" I asked the Face of Trust, who was once great friends with Worthiness.

"I'm not sure. She's been visiting her pocket a lot," Trust informed me, her sea-green gaze forlorn as she stared out into the nothingness of the Unknown.

"Has she said why? Do you think she's there?" I groaned. "We need her *here*. New fears are emerging and she needs to be a solid presence for the Host."

"I don't know." Trust shook her head. The sea glass dangling from her seashell crown tinkled softly. "She left soon after sprinkling a bit of worth into my pocket." She paused, gaze lowering. "But all the worth she gave vanished with her. My pocket hasn't been the same since."

"Why would she forsake her purpose here?"

"Something from the outside world must be affecting her," Trust rationalized, fidgeting with the tangled knots in her long and perpetually wet auburn hair.

I groaned again. "Alert me when she returns. I need to talk to her."

She nodded. "I will."

I flew away, annoyed that I'd once again need to resolve issues that were not my own.

A week passed.

The Face of Worthiness had not yet returned.

"No sign of her?" I called down to Trust during my nightly trip across the sky.

The Face of Trust shook her head.

A month passed.

It was the start of our fourteenth year and the Face of Worthiness was still missing.

I did not bother asking Trust, as she knew no more than me. Instead, I focused on locating the cause. I spent my spare time interrogating the remaining Faces, searching for a reason. Attempting to understand why such an important Face would abandon her post.

No one could help.

I dove into her pocket to investigate for myself.

The ocean was calm, the colors were bright; everything seemed alright. A soft melancholic melody echoed each time a surface bubble popped. I went to the sound and found a singing clam right below the water's surface.

I did not intend to find a new treasure for my collection, but this little singing clam with its pristine white shells was perfect.

I needed to make it mine.

This was my most risky acquisition because something lived inside. As I retrieved the clam, it stopped singing through its closed shells. I hid it in my pocket and flew out of the Pocket of Trust, careful not to let the other Faces see my newest souvenir as I flew home to the Lunar Spire.

The little clam stayed shut all day.

I let her be; I did not try to pry her shells open—I liked her just the way she was.

At dusk, right before I had to carry the moon across the sky, the tiny being inside the clam sang to herself through closed shells.

Her voice was so sweet.

She mumbled a whimsical tune.

"Hello, there," I whispered, holding the little clam close to my lips.

Her singing stopped.

"I will always keep you safe," I promised. "You are perfect, and I will keep you that way. You can trust me."

She whimpered, so I placed her back into her glass bowl of salt water.

A year passed.

The Face of Worthiness was officially gone.

I had lost this battle.

Discontent with my failure, I found solace in my little clam. Her calming songs soothed my angered spirit and reminded me to stay focused on my task: catching every nighttime fear.

Halfway through our fifteenth cycle, a new pocket formed. The arrival of the Face of Anxiety forced me to refocus my energy. She arrived in a screeching whirlwind, casting a glittering cloud of doubt over everything. Beautiful in complexity, suffocating in actuality. We all worked extra hard to keep her dramatic reach from escaping her pocket, which was an unnavigable mess of shimmering dust and nets. She never sat still—she flittered nonstop around her pocket, continually weaving her dazzling nest of discord.

As our sixteenth cycle approached, I took stock of our mind's health.

Everyone performed their jobs—I carried the moon, Day carried the sun, and Time counted the seconds, minutes, and hours in an orderly fashion.

Still, Worthiness was missing, and her absence cast an ever-growing melancholy over everything. A sense of futility had washed over the sandclock and infected each pocket. I needed to know why she had left. I needed to understand how a perfectly confident creature became defective.

With the arrival of new unruly Faces, too much was at stake to let another day pass without relocating our sense of worth.

A note from the Fox

I imagine you have questions.

I would, too.

It's a strange concept to think that so many characters and stories can exist in one mind, but the human brain is a miraculous place, and every person has boundless worlds within them, each shaping their unique identity.

You have worlds within you, too.

Though your inner world differs from Jane's, we all share a few similarities: the core Faces—Day, Night, and Time. Even then, these Faces manifest differently in each of us, but they are always there.

I will show you how these core Faces developed within Jane Doe.

I will also show you how one monster—one ailment—tore them apart.

But first, a little about them:

Night represents who a person is when no one else is around—this is how Night works for every mortal. In my Host, Night possesses a deep desire for control, an infatuation with the illusion of perfection. Through him, Jane Doe processes her darkest fears, her most dangerous thoughts. If he loses courage, so does she.

Day represents how a person presents themself to the world—again, this is how Day works for every mortal. In Jane, Day embodies and embraces the sun she loves so dearly. A beaming ray of light so bright, she is a source of joy to all those who know her.

That was, until Malsana arrived and infected every facet of Jane's identity.

You already know how she poisoned my thoughts.

Well, she did the same to Day.

The subtle change went unnoticed by most at first. Only Night seemed concerned by the shifting tides within our Host's mind.

I was no longer there to help, and Night would surely argue that my absence amplified our struggle.

I would argue that he was correct.

But that is neither here nor there—I was absent, and the world kept spinning without me. In fact, none of this was known to me until the day of discovery during our 24th year.

On the day of discovery, years after Malsana's arrival, I found the burned-out fuse I had discarded when I first escaped into my foxhole.

Though I did not understand at the time, the memento belonged to me. I did not recognize it; I had blocked those memories from my mind.

Charred fuse in my paw, a strange sense of familiarity washed over me, and I was taken to a foreign place that felt like home.

Memento #4

When: The 16th Cycle
Where: Jane's mind—Pocket of Worthiness
Who: Jane Doe without worth

There were many ways to disappear.

I chose the road lined with darkness.

In a world so bright, so fluorescent and clear, the only place to hide was among the shadows. I spent years thinking I was too good to fade, too strong to flinch beneath the surging currents of excellence. I was as bright as the rest. I was worthy of the confidence I carried.

But I was wrong.

It was all a lie.

I was no better than the weakest among us.

Like them, I was a false example of perfection.

The sickness arrived in waves. It started small and eventually grew to a size I could no longer contain.

Was I in the middle of this madness or nearing the end?

There was no way to tell. I could only hang on and hope to outlast the worst of myself.

No one around me saw my fight, and the few who did were too embarrassed to help. Any mention of my deterioration, any awkward attempts to point out how I was losing my glow, sent me into a fit of rage. I'd scream until my throat bled, I'd fight without surrender, I'd break everything around me—I'd rather lose everyone than acknowledge that I needed help.

To keep me close, those who loved me most stopped trying to help.

The shadows became my greatest friends.

Only the moonlight knew my secrets.

Another day, another failed attempt to heal.

I swallowed the black marble pills that soothed my pain.

"Jane," my mother shouted from the kitchen. "Come eat!"

Prepared to fake a smile, I stared at myself in the mirror. The neon green rings around my lavender eyes had lost their luster, and the muscles in my glass face had grown stiff. I massaged the corners of my lips until my smile stretched with ease.

"Your food is getting cold," my mother shouted.

I raced down the stairs and took a seat next to my father. Nose buried in the *Neonite Chronicles,* he did not notice my arrival.

Hunched over my bowl of electrons, I dug in. One hand holding the spoon and the other knuckle-deep in the lightning converter, a steady stream of volts traveled through my fingers, up my arm, and into my chest, spreading throughout my body and igniting my glow. I had woken up feeling dim—this little boost reinvigorated my lavender light and cleared the comfortable fog I so enjoyed.

"Have you seen your cousin Liana?" my mother asked as she barged into the kitchen.

"No, not recently. Why?" I took another bite of electrons.

"She has changed."

"What do you mean?" I asked.

"Her glow has faded."

"We can't all be perfect," I replied.

"It's not about being perfect. It's about survival. You managed to overcome a spell of darkness. Perhaps you can talk to her."

"Not all darkness is created the same."

"Still, your ability to overcome might inspire her to do the same."

I took another bite, unwilling to admit I was far from fixed.

My mother touched my long, flowing lavender hair and gazed at me intently. "Can you at least try?"

"I will," I promised. She kissed my forehead and then left the room.

I was alone in the kitchen again with only my father, who silently hid behind the illuminated chronicle. The letters glowed in every hue, captivating his full attention.

I thought of my cousin.

There were many ways to lose one's glow — a fuse could break, be misplaced, or poorly cared for — but the worst way, by far, was to have it stolen by a snatcher. Being in high demand on the black market, functional fuses were a high-ticket item, and the snatchers relentlessly acquired such purity.

"Do you think it was a snatcher?" I asked my father.

My voice startled him out of his daze.

"Excuse me?"

"Liana's fading glow … do you think a snatcher got to her?"

He gasped. "What horrors leave your lips? The mere suggestion is offensive."

"It *is* a possibility, though."

He clicked his tongue and returned to the news. He preferred distant troubles over those plaguing his home.

I had to visit my cousin, if for no other reason than to remind her she wasn't alone.

After eating the rest of my breakfast, I ran out to the garage. I mounted my batt-bike, fastened my helmet, and kicked into gear. The expansive wireways of Neonite were a maze to navigate, but I knew the way. I latched onto route Ne10 and used the terrestrial energy to zip forward.

A blast of lightning had created this world, and that everlasting bolt of fire existed at Neonite's core to this day. It released endless surges of energy, which we consumed with every breath. I absorbed that electricity now, pushing my fuse to its limits to travel faster.

When I arrived at Liana's home, hers was the only dark house on the street.

I entered cautiously, afraid I might walk into a nightmare. Upon entering the darkness, I did not feel fear—I felt sorrow.

Liana sat in a dark, quiet room, staring blankly at the wall.

"Cousin," I said in greeting, announcing my arrival. "I hope you don't mind that I let myself in."

It took her a moment to register my words. When she finally turned to look at me, she moved slowly. Her empty expression never shifted.

"Hey, Jane," she replied, her energy low.

We, as a species, were fragile. We were made of glass and noble gas—vacuum tubes encased our bodies, and the charge of our world helped us glow. I was made of argon, so I emitted lavender light, but the color possibilities among my people were endless. Some glowed blue, others green. There were gold, pink, and orange people, too. Our noble gas determined our color, as did the tint of our glass casings. Inside our bodies, we each possessed a fuse that kept us safe from unexpected electricity surges. Without the fuse, it was tough to maintain a steady glow—you could burn too bright or not at all. The fuse determined our worth.

"Was it a snatcher?" I asked cautiously.

She shook her head. "Just the normal wear and tear of being alive."

"Well, that's a relief. Can't do much about a stolen fuse."

"How about a broken spirit?" she asked.

I looked down at my hands. "I'm still here, and I've been broken for years."

"You're good at faking it."

"Not at first," I said, struggling to ignore the harsh thudding in my chest. "Surely, you remember."

"Yeah, I was young, but I recall. How'd you heal?"

"I haven't healed. I've just learned how to cope."

I caught myself picking at my fingernails as I spoke and immediately shoved them into my jacket pockets.

"Learning to cope sounds exhausting," Liana replied.

"It is, but it's better than the alternative."

"What's that?"

"A constant barrage of people asking if you're okay."

"It's horrible. My parents are so worried they won't leave me alone."

"Where are they now?" I asked.

"Working. I don't have class today, so I'm home alone. A blessing and a curse—no one to bug me, but only my deteriorating thoughts to keep me company."

"Is there something specific that's been bothering you?"

"Yes and no. I feel like I don't belong here."

"Where?"

"Inside my own body."

I grimaced—this was exactly how I felt, too. "I understand."

"Please teach me how to cope," she begged.

I thought of the little black pills in my pocket.

"There are many ways to disappear," I began.

"Disappear?"

I nodded. "To become out of reach from your pain. When you run, when you hide, the suffering cannot find you."

"But it's inside my mind," she argued. "How can I possibly outrun that which lives inside of me?"

"By changing the landscape of your mind."

"How, though?"

I reached into my pocket—the pills were smooth against my fingertips.

My younger cousin looked up at me, her gaze pleading.

She wasn't ready for a solution like this.

She was too young.

"Distractions," I said. "You need to find a new vice to consume you."

She slouched over, displeased with my answer.

"That sounds like work."

"There are no easy fixes," I lied, then considered it might actually be the truth—my method of coping surely hadn't repaired my mental state. In fact, it was making my condition worse.

The pills rolled between my fingers, coaxing me to swallow their foggy bliss.

Maybe it was time to follow my own advice.

"I'll try," Liana conceded.

"That's all anyone can ask of you."

I pulled her in for a hug, lifting my hand out of my pocket.

The pills tugged at me to return.

Liana burrowed into my embrace—I wouldn't ruin her, too. These bad habits were mine to keep.

I left the house, but before departing, I peered through the window at Liana, checking to see if my advice had helped.

She sat on the couch, staring at the wall, orange glow flickering in the darkness. She was trying to make herself feel better, but struggling.

"At least she is trying," I said to myself.

I reached into my coat pocket and sifted through the loose pills. Black marble pill in hand, I swallowed my disquiet, my displeasure, my discomfort. After a quick surrender to the chemicals, my mind was consumed by shadows.

Embraced by my comfortable fog, I hopped onto my batt-bike and hit the wireway. Ne10 was long and liberating. The electrically charged air lashed my face, forcing me to feel through the steadfast haze encasing my mind.

Like fuzzy orbs of light, others zipped past me, passing in blurs of neon color. Fuchsia, cyan, violet, and turquoise rocketed down the wireway on their batt-bikes or in their batt-cars, heading toward unknown destinations. I imagined their purpose, assuming they each had great meaning in life: families to love, friends to visit, careers to pursue. I was somewhere in between. I had a family, I had friends, but my purpose for living was lost. It eluded me, and I lived each day with no direction.

I supposed graduating from Elettrica Academy was my most pressing goal. I showed up to class, but I was never truly present. I struggled to see the point, to understand my end destination. As I was on this wireway, I was in my schooling—on a fast track to a nameless fate, and I wanted off the ride.

I didn't know where I was heading now. The thought of returning home felt suffocating—I'd be interrogated and asked questions I did not have the energy to answer. I could call a friend, but I hated to bother them. I was on a tear and my company would be depressing.

My only option was the freedom of the road.

I'd keep driving until I outraced my demons.

I drove as far as I could, aimlessly zipping up and down the wireway until I became too tired to carry on. Enough time wasted, the road had emptied of other drivers and the sky had turned black. I was the brightest light for miles.

The city of Neonite glowed in the distance, dimmed as it always was after hours. I zoomed toward the metropolis, prepared to surrender for the night, when my bike began to sputter.

The charge tank was nearly empty.

Cursing under my breath, I searched for a nearby charge station. I sputtered past countless proton markets and electron dealerships before locating a spot to charge my bike. It was a seedy part of town, but it would suffice. I pulled up to the electric vestibule, plugged in my bike, and waited. It would take at least fifteen minutes to get enough of a charge to make it home.

I swallowed another black pill.

"When did you lose your way?" a voice shouted from the darkness.

I looked at the source and discovered a man staring at me from the shadows.

"Excuse me?"

"What was the catalyst?"

The fog in my mind thickened, attempting to protect me from this foreign assault.

"I don't understand. Are you a snatcher?" I trembled, terrified.

He stepped out of the darkness, revealing his full form. Giant black falcon wings adorned his chiseled body made of flesh and shadow. Partially translucent, I could almost see through him.

"What are you?" I asked with a gasp, realizing my former assumption was wildly incorrect. Was my altered mind playing tricks on me? Had I taken too many pills?

His dark green eyes bore into me.

"I am the Face of Night, and I am here to save you."

"From what?"

"Yourself."

I scoffed. "I'm fine as I am, thank you very much."

"You are wretchedly misguided. Why don't you love yourself?"

"I love myself."

"If you did, you wouldn't need chemicals to feel whole."

I was mortified.

"Go away," I demanded.

"I know all your secrets. I catch them as you sleep each night."

"Stop." The charging meter still churned—I did not have enough power to get away.

"Only one secret eludes me, and that is the cause of this catastrophic spiral."

"It's just easier to cope when I cannot feel."

He shook his head. Shadows of the night danced around his pointedly carved facial features.

"Where did your worth go?" he asked.

"I don't know," I sobbed.

His expression tightened. "Don't worry. I will find her."

He rocketed into the sky, wings pounding the electric air, and disappeared into the night.

I was alone again. My faint lavender glow was the brightest light around.

Panicked, I paced as my bike refueled with electricity.

My worth? Why did he wish to know such a thing? And why did it matter so much to him? Pained, for he had awoken a part of me I had forsaken.

Was it a lack of self-love that got me here?

The pills weighed heavily in my pocket.

One more might be too many. Still, they beckoned me to play.

A risky gamble—to feel everything or nothing.

My eyes glistened with remorse.

I chose nothing.

Pill popped, I unplugged my bike and raced into the night. Dizzy from the overstimulation, heaving from the chemicals. I crashed my bike in the yard of my parents' ultra-violet house.

I wasn't sure how I got there, but I was home.

I stumbled inside, desperate to hide, and successfully made it into my room without being noticed.

One more pill to ensure a victorious escape.

There were many ways to disappear.

I chose the road lined with darkness.

A note from the Fox

I didn't know it at the time, but that Pocket, that place, was the home I had forsaken.

Like me—because of me—Jane only craved Malsana's black marble lies.

There are few words to describe the disappointment I felt after fully comprehending the extent of my crime, but I suppose saying that I was crushed would suffice.

My absence had caused the loss of Jane's self-worth.

On that day of discovery, I was forced to choose: ignore or accept.

Though I did not understand my involvement quite yet or how these mementos related to me, the gradual return of my awareness forced me to carry on.

I had to do better.

I could not continue hiding.

The neon lights of my forsaken pocket lingered in my vision, outlining the dark tunnel I navigated.

Determined to learn what happened next, I gently touched the black feather propped behind my ear and returned to the Lunar Spire.

The Face of Night would show me the way.

Revisiting Memento #3

When: The 16ᵗʰ – 17ᵗʰ Cycle
Where: Jane's mind—Lunar Spire, Northern Unknown
Who: The Face of Night

I left the pocket of neon lights more agitated than before.

The Face of Worthiness was not there.

Not only was she not there, but her absence had vanquished all sense of worth among the inhabitants.

The Host lived within that pocket—I spoke to her while I was there and found she was affected, too.

I had made no progress.

My furious gaze shifted to the empty throne tangled with overgrown foxglove vines. The blossoms, once vibrant with a neon glow, were now colorless.

Worthiness was nowhere to be found.

Our perfect existence threatened, my fury roared.

The Face of Day flew overhead, casting light on the village of time.

I aimed my flight toward the Face of Fear.

"No," he boomed, voice echoing as I approached.

"Tell me what is happening out there," I demanded. While I controlled certain aspects of the mind's inner workings, I could only see glimpses of the outside world during the night.

"Everything is fine," he droned. Black ink smeared the bottom half of his stark white face.

"The Face of Worthiness is still missing, and these nighttime terrors grow stronger every year."

"With time comes strength. You are no longer dealing with infantile fears."

"Make them stop."

"That's not how this works."

"You are the Face of Fear! It's the one thing you *can* control."

He shook his head. "I *am* the fear. I embody every single fear our Host feels. But I do not give them life, nor can I cease their existence."

"Useless."

"You think perfection is the goal, but the true marker of success is growth."

"I cannot do my job if you allow hostile, intelligent fears—or sickness disguised as fear—into the sandclock."

"I will not thwart our growth." He shrugged, disinterested. "Do better."

Furious and seething, I pounded my wings against the daytime air and hovered in place, debating how to get what I wanted from this insolent Face.

"If you *are* the fears, then at least tell me what is coming. Help me prepare."

He frowned, a crooked scowl on his decaying face. "Perhaps you ought to start by delivering what belongs to me."

"What?"

"The fear inside your gut. I can see it fighting for life within your shadow."

I looked at my stomach. The sickness I thought I had consumed and regurgitated years ago still glowed faintly.

"How?" I asked, outraged as I dug my talons into my gut. Shadowy flesh ripped open, I extracted the sickness.

The wisp of charcoal dust turned to a black marble in my grip.

"Has it been inside me all this time?" I asked as I tossed the marble to the Face of Fear. It landed in his palm.

89

"It is a potent ailment."

I thought of the Face of Worthiness.

"Have I unknowingly infected everyone here?"

"Possibly. It appears you've extracted all of it from yourself now, though."

"Where did it come from?" I asked.

"That is the wrong question," he replied.

"Then, why?"

"The outside world is cruel. Our Host has known too much, too young, too soon." His foggy eyes showed sympathy. "This breakdown was inevitable."

"No, she cannot break," I objected. "Can't the Face of Joy intervene?"

"She has tried many times. Everything that once brought joy is now tarnished by sorrow."

"Then tell the Face of Sorrow to back off."

"He did not cause her sorrow—the universe delivered it to her. Like me, the Face of Sorrow only embodies the emotion. We can sway it, perhaps, but we cannot control it."

"What do I need to do?"

"Prepare for shutdown."

"Shutdown?"

"New Faces will emerge, likely nefarious in nature. You must continue functioning as normal, as must the Face of Time and the Face of Day. No matter the changes or developments to come, the three of you control her ultimate fate."

Fear looked away, his murky gaze staring at his faraway pocket of terror in the distance.

I would have to face the unknown alone.

I flew to my tower room of the Lunar Spire and rushed to my chest of treasures, opting for the little clam over the mummified sunflower.

"Talk to me," I begged. "I need a friend."

The little clam stayed quiet.

"Will you ever open up to me?" I asked.

Though her shells remained closed, I received my first reply.

"You wouldn't like me." Her tiny, meek words came out as a melody.

My expression tightened. "Let me take your fear, like I do all the others."

The little clam quieted again.

I surrendered.

"I will wait until you are ready."

I returned her to her saltwater bowl, knowing I would have to navigate the forthcoming storm alone.

The day passed quickly and Luna was once again in my grip. I tried to explain the coming change, but she wouldn't listen. She wept the whole night, refusing to be a friend when I needed one most.

At the Solar Citadel, I let her go and she disappeared into the Southern Abyss.

The Face of Day's eyebrows pinched with concern. "You are paler than usual."

"Change is coming," I warned.

"I feel it too," she confessed. "I plan to greet it with a smile."

"I spoke to the Face of Fear; this change will test our strength."

"I am ready," she insisted before rocketing into the sky with the sun.

Maybe I was wrong to worry—no one else seemed concerned.

I soared to the Tower of Time to address the Face of Time, but as usual, he was locked away—inaccessible, as Father Time had designed.

I flew as close as I could to the glass tower, shouting and pounding my wings dramatically, but nothing could break the glass soldier's focus. He was good at his job—he never let time glitch.

In all our years together, I never once spoke to him. I often wondered if he even knew why he kept time or for whom. But he worked without fail and with perfect precision—he never faltered, and I respected him for that.

He, too, could not help me face the battle to come.

Why did change scare me? Why did the threat of something new send my nerves to war?

Each night I carried Luna across the northern sky I felt the presence of fear intensify. It amplified ever so slightly—its growth so minor most would not notice.

But I did, and the fears I caught grew nastier each night.

They fought me, ripping at my shadowy insides, tearing at the woven net in my gut. They gnawed my translucent webbing, making my job agonizing.

They wanted to live freely outside the Pocket of Fear, but I battled them night after night until the red dawn arrived and changed everything.

In our seventeenth year, Chaos arrived with a bang. Red smoke and deafening alarms startled us all. Within the explosion was a shadow creature with beaming red eyes.

"I am Mr. Darclove," he announced as I delivered Luna safely to the Solar Citadel. "I am the Face of Chaos."

I looked at Day, who was lifting the sun into the sky.

"Welcome," she shouted down to the Face of Chaos. "I hope you come in peace."

Mr. Darclove smirked. "We are family, are we not?"

I launched myself into the morning sky, unable to remain quiet.

"Family is a strong word," I answered.

Mr. Darclove turned his attention to me.

"But we share so much," he replied, his tone sinister. "I see myself in both of you."

"Impossible. We are constants, while you could very well be temporary."

"I'm not going anywhere," he stated calmly, claiming the spiked ivory throne that materialized for him. A void swirled in the distance, out in the ether among the other pockets. It churned and twisted near the Pocket of Time, swallowing up the existing pocket and replacing it with chaos.

Mr. Darclove smiled as his chaotic roots secured to our Host.

"You cannot seize a pocket that is not your own," I argued.

"Father Time gave me permission."

"I don't believe you."

"It does not matter what you believe," Mr. Darclove replied.

My gaze turned to the Tower of Time—the glass soldier did not seem to notice that his home pocket had been seized—then back to the newly formed Pocket of Chaos, which hovered between fear and anger. I then turned to the sun and saw that Day had shimmering flecks of red circling her body.

"What did you do to her?" I demanded of Mr. Darclove.

"It wasn't me. It was you," he replied. "You couldn't catch everything I sent your way."

Soaring closer to this new, nefarious Face, I noticed a cricket sitting on his shoulder. It had black marble eyes.

"What is that?" I growled, pointing at the insect.

"This is my little friend. Her name is Malsana. Isn't she lovely?"

"She is a monster. She belongs in the Pocket of Fear."

"She is mine now."

"When did you free her? How did you get her past the Face of Fear?"

"I have been here longer than you realize. Invisibly observing and strategizing."

"And infiltrating?"

He smiled. "It's all part of the greater plan."

"Whose plan? Yours?"

"I would not be here if our Host did not welcome me."

He was right.

The former Pocket of Time was now enveloped by an ominous storm cloud.

"What will you call it?" I asked.

He sat with my question for a moment.

"The Fringe."

A note from the Fox

Chaos had finally shown his Face.

I told you—things would worsen before they improved.

At this point in my discovery, Mr. Darclove's hold over us was strong—he had orchestrated Malsana's infiltration within every pocket before he revealed himself. Her roots dug deep into Jane's mind. The sickness Malsana inflicted initially manifested in the outer world as disordered eating, and inevitably grew into other mental health struggles.

The Faces only saw glimpses of the damage on the outside, for the mess that unraveled within was all-consuming.

I was gone for too long.

On the day of discovery, when I relived the torment we had endured through the mementos, I noticed that everything was presented in a shroud of chaos, confusion, and denial.

It's hard to recognize and remedy the destruction while you're living in it, but my God, did Jane try.

Through the Face of Night, she battled to hang on to her understanding of wrong versus right, but with so many parts of herself infected by Malsana, the thin line separating reality from her delusions often blurred.

She withered away, her only defense a strong shield of denial.

Our strength morphed into stubbornness as we lost control, and in order to regain control, we had to shift our conviction to match Malsana's. We had no power when we fought her, so we played along. We surrendered our mind, body, and spirit to the monster.

As I'm sure you've already gathered, that was a losing strategy.

The more Jane succumbed to the sickness, the further she spiraled, and without warning, Malsana's whims enslaved her.

It sabotaged everything, including her relationships in the outside world.

The loss that echoed loudest existed within the next memento I found: a rustleweed.
Its sharp thorns pricked my paw as I lifted it to my snout and sniffed—evergreen and honey.
The potent aroma infiltrated my consciousness, and before I could drop the invasive weed, my mind drifted to a land of shadows.

Memento #5

When: The 13ᵗʰ Cycle
Where: Jane's mind—Pocket of Chaos, formerly the Pocket of
Time
Who: Jane Doe within the Pocket of Chaos

I placed my hand over my chest.

Gone.

He took my heart when he left.

Panicked, I sat up in the black of night, searching for his hand, but I was rendered blind—I could not see through my own darkness; I was lost amid this nightmare.

Darkness consumed my body.

I felt my way to the light, clawing at the sheets that still smelled like our love: evergreen and honey. When I reached the end of the bed, the scent was replaced by cedar sheetrock.

I flipped the switch and light flooded my bedroom.

The bed was empty.

He was truly gone.

I looked down at my chest. A hole gaped where my heart used to be. A single heave and my knees buckled. On the floor, I wept.

He had left without saying goodbye.

The walls tightened around me, creating a prison out of my home. I tore through the hall, dizzy from sorrow as I felt my way toward the washroom. My hands kept me balanced as I ricocheted back and forth, stumbling like a wounded animal toward reprieve. A trail of darkness streaked from my fingertips, smearing my heartache along the walls.

I was disappearing—my figure was fading, my shadow body dissipating, and I was becoming no one.

Hurling what was left of me into the bathroom, I turned on the light and stared into the mirror.

Made of vapor and dust from the dark side of the moon, I looked the same—a shadow figure like I had always been, but now my green eyes glowed red. I blinked rapidly, hoping to clear my bereaved rage, but it would not fade. I was thoroughly changed.

I now saw the world in red.

A hole lined in smoldering crimson sat in the middle of my chest—a scar of betrayal. Forever a reminder that I would never be the same.

One breath. Two. My dirty hands gripped the sink, holding me upright while I tried to think. Blurry from the horror, dizzy from the pain.

Three breaths. Four. My red eyes lifted, glaring at my reflection. I no longer recognized myself.

Jane Doe was gone.

I had become a monster with no name. My gaze lowered to my hands, gripping the sides of the sink.

I'm still here with you.

I looked up to find Malsana staring back at me in the mirror. Her black marble eyes glimmered with empathy as she scanned the hole in my chest.

He didn't deserve you.

"How could he do this to me?"

He was jealous that you loved me more.

"I loved you both."

He wanted you to choose.

My breathing grew heavy as my anger intensified. "I choose you."

He knew you would choose me over him.

"Doesn't justify him stealing my heart when he left." I took a step back and gasped. My disappearing shadow looked fuller than ever. "When did I get so big?"

You have gotten a little hefty, haven't you?

"I am disgusting."

Nothing a little restriction can't solve. I will help you.

"I don't know what I would do without you."

I stepped away from the mirror, leaving Malsana but hanging on to her words of support. She was a true friend, my only friend. She'd never betray me.

The burning in my chest remained, matched closely by the subtle sting in my reddened eyes. I existed in agony, carrying on despite my rapid transformation.

The morning gray arrived, deepening the damage. My shadowy neighbors' piercing green eyes stared unforgivingly, judging my transformation. No one asked why or how. No one asked if I was okay. They simply cast their disapproval my way, disinterested in understanding my change.

Did I sit at the root of my suffering? Was his betrayal my burden to carry?

I turned to my friends, who said I was to blame. Their ruthless reasonings echoed in my head.

"You chose ruin over love ... of course he left!"

"He could not stay with someone who desired destruction over happiness."

"You became unworthy of his love the day you began entertaining the monster in your head."

I did not wish to hear any more—they were wrong—so I slipped further away from them and deeper into my isolation. I was the only one who truly understood my suffering.

Love and friendship lost to my enraged sorrow. My red eyes grew brighter each day.

I could not count on the friends who knew me best, so I turned to acquaintances who might lend a kinder ear. Perhaps they would tell me what I wanted to hear—he was wrong to leave, I deserved better, of course I wasn't to blame. I sought out every familiar face, and not one of them assuaged my fears. Most did not trust my red eyes and shooed me away. Others pretended they did not know me, and a few tried to explain that I was too damaged to trust, too sad to stay.

"Too sad to stay?" I asked my neighbor, a kind old lady who did not pretend I was a stranger.

"Cheer up. Your sorrow is infectious. It brings everybody down, and I'm sorry to say, that means no one will want you around."

I understood, but it seemed unfair. How could I heal in isolation? How would I mend without one single friend?

Conviction returned, I marched with determination to retrieve my heart.

Five fist-slams against the wooden door.

"Norden!" I shouted, hating the sound of his name leaving my lips.

Five more fist-slams.

"Let me in!" I demanded.

His shuffling shadow feet reached the door. The knob turned, and my forlorn heart fluttered as my lost love peered through the small crack.

"What do you want?" he asked, eyes staring at the ground.

"Don't act stupid, Norden. You know what I want."

"I can't be what you need."

"Give me back my heart."

"I cannot do that," he confessed, still refusing to make eye contact.

"Why not?"

"Someone needs to save you from yourself."

"It doesn't belong to you!"

"I don't trust what you'll do with it while that monster is in your head. I know you'll come back to me one day ... I am keeping your heart safe until then."

"Give it back!"

He lifted his gaze, looking directly at me for the first time. His pretty green eyes had turned yellow. My anger shifted to shock.

"They were red a few days ago," he explained. "I only just managed to get them to shift to yellow this morning."

"*You* left *me*," I rationalized. "What could have possibly turned you red?"

"You chose that monster, the one you call Malsana, over me time and time again. Watching her destroy you destroyed me. I only left because you gave me no other choice. If I had stayed, that monster would have inadvertently ruined me, too." He shook his head. "Seems I didn't leave soon enough. You still managed to break my heart."

Furious and unable to listen with a clear mind, I spat, "Give me back my heart, you thief!"

Tears welled in his eyes as he let out a sad laugh. "I lost you long before I left."

He turned, leaving the door cracked open, and returned a moment later with my heart in his hands. He extended it toward me.

"Don't be reckless with it," he warned. "You only get one."

I snatched it from him. "You don't get to tell me what to do."

Norden shook his head and closed the door, thoroughly giving up on me.

Too angry to care, too enraged to see the destruction in my wake, I shoved my heart into the hole in my chest where it no longer fit. It rattled against the hardened edges of its cage as I stormed away, collecting new scars with every step.

Darkness comprised the landscape. Darkness consumed my shadow body. Only the scarlet glow from my red eyes kept me going, guiding my every step. I found comfort in the chemicals altering my brain. I found joy in others' suffering. I was a cancer, a festering sore among the masses. Makellos Metropolis no longer welcomed me—I did not blend in. I did not fit. I returned to the mirror and asked Malsana how to mend my broken bits.

Give them away, she said.

"I don't understand."

There is a place beyond the city, past the outskirts and the barren desert. At the edge of this world, you will find the Fringe. There, you will find salvation.

"How do you know what's out there?"

It's where I come from. It's where I lived before finding you.

Having run out of options, I packed a bag and prepared to find healing elsewhere.

Makellos Metropolis to Verblichen Village; I decided to visit my family on my way to the Fringe. Perhaps they might see past my red eyes.

Among the tall boulders and rustleweeds were deep caves situated within the nooks of piled rocks. I found my family's emblem stamped onto a familiar boulder: my great-grandfather's handprint was pressed onto the stone with yellow paint and surrounded by orange prints of each shadow who came after. In the lower-left corner, I saw my own mark. My hand had been much smaller when I called this place home.

Beneath the towering boulders was a gap. I shifted through the tiny opening and found a siege of wary green eyes locked on me. Unlike those in Makellos, these eyes held a faded glow.

"Who are you?" my uncle demanded.

"Intruder!" my grandmother screeched.

I stood as still as possible, fearful of scaring them further. My brother stepped forward, his eyes a worrying shade of yellow. He had been hurt; he was damaged, too.

"Hello, Süden," I greeted in a calm voice.

My brother did not flinch at the revelation. He simply stepped closer to feel my energy.

"She is familiar," he finally told the rest of our family.

My younger sister, Berdine, stepped into the faint sunbeam streaking through the rocks piled above. Eyes the purest green, she examined me with solemn kindness. A glance at the damage around my heart, then back to my red eyes, and her green gaze shimmered with sorrow.

"I miss you, Berdi," I said to my sister.

"Jane!" she exclaimed as she lunged and wrapped me in a hug. Before her love could save me, my mother pulled her away.

"Who did this to you, my dear Jane?" my mother asked.

I fell to my knees.

Berdi yanked free and knelt beside me.

"I am broken," I declared.

"You don't have to be," my mother said from a safe distance.

My shoulders shook with grief. "I am lost."

"She's gone," Süden commented, his yellow eyes blazing. "I know what it's like. She let it take too much of her."

"Vaterzeit," Berdi cried. "Help her."

My grandfather stepped forward, gray and fading, and lowered his icy green gaze.

"I cannot undo her suffering—it would require altering the minds of everyone who caused her pain, and I cannot do that."

"Turn back time to before she turned red," she begged.

"The sandclock doesn't work that way."

"Make it work that way!" she demanded.

He shook his head. "Chaos has consumed this place. It will always end this way. Her choices will never change. Using the sandclock on her now will only make her relive the pain."

"We must let her go," Süden persisted.

"How could you forsake me?" I challenged, voice raw.

"It's not about me," Süden replied, "or her, or him, or us, or them. It's about you. Only you can heal yourself. And it appears you've let the damage spiral into something else."

I looked down at myself, unable to see what he meant.

He went on, "You are the master of your fate. You control what you become."

My mother placed her hand on Berdi's shoulder, coaxing her to step away.

She obliged, aware that Süden spoke the truth.

"I hope you find yourself," my mother said. "I hope you can fix your broken bits."

Berdi's shimmering green eyes never broke contact with mine.

"I'm sorry, Jane," she said, her wasted love for me spilling from her eyes.

"I'm not welcome here?" I asked, looking at my elders.

"No," my mother answered. "You must go."

Wildly alone, with no one willing to hold my hand as I navigated this new darkness, I unraveled into the pits of my being—a place so cold I found myself terrified by my own depths.

Without saying goodbye, I departed, leaving my treacherous family behind.

How could they forsake me? How could they let me battle these demons alone?

I swept through the small entryway out of their cave.

The place I once called home, I no longer recognized.

I was not welcome.

I was not wanted.

The red within me grew stronger, brighter.

Hurt consumed me.

Rage smothered me.

With nowhere to go, I tried to disappear. I tried to swallow myself whole and become one with the night, but the safest hiding place was gone. I could no longer withdraw into myself. I was too small, too weak—my starvation had shrunk my shadow body to an unredeemable size. The smaller I became, the worse my irrational outlook became, but it was the only way to numb my heartache. When my whole body ached with hunger, I felt the sting of my broken heart less.

I could not hide, I could not blend, I could not mask my suffering. Like a neon billboard marring my name, I was a beacon blaring the worst of me.

I paused beside a small lake—a magical sight within the barren wasteland. Kneeling on the sand, leaning over the water, my reflection forced me to pause. Black marbles had replaced my red eyes.

You still have me, Malsana reminded me.

"You're all I have left."

You are doing great.

"I am so frail."

The pain makes you stronger.

I nodded, eating up her words—the only sustenance I craved.

She continued, *Keep going. There are others like you on the Fringe. You are not alone.*

I walked for days, pretending I was okay, but really, I was drowning. Alive, yet submerged. Somehow breathing despite the lack of air. Lost in a wicked sea of despair, swallowed by the squall—just a ghost among the living. My infectious sorrow spread like a disease, taking root in places I never thought it could reach and ruining every last part of me. I forgot how to smile. Forgot how to appreciate the little joys around me. I walked for miles, out of the boulder fields and into the desert where only sand and rustleweeds existed.

I escaped the shadows of my former years. Releasing the concept of friendship and love—I could have neither as I was. My brother had said only I could heal myself, but I wanted help. I wanted someone to love me through the pain.

At least I had Malsana.

Miles and miles and miles, till the world's edge forced me to halt. I had come to the end. Ahead of me, a cliff dropped off, bottomless with nothing beyond—no land, no water, just fog.

I teetered at the edge, ready to fall.

"Nameless men claim nameless fates, damned to darkness in the ether."

I looked down at my feet—a single rustleweed sprouted in the harsh terrain.

"Are you talking to me?" I asked, afraid that my mind was truly lost to delusion.

"Heal before you go," the weed replied.

I took a step back, terrified of what consequences my thoughtless surrender might bring. I had to be more careful; I had to stop losing myself to each all-consuming moment.

Clarity resumed, for now, I backtracked away from the cliff and returned to the desert. Flat acres of dust surrounded me in every direction.

Nothing and no one, just like me.

I paused—perhaps I could heal here.

I closed my eyes and saw Malsana.

You are home.

Surrounded by infinite dunes, unsure what would come next, I rested my body on the sand. The unforgiving sun scorched my shadow, piercing through me as day turned into night. As its final beam disappeared over the horizon, the dark of night revealed countless red eyes staring at me.

Cautiously, I stood, wary of their arrival. Were they like me? Or were they worse? Would I be welcomed? Or shunned?

Unafraid, for nothing could be worse than what I had already endured, I walked toward them.

"Welcome," a faceless man with beaming red eyes greeted.

"What is this place?" I asked.

"The Fringe—where all the Redeyes gather."

"Redeyes?"

"The unlovables," he explained.

"I made it," I expressed, words barely escaping under my breath.

One thousand red eyes watched me carefully, trying to determine whether I was one of them. Like me, they had lost pieces of themselves along the way. Like me, they saw in red.

"Stay," they mumbled in unison, repeating the word until their voices became a chant. I was engulfed by their reception.

I took a deep breath and a smile crossed my face.

"Do you have a mirror?" I asked.

The closest Redeye smiled. "You can thank Malsana later."

Shocked by their full understanding of my request, I was rendered speechless as they escorted me across the barren landscape. We stopped at a familiar sight, a different drop off the side of the world, but the same end.

Angular cliffs lined the edge—a fall to certain death, even for a shadow. They took me to it and together we stood with our toes curled over the sharp bluff. This time, I did not wish to jump.

Tranquility washed over me.

I let the expansive emptiness surge into my hollow body. It filled me, provided comfort, and suddenly, I didn't feel so alone. The Fringe held great beauty despite its dangerous nature, and in that, I found hope.

The clouds cleared and revealed the splendor beyond the fog: enormous spires of drip-dried sand hardened in the unforgiving sun. These narrow rock towers of all sizes lined the other side of the canyon. I had found glory in a kingdom beyond the dregs of society.

A jarring discord turned my attention south. One hundred ravenlocks screeched their morning hymn as they dispersed from a cloud of smoke and bone dust. Within the shroud of darkness atop a rocky mound sat a throne made of charred ivory blades, and upon it sat a giant shadow with blood-red eyes glaring through the veil of night.

"Who is that?" I asked in a whisper.

"Mr. Darclove."

I swallowed my apprehension and craned my neck to get a better look. On the shoulder of this behemoth man sat a falcon with black marble eyes—the same eyes as Malsana.

"He's been waiting for you," the Redeye explained. "The damned, the broken, the outcasts. The unlucky, the shunned, the rejects. He waits for all of us."

A hand pushed me from behind. "Go to him."

I had nothing left to lose.

I walked to his ivory-bone throne, staring up with trembling anticipation.

"Welcome to the Fringe," he greeted, voice echoing off the empty cliff chamber. "Welcome home."

"I have no home."

"This is your home now," he declared. "These are your new friends, and soon, you will see us as family. You are a Redeye now." He smiled through the shadows. His golden, dagger-tipped teeth gleamed in the blinding reflection of the sun. "I will protect you."

"I cannot undo all I have become, all I have suffered. I am broken."

"We can erase your pain. We can fix you." He surveyed me with great contemplation. "Let me carry your burden."

109

"How?"

"Give me your broken bits."

My hands instinctively covered my damaged heart.

Mr. Darclove waved his hand and a mirror appeared before me. In it, I saw Malsana.

"I just got my heart back. I can't give it away so soon. It isn't healed yet."

You can trust him.

"How do you know?"

He sent me to you. He sends me to all the lost souls. I guided you here to be healed.

"I'm afraid."

Have I ever steered you wrong before?

I shook my head.

With a deep sigh, I announced, "I am ready."

The mirror disappeared and I faced Mr. Darclove's fierce red glare again. Hands extended, he awaited the delivery of my heart.

I reached into the frayed and tattered hole in my chest, where my heart no longer fit perfectly, and extracted the battered organ. Ready to heal, I handed it over to Mr. Darclove.

He accepted my offering by shoving my bruised heart into his mouth and swallowing it whole.

I gasped.

"It will be safest here," he explained.

I shivered. The hole in my chest seared as the hot, sandy air whipped through the exposed wound.

Red eyes vacant of emotion, Mr. Darclove declared, "Jane Doe is gone. From now on, you will be known as Redeye Heartstone."

He picked up a smooth stone and floated toward me, descending over the rocky mound and across the sand field separating us. When he reached me, his height dwarfed my fear. I was in awe.

He kissed the stone, then placed it gently into the hole within my chest.

Impossible, I thought, but my doubts faded as my hand caressed my stone heart, amazed at how perfectly it fit. My reservations turned to wonder.

Redeye Heartstone.

A new name, an identity yet to be defined. I had grown accustomed to the name Jane, but that girl was gone.

The falcon on Mr. Darclove's shoulder screeched.

"I recognize its eyes," I said.

"That's because part of her lives in you."

"I see her in my reflection."

"Malsana is a friend to the broken. Just as I am." Though Mr. Darclove's words were kind, his red eyes gleamed with menace.

"I am happy she led me here." I placed my hand over the stone in my chest. "I am grateful to be whole again."

"Stick with us and you'll stay this way."

The promise was enticing—almost too good—but I stayed, willing to see if his words held weight.

I lived on the Fringe for more suns than I could count and, in time, learned that his promise was true. Among the Redeyes, I rediscovered happiness. With them, I was accepted.

We were alike, after all. Damaged and forsaken by everyone except Mr. Darclove. He was our savior; he was a true ally to the Redeyes. He was a confident voice for the weak, a focused mind for the frayed—he lived to rebuild the broken.

So I let him.

I let him take my broken bits and rearrange them. He made me whole again, with purpose and determination.

Without him, I would have fallen off the edge.

Without him, I would be no one.

Though I still saw in red, I was not alone—everyone around me saw the world as I did.

It wasn't long before I could no longer imagine my life elsewhere.

I was happy here.

I belonged.

Beyond the sand field, within sight of Mr. Darclove's throne, stood the camp where we lived. Each Redeye dug themself a hole and built an awning overtop made of rocks and dried clay. It took me a few days to dig a hole deep enough to reach wet clay, and a few more days to figure out the correct mixture of clay and sand to make concrete, but I was settled now. I had a home within the Fringe.

"Cast aside your woes," Mr. Darclove declared at his nightly assembly. Malsana, his marble-eyed companion, cawed as she flew through the sky. "All that you have survived has brought you to me. Because of your pain, you are stronger. Because of your hardships, you see more clearly. We are a family and we protect our own."

The Redeyes cheered.

Mr. Darclove went on, "Stick with me, and you will never know suffering again."

Joyous cries erupted from the crowd and red light from his devoted followers' eyes shone brightly upon him, illuminating his devious smile.

Mr. Darclove and Malsana disappeared into the cloud of smoke surrounding his throne and left us in a hopeful state of contemplation.

"A life without suffering—do you think it's possible?" I asked Redeye Bullgrave.

He glanced at me, fidgeting in place as he considered my question. "I certainly hope so."

"Which broken bits of yours did he take?"

"My mind."

My eyes widened. "How do you think without a brain?"

"He only took the grieving parts. He replaced those bits with stones. I haven't cried since."

"He was a weeping fool prior," Redeye Woesome jumped in. "Mr. Darclove set him straight."

"And what about you?" I asked.

"My memories were a menace, so I gave him the worst of my past." Redeye Woesome paused. "All I have left are these scars on my wrists."

"How'd you get them?"

"I gave them to myself."

"Why?"

Redeye Woesome shrugged. "I can't remember. Those are the memories Mr. Darclove took."

"Do you ever wonder?"

Redeye Woesome shook his head. "No use wondering when I know I'm better off now. Why try to dig up a hurtful past?" He lowered his gaze and turned away, unwilling to banter further. My questions were dangerous—I realized this as he walked away. I turned to Redeye Bullgrave.

"I didn't mean to pry."

"It's okay. He will be fine."

Redeye Bullgrave departed, leaving me in solitude at the edge. My feet dangled over the side—bottomless energy radiated up through my shadow. I wondered if I'd always feel this way.

I looked east toward the city I once loved. I couldn't see it from here, but I felt it in the distance. Stripped bare, guts and bones, I was someone else now. I liked this new version of myself. Resurrected from the ashes, the memories of who I used to be began to fade with the flickering flames of yesterday.

Night came and went.

An alarm startled me awake. I sat up slowly and located the source of the noise—Mr. Darclove stood atop his rocky tor, mouth agape, red eyes flashing, and sirens echoing from the pit of his gut. Malsana tore through the sky, beady black eyes reflecting the red warning on their shiny surface.

The Redeyes stood in a line, blocking Mr. Darclove as a shield of shadows. I was the only one left sleeping in the dusty desert.

I was alone, facing a menacing wall of Redeyes.

From behind, green light struck the wall of shadows, illuminating their veiled faces. Darkness temporarily vanquished, their harrowed expressions were vile.

I turned to look for the brave but foolish intruder and found a girl slightly younger than me standing in a brush of rustleweeds.

"Welcome, Berdine," Mr. Darclove announced.

The stone in my chest tripled in weight—I wasn't supposed to feel, yet I felt myself breaking.

"Why are you here?" I demanded, marching toward my sister.

"I missed you."

"Go home. I'll find you there."

Berdi was not listening. She spun in a circle, mouth agape as she admired this foreign place. Distant, mysterious, misunderstood — the allure of the Fringe captivated her attention. Malsana in hawk form circled above, black marble eyes locked on Berdi.

The green light of Berdi's innocent gaze illuminated Mr. Darclove's sinister smile.

"Tell her to leave," I insisted.

"All are welcome here," Mr. Darclove replied, his voice calm despite the growing tension.

"She isn't a Redeye!"

"Look again."

I turned to face my sister.

Malsana perched on Berdi's shoulder with her wings wrapped around my sister's face.

"Get off her!" I shouted, shooing the shapeshifting monster away. Malsana screeched as she catapulted off Berdi's shoulder, twisting into a mourning dove as she flew back to Mr. Darclove.

Berdi's eyes were closed.

"Are you okay?" I asked.

She breathed heavily.

"What did she do to you?"

"She asked me what I wanted most," Berdi answered.

The stone in my chest anchored me in place.

"And what did you tell her?"

"I told her that I wanted to be like you." Berdi slowly opened her eyes and looked up at me.

Green eyes gone, she beamed a fearsome red.

"No, no," I stammered. "Why?"

"I didn't want you to be alone."

Innocence ravaged by destruction—what had I accidentally inspired?

"You have to go home," I urged, hoping her red eyes would heal if she didn't linger here too long.

"The Fringe is her home now," Mr. Darclove bellowed. "She is a Redeye."

My muscles tensed.

"Don't be mad," Berdi whispered. "We can be together now."

Loud cheers boomed all around.

I collapsed to my knees.

The Redeyes surrounded us, praising Berdi with welcoming shouts and hollers, hugs, and friendly shoves. They welcomed her just as they had welcomed me.

Berdi tentatively glanced back at me, but the raucous celebration consumed her concern, and a giant smile spread across her face as the cheering crowd enveloped her.

Red lines of fury streaked across my vision. When they finally faded, I crawled out of the joyous huddle and peered over the edge of the Fringe.

Thick clouds of mist blocked the long drop, and I saw my reflection in the vapor.

Malsana stared back at me, her marble eyes unfriendly.

"What have you done to her?" I demanded.

Nothing I haven't already done to you.

"Let her go!"

Why can't I be friends with your sister, too?

"She didn't need you like I needed you. She was fine before you entered her mind."

Some might argue you were fine, too, but you weren't. Neither was she. I will help her, just like I helped you.

Suffocating panic clenched my stone heart.

Caught up in the furious excitement of my fellow Redeyes, I lost myself once more. They cheered and celebrated, elated by my sister's recruitment.

Redeye Bullgrave grabbed Berdi's hand and thrust her fist into the air, declaring victory, and the Redeyes cheered louder.

She was one of us now.

Days passed in a blur.

I felt dead inside—my sister's transformation into a Redeye shook me to my core—but I had to stay strong. As much as I had grown to enjoy and accept life on the Fringe, it wasn't a full life; it was merely a means of survival for the broken.

Berdi wasn't fated to this desperate place like I was—I had accidentally led her here.

She deserved better.

I had to find a way to save her.

To endure, I numbed the guilt coursing through me. I held on tight to the feeling of nothing. I feared where I'd land if I let go.

I could not recall when the celebration ended, only that I had existed in silence for a week after her arrival. So much to process, so much to digest. Berdi was tied up with the Redeyes, who had taken her in as they had done for me. As the days passed, Berdi's VIP treatment faded, and her attention returned to me. Though I clung to my detachment, it slipped further out of my grip every time Berdi asked if I was okay. I couldn't hang on much longer—the truth clawed at the door.

Berdi jogged up to me on my eighth day of silence.

Out of breath, shadow body shrinking from her newfound obsession with exercise, she doubled over to catch her breath before speaking.

"This heat is brutal," she said.

"Why do you choose to run in it?"

"She speaks!" Berdi exclaimed.

"Answer my question."

"I run because it makes me feel good. Malsana encourages me to run daily."

"It's making you sick."

"Impossible."

"Have you looked in a mirror?"

"Have you?" she snapped. "You're no better than me."

She was right—I was just as frail, just as weak, just as small.

My stone heart trembled. "I'm beginning to think Malsana is not our friend."

"She is our greatest friend," Berdi countered. "She saved you from heartbreak. She saved me from loneliness. Do not forsake her."

Berdi scoffed before racing away, visibly agitated that I was ruining her fun. But the joy she felt was an illusion. The comradery from the Redeyes was a distraction, their acceptance a diversion. Consumed by their love, she did not notice how Malsana's friendship destroyed her. She wore a proud smile as her shadow withered away into nothing.

I looked down at my skinny shadow fingers.

Was I as lost as my sister? Was I as disillusioned as her?

Fist clenched, I refused to believe I was not in control. I chose this fate, whereas Berdi had followed me blindly.

I had to help her.

She is better now than she was before.

"Where are you?" I asked, unsure how Malsana spoke to me without a reflection. I spun in a circle, trying to locate the monster, but she was nowhere to be found.

I'm in your head.

"I thought you lived in mirrors."

I am everywhere.

"Leave my sister alone!"

Stop feeding me, and maybe I will.

Panicked, I took her words to heart. Not only did I stop giving her life in my thoughts, but my restrictive food intake worsened. No appetite, no hunger—I would starve Malsana until she agreed to vacate my sister's mind.

I stopped smiling. I stopped saying "thank you" whenever someone complimented my ever-shrinking figure. I turned off, no longer willing to pretend.

Malsana's grip on me grew stronger. Though I continued to starve, it seemed my deprivation only empowered her. I was losing this battle of will.

Not only did I shrink at a rapidly concerning rate, but Berdi was withering away, too. Every day that passed, I became more aware of my failure.

I had to try something different.

In the dark of night, while the other Redeyes slept, I snuck out of camp and set my sights on Verblichen. There, I could consult with my family. Perhaps they'd suggest an idea that would help me save Berdi.

I tore through the desert, crushing rustleweeds with each step. My shadow feet bled gray as thorns ripped through my smoky flesh. I couldn't feel the pain—the emptiness of my stomach was all-consuming.

"The Face of Guilt," a crumpled rustleweed declared. "Finally! A fate defined."

"No, I will shake this reflection and do better. I will make things right."

A field of tall boulders lined the horizon—I was almost there.

The enormous rocks towering over my childhood home came into view. I ran to them, desperate to feel the parts of myself I had lost.

The wall was adorned with the handprint of every shadow who claimed our family name, but where my print once lay were streaks of red. An attempt to erase me, a warning that I was not welcome.

I could not stop now. I had to remedy the horror I helped birth. I twisted my shadow until it fit through the small entranceway into the cave.

My mother screamed at the sight of me.

"You took Berdi from us!" she bellowed between uncontrollable sobs.

"I am going to fix everything," I swore. "Where is Vaterzeit?"

My mother hesitated, her cries temporarily silenced. Eyes narrowed—she understood my intentions. "You cannot undo what you've done."

"I can try."

She shook her head. "I'm no expert with sandclocks— the dark magic is tricky to control—but I am fairly confident that they don't work that way."

"Let me talk to Vaterzeit."

My mother lowered her gaze and slouched forward as if I had placed upon her the greatest burden.

"Is it me?" I asked.

She nodded. "I brought chaos into the world."

She disappeared into the cave's darkness, leaving me alone to stew in her lingering disappointment.

Vaterzeit appeared a moment later, straddling the darkness, hesitant to come too close.

"I do not wish to cause you distress," I promised.

"I heard your desires. I cannot help you."

"Why not?"

"You are marked by chaos. You have befriended a fear monster. Time has morphed your face into the image of mayhem and guilt."

"That's not who I am."

"That's who I see standing before me."

"Then it's not who I want to be."

Vaterzeit digested my claim, green eyes fierce with skepticism. "I know you wish to use the sandclock to turn back time and alter the timeline, but it will not work. That monster will always arrive at your door."

"I will refuse her friendship."

"You won't."

"I will!"

He crossed his shadow arms over his chest. "Only the wardens can tame the fear monsters."

"I am strong enough."

"It's not about strength. It's about wisdom and willingness."

"I will do better." My red eyes filled with determined tears.

Vaterzeit shook his head. "Unfortunately, you won't. You aren't ready to let her go."

"How do you know?" I asked, afraid to be honest with myself.

"We have been here before. You have tried to change the past numerous times through the sandclock, and we always end up here. You always choose Malsana."

"How do you know her name?" I asked, appalled that he knew my most coveted secret.

"Like I said, we've been here before." He sighed. "Your secret is safe with me."

"I need to save Berdi."

"To save her, you must save yourself. Fix yourself in the here and now, not in the past."

I struggled with this notion. Though I was becoming more aware of my deterioration, I wasn't quite ready to heal. I hated Malsana for what she had done to Berdi, but I still loved her for all she had given me. Reckoning between the two wasn't a battle I was ready to fight.

"Let me try the sandclock one last time," I pled.

Vaterzeit did not answer. Instead, he led me to the family garden of rustleweeds. I paused before getting too close.

"Sit," Vaterzeit instructed. "Time travel is messy and often results in more problems than solutions. There are other ways to heal."

I knelt beside him as he tended the garden, pushing dusty dirt around and creating healthy piles for each rustleweed to grow. The weeds hummed a song I did not recognize as Vaterzeit worked.

"Rustleweeds carry wisdom," he explained.

"They spoke to me a few times in the desert. Their words were harsh."

"The truth isn't always kind."

Vaterzeit patted the thick mounds of dirt around the healthiest rustleweeds, then turned his attention to a frail weed near the back of the patch.

He continued, "I have harvested and nurtured a rustleweed for each member of my family. This one is yours."

"It looks sick."

"That's because it mimics the life of its assigned shadow."

"I am not sick," I protested.

"You do not see clearly." He dug his fingers into the soil beneath my dying rustleweed and extracted it from the ground. "Are you ready?"

"For what?"

"Clarity."

Before I could reply, he snapped his fingers, and the stone in my chest caught fire. It fell to the ground with a thud. Cold air whipped the nerves lining my wound—it hadn't healed. It was still raw. Vaterzeit quickly shoved the mound with the withering rustleweed into the hole in my chest. Its roots latched onto the edges of my wound, slithering and burrowing into my body.

"It hurts," I protested.

"The truth often does."

A web of rustleweed tendrils filled my hole, and at the center was a miserable-looking weed.

"How will this help me?" I asked, still grimacing as the roots dug deeper into my body.

"It will shred the veil you hide behind."

"I don't understand."

"Denial only worsens your condition. You don't have to come clean to me, or anyone else, but you must be truthful with yourself."

My rustleweed settled into place and the pain ceased. I expected to feel different, but I felt the same.

Vaterzeit sensed my confusion. "The answers will come."

I returned to the Fringe.

The sight of my sister running tireless laps around Mr. Darclove's tor greeted me. Obsessed, consumed—she ran until she was depleted. I waited until Berdi collapsed to her knees.

"I'm worried about you," I said.

"You shouldn't be. I feel better than ever."

"You're shrinking."

"I'm still not as small as you."

I cringed—she was right. I was a terrible influence.

"You should not strive to look like me."

"Why not? You're beautiful."

"I am sick."

This admission shocked us both—I had never admitted these words to myself or anyone else.

Berdi stepped back. "Sick, how?"

I shook my head. "I'm not sure."

Be honest with yourself, a voice I did not recognize said.

"Malsana?" I asked.

"What about Malsana?" Berdi asked.

A bolt of realization struck my rustleweed heart.

"She is the cause. She is to blame," I said.

"You aren't making sense."

"It was her all along."

Berdi frowned, then asked, "Were you happy here before I arrived?"

"No, I was empty. Now, I am filled with guilt."

"Why?"

"Because I led you here."

"I like it here."

I shook my head. "I cannot watch you wallow in your own destruction as all the other Redeyes do ... as I do. You don't deserve this fate."

"You seem different today than you did yesterday," Berdi commented.

"I think I'm waking up."

Morning turned into afternoon as I waited patiently for Mr. Darclove to return to his tor. I paced, my guilt rapidly transforming into anger. As the sun began to set, a cloud of smoke swirled at the top of the rocky mound, delivering Mr. Darclove to his throne.

Malsana sat on his shoulder as an iguana. Black marble eyes fixated on me, she sensed my disassociation.

"Hello, Redeye Heartstone," Mr. Darclove shouted from the top of his jagged hilltop. Masked in a cloud of smoke and bone dust, I could not see the intent within his stare. Ravenlocks screeched in protest as I approached.

As the smoke cleared, his red eyes zeroed in on my chest.

"You have changed," he said, his tone sinister.

"I am beginning to see things clearly," I answered honestly. Though my mistrust for Malsana grew, Mr. Darclove still kept my broken heart safe.

"Will you forsake us?" he asked.

"I am more lost than ever."

"It appears so. Never forget what the Fringe has provided."

I shook my head. "This place is a lie."

"You are mistaken," he replied confidently. "You were broken when you arrived and I fixed you." He stepped out of his cloud and revealed himself, red eyes soft and arms open.

"*You* are mistaken." I pointed to Malsana. "*She* broke me. I never would have needed this place if it wasn't for her."

"Malsana only enters the minds of those who welcome her. If you had said no, she would have left you alone."

"How was I supposed to know she'd infect me with delusions and lead me down a path of self-sabotage?"

"Her love manifests however *you* choose."

"Well, I'm choosing to forsake her. I reject her friendship."

"It's a one-way invite. Once she's in, she never leaves."

Forgive yourself, the foreign voice said within my head.

I struggled to curb my fury.

"You're in on it," I shouted at Mr. Darclove. My thoughts spun in vicious circles. "Did you send her to me? Are you the reason all the Redeyes are here?"

"You think I am to blame?" he sneered. "Look at what you've done." He swept his arm toward Berdi, who looked skinnier today than she had yesterday.

"No!" I shouted. "I didn't want it to be this way."

I stumbled as I backed away, tripping over my shadow feet as I tried to run from myself.

Malsana shifted into a bear and chased after me. I could not outrun her goliath form, and she snatched me by the neck. Lifted off the ground, I fought and flailed, but to no avail. Malsana carried me back to Mr. Darclove's throne.

"You aren't welcome out there," he stated simply, unperturbed by my desperate desire to escape him.

With Malsana's teeth still clamped into the back of my neck, blinding pain ripped through me, but I would not give up.

"You are the cause of my suffering! Let me go," I shouted, thrusting my fist over my head and punching Malsana in the eye. Bellowing in agony, she shapeshifted into a mouse and dropped me.

I ran.

Where do you think you are going? Malsana seethed inside my head.

"Away from here."

You can't evade me; I live within you.

"Shut up!"

Be compassionate with yourself, the other voice advised.

Malsana cackled, her evil laugh reverberating with each long leap of my escape.

I stopped along the cliff, too close to the edge, my chest searing from the trauma I neglected for so long. The wound had rotted and decayed—it would be much harder to heal now. I covered it with my hands, hoping to shield it from the horror I had inflicted. It was my fault that I was in this nightmare, my fault that I had not healed long ago.

Be gentle with yourself, the other voice inside my heart encouraged.

I placed my hand over my rustleweed heart, aware now that the other voice I heard came directly from me.

"I have to save Berdi."

To save her, you must save yourself.

"How?"

The love and healing you wish to give to her, you must also give to yourself.

I wasn't ready to let go. I wasn't ready to heal.

Though I no longer lived in denial—I silently acknowledged my sickness—I wasn't ready to forsake my secret friendship with Malsana.

I am your greatest friend, Malsana said, returning to the forefront of my mind and silencing my rustleweed.

I bartered with Malsana. "Please, let my sister go."

If you want me to leave her, I'll have to take more of you.

"Fine, anything. Just let her go."

You'll need to make more room for me in your heart.

I placed my hand over my rustleweed.

"You promise to release Berdi?"

I promise.

I wiggled my fingers into the hole in my chest, digging into the many roots of my rustleweed.

A gentle pull removed my rustleweed.

"I will come back for you," I promised, bending to plant my rustleweed where I knelt.

No, Malsana objected. *Discard the weed.*

Tears spilled from my eyes.

"You want all of me?"

It's only fair.

A life for a life.

"I hate you."

You love me.

She was right. Though I finally saw her for what she was, I could not lessen my dependence. I needed her; I needed the control her influence provided.

I walked to the edge of the Fringe, the shriveling rustleweed in my grip.

"I'm sorry," I confessed as I tossed the weed into the abyss and watched it fall.

Wisdom forsaken, for I was not yet willing, tears fell from my eyes as I ruined another part of myself for Malsana.

"I see you for what you are now," I seethed.

In time, you will forget.

"Never. My rustleweed might be gone, but I will hold on tight to the brief wisdom it gave me."

Malsana laughed. *The longer you let me stay, the harder it will be to let me go.*

"All I care about right now is saving Berdi from you."

She is as free as I can let her be.

"What do you mean?" My gaze darted toward my sister, who had paused her daily workout to assess her surroundings. Her eyes were now yellow.

Like Mr. Darclove told you, my arrival is a one-way ticket. I removed everything but my black marble roots. I will always be there.

"Remove those, too!"

I can't. They are rooted in her mind. She will always remember me.

Berdi looked frightened, as if all memory of how she had gotten to the Fringe had vanished.

I shouted to my sister, "Go home!"

Hearing my voice startled Berdi from her terrified confusion. She began walking toward me.

"No," I demanded. "Go home!"

"Come with me," she begged.

"I can't. Not yet."

Misty tears poured from her yellow eyes. The vapor created a haze around her shadowy figure as she ran away from the Fringe.

I closed my eyes; I did not want to watch her go.

Darkness greeted me—the only solace I had left.

At my feet, I could feel the long drop into the abyss. The lonely end I so callously delivered to my rustleweed; perhaps the fate I delivered was also the fate I deserved.

Be gentle with yourself.

It wasn't Malsana this time—the voice came from somewhere else. I looked down at the vacant, raw hole in my chest and saw the few seeds of wisdom my rustleweed had left behind beginning to grow.

Honesty.

Forgiveness.

Compassion.

Small budlings forced their way through my wound's scabbed and scarred lining.

They would grow. They would blossom. It would take time, but they were there, and they'd always be with me.

Though not yet ready to fully heal, I was no longer in denial—a small, but mighty accomplishment.

I took a deep breath.

These were the seeds of salvation.

A note from the Fox

Jane chose Malsana over Norden; she chose ruin over love. She did this with every relationship in her life: friends, family, lovers—Malsana always came first. And while Jane was no longer in denial at this point of her story, she still clung to the toxic comfort Malsana provided. Aware that she needed to let the monster go, but not yet willing to make the hard changes required to heal, Jane continued choosing Malsana over everyone else.

This recurring decision ate at her from the inside, rotting her perception of love and friendship—not only the type of love she could give, but also that which she felt worthy to receive.

Another notch in Malsana's belt, another trophy to add to her collection.

Like a wilted blossom surrounded by thriving wildflowers, Jane battled futilely against the sunlight. Nourishment, energy, a source for survival—she wanted none of it. A spotlight on her shortcomings, the sun tormented her daily.

I wish I had been there; I wish I had helped.

Looking back on it all, Day did her best to smile despite Jane's potent deterioration—I'd argue that she went as far as to turn a blind eye to the Host's destructive new habits.

If she smiled, so would Jane.

As the Face of Day, her skill at faking being fine only enabled the rampant obsession plaguing Jane. She became convinced she was fine and would listen to no challengers of her stubborn delusions.

A vicious game—one I only now recognize after years of reflection.

The only Face who refused to back down from Jane's dangerous and ill-prepared quest to control Malsana was Night.

When I returned to the black feather memento on the day of discovery, I witnessed Jane's plight once again through this facet of her personality—the only part of her that was determined to remedy her unraveling.

Revisiting Memento #3

When: The 18th Cycle
Where: Jane's mind—Lunar Spire, Northern Unknown
Who: The Face of Night

Enraged, I soared back to the Lunar Spire, pacing as I waited for sundown. When the Face of Day arrived with the sun, I raced to her. She let the sun drop into the Southern Abyss and I took her hands.

"How do you feel?" I asked.

"Weirded out," she replied, yanking her hands from my grip. "What's wrong?"

"The fear is still inside of you. I saw it dancing along your porcelain as you flew across the sky."

Day took a step back, appalled.

Now that Chaos was here, we could see it more clearly. The fear crawled all over her, scuttling across her porcelain-coated flesh like tiny insects.

"Get it off me!" she screamed.

I grabbed her hands again, pulled her close, and enveloped her in a hug. I did all I could to take away the fear.

When I let her go, she appeared to be cleansed.

"Is it all gone?" she asked, her voice desperate.

I examined her. "As far as I can see, yes."

Day shook her arms, still repulsed by the fear that had secretly latched onto her for so long, and then screamed.

"I'm trying to stay positive," she shouted, "but how can I when I have no support?"

"I'm doing my best."

"You let it infect me!" she accused.

"I tried to keep you safe."

Tears wet her forest-green eyes, which brimmed with anger. For the first time, I noticed the fine lines that had recently formed across her face.

"How did you get those cracks?" I asked.

"You failed us."

She marched to the sun etched on the wall and disappeared through the portal.

I cursed beneath my breath, wholly aggravated with myself.

Luna emerged in her tiniest form, weeping as she appeared to fulfill her purpose.

Further confirmation: I broke everyone around me.

"Tell me why you are so sad," I begged. "Is it my fault?"

The girl inside the moon held my gaze, and for the first time in a long time, I saw her clearly. Her large, spherical eyes shone brightly as her crying ceased.

"We were never meant to be apart."

"I'm with you every night."

"Not you," she corrected. "Me and Solís."

"The sun?" I confirmed.

She nodded; her unkempt black hair fell in front of her face. "We were sent into this mortal mind to heal, but it's beginning to feel like a punishment for the love we shared many lifetimes ago."

"You are the moon, and he is the sun," I stated as if it were logical. "Of course, you cannot be together."

She shook her head, disappointed by my reply, and retreated into the moon's center where she wept in solitude.

"I'd be happy to listen if you ever want to tell me more," I shouted to her.

Her moon-disc eyes lowered. "I have already said too much."

Without the moon, time would halt.

Without the Face of Day, our Host would descend into darkness.

Everything was falling apart, and I was beginning to lose track of which breaking piece to catch first before it shattered.

I carried Luna across the sky, pondering this precarious dilemma.

Sight of the Soldier of Time teetering precariously at the end of the hour hand stripped me from my thoughts.

Expression forlorn, posture slouched, he looked like he wanted to jump.

We could not lose him, too.

I had to stay with the moon.

I could not rush to his aid.

"Help him!" I shouted down to the Faces sitting along the Ring of Thrones.

Sorrow looked at me first—the back half of her body was a never-ending rainstorm of teardrops. No matter how many droplets fell, her front half remained whole. Her teal eyes held the heaviness of a thousand lifetimes as she considered my frantic plea.

"Help him!" I repeated.

"Who?" Sorrow asked.

"Time."

Sorrow shook her head. "My help would make him worse."

"Joy, Trust, Control—anyone! We have to stop him from making a grave mistake."

"He doesn't need us," Joy replied, watery hopelessness shimmering in her emerald eyes. "Look again."

I returned my gaze to the tower and found Day talking to Time.

The panic in my gut eased.

Though she struggled, too, her patience for imperfect creatures was exactly what Time needed.

Day was the right Face for the job.

We survived the night without injury, and I thought we were in the clear, but the following evening, the startling jolt of time hiccupping ripped me from my temporary relief.

For the first time since the start, the Face of Time had faltered.

Luna lurched downward, dragging me with her. I pounded my wings against the cool night air, refusing to let her fall.

"What is going on?" I shouted, furious.

The Face of Time quickly recovered and time resumed.

Though he remedied his mistake, my concern for this mind's safety amplified.

The looming threat of disaster scraped viciously at my nerves.

Sunrise came and Day lifted the sun into the sky without looking at me, so I returned home through the portal.

I rummaged through my treasure chest, searching for the last remaining item that could comfort me.

"Little clam," I said softly, "can I hold you?"

Her slumbering melody muffled to a slow stop as she awoke.

We shared a long silence before she sang a lively, vibrant song through closed shells.

I lifted her and held her close. She remained unbroken, still perfect in my care.

"Everything is falling apart out here," I confided.

The little clam did not speak, but her song shifted to one of compassion.

"Are you happy with me?" I asked, terrified to express vulnerability.

Her melody turned melancholic, and the rejection stung.

I determined I would make her happy without letting her go.

"Would a trip home make you happy?"

Her sad song brightened and her answer was clear.

I smiled—I could stomach this compromise.

"I can do that for you."

I emptied her water bowl, placed it into a small satchel, and safely contained the little clam in my grip. We took off, soaring into the sunlit sky. I circled the sandclock twice, admiring the intricate workings of time below.

The creatures of time created art as they worked. The Bitlings and Jiffies docked the seconds and minutes, pulsating in and out like a heartbeat—the Bitlings moved fast with each second while the Jiffies moved slower with each minute. The twelve Circlettes guarded their huts along the outer edge of the village, lighting up twice per day—once during the day and once during the night. The Face of Time lived in the tower that wrapped around the neck of our sandclock, ensuring that all the grains of sand fell without error.

Whenever I felt burdened by my chains to the moon, I reminded myself that I was freer than the creatures of time could ever be.

I could leave, I could explore beyond, I could think about things other than time—they could not.

High above, I appreciated the liberties I was allowed. Leaving reminded me how lucky I truly was.

I flew over the Ring of Thrones that sat on the edge of the village and into the ether where the pockets floated. Past Joy and Sorrow, I found Trust. The lustrous orb beckoned as I flew through its haze and into the world within. The glossy fog faded and colorful tranquility greeted me. The world was mostly water, with a few small islands of lush forestry.

The little clam came alive in my grip—though she never opened her shells, she still cried with delight as the scent of her home reached us.

I descended until I hovered just above the sea. I lowered my talon grip, letting her dip beneath the water. When I lifted her out of the sea, she sang a joyous tune.

My heart swelled—I was making her happy.

We spent half the day there, soaring around, stopping on one of the tiny islands, and wading in the shallow waters. The little clam's iridescent shell looked brighter, more polished. Somehow, her already perfect beauty amplified.

Being a cousin to time, I sensed the hour.

"It's five p.m. We have to head back."

The little clam stopped singing.

My heart ached. "Do you want to stay?"

She sat with my question a moment.

"Am I your only friend?" she asked in song, keeping her shells closed.

"Yes." The answer stung.

"Then I will stay with you."

Her great sacrifice humbled me. "Thank you. Now that I know the joy your home brings, we will visit more often."

She hummed a happy melody.

My soul rested easy as we flew back to the sandclock. While everything else fell apart, this one thing fell into place, and I held to its potential firmly.

Many nights came and went with Luna in a state of irreversible despair.

Time continued glitching.

The Face of Time was losing his grip, and it grew harder and harder to carry the moon through the sky. My back muscles strained to hold the moon's sudden heaviness each night, and they screamed in sore agony each day.

Unable to control the chaos unraveling around the sandclock, I found joy in escaping with my little clam during the day. We traveled to the Pocket of Trust regularly, and it quickly turned into a haven from the turmoil at the sandclock, a shelter from the storm brewing inside our Host.

I performed my job every night with meticulous accuracy, absorbing every single fear that materialized and delivering them to the Face of Fear, and then happily retreated during the day. We became comfortable in our isolation, and I found myself enamored by the little clam.

"You are my first love," she sang.

"You are my greatest love," I told her.

Her song echoed my sentiment.

"Why don't you ever open your shells?" I asked.

"I don't like to."

"I understand," I offered. "I like you just the way you are."

And like that, we existed blissfully, relying on each other to survive the darkening days.

The Face of Day also performed her job with precision, but I sensed she was slipping away. Though I tried talking to her, she still did not forgive me for letting the sickness touch her.

On a peaceful dawn near the end of our eighteenth year, I forced Day to address me. I grabbed her by the wrist and refused to let her go. The fine cracks all over her body had tripled. Though small and shallow, they indicated that she was suffering, too.

"I have a job to do," she argued.

"Talk to me."

"About what?"

"You never smile anymore."

"I save my smiles for the day, for when it matters."

"If the fear is still inside you, I can help."

Her bright forest-green eyes stared at me with deep hurt. "It's part of me now."

She yanked her wrist from my grip, and I noticed a new fissure running up her porcelain arm. This crack was unlike the others—it was deeper and filled with gold.

"How'd you get that?"

She looked down at her arm. "It doesn't hurt."

"Be careful. The sun will burn you alive if your protective porcelain casing breaks."

"I'm fine," she insisted.

"You're covered in cracks. The Face of Time keeps letting the seconds glitch … everyone is falling apart."

"I have befriended the Face of Time. I will fix him."

"How can you fix him when you can't even fix yourself? I've seen how he waits for you—you're making him worse."

"I don't see *you* trying to help him," she snapped while lifting the sun and rising into the sky.

I watched her fly away, unable to help.

She was right. I had to help him be strong on his own, without her.

As I flew over the Tower of Time that night, I was determined to make the glass soldier see reason.

"Stop worrying about Day," I shouted down to him.

"I don't need advice from you," he shouted back.

"She cannot help you," I squawked as I carried the moon through the sky.

"You know nothing."

I laughed. "I know more than you ever will."

"Then tell me."

"I'm too busy fixing your mess."

Time stopped.

Enraged by my words, the glass soldier halted the progression of time.

Halfway through the sky, I was rendered immobile where I hovered. I slipped a little closer to the ground with each second held hostage.

"Stop!" I insisted. "The moon is too heavy."

"Tell me why she won't come back."

"You'll ruin everything," I urged. "Let me go."

"Tell me why!"

"I'm trying to help you—to save you and me and everyone else."

"I don't understand."

"She is obsessed with broken things. They make her feel better—they make her feel less broken." I scoffed at his blank expression. "She *will* come back for you, but you must reject her."

"She is my only friend." His fists clenched tighter and time's progression halted.

My large feathered wings quivered as I fought to stay airborne. "She will try to fix you to make herself feel whole. She is selfish. Let her go."

The glass soldier's fists released and time resumed.

"You were designed to be alone," I reminded him as I battled the moon's weight and worked hard to make up the time lost.

A terrible interaction—I cursed at myself. My patience for brokenness was limited; why did I struggle to be kind?

I finished out the night, set Luna to rest, and prayed I hadn't caused more damage. The sun rose into the sky, initiating the start of day, and I observed the world from above. Everything on the sandclock was brighter during the day, including the Ring of Thrones, where each Face sat.

Joy, Sorrow, Anger, and Fear sat stoically in their assigned spots.

Trust relaxed on her throne of shells and sea moss—a welcome sight among the others.

Mr. Darclove was not there—he often wasn't. He chose to exist within his pocket: the Fringe. There, he could reign freely and with reckless abandon, whereas on the sandclock, his wild and unpredictable temperament held less influence. I welcomed his frequent absence. It gave me one less thing to worry about.

Worthiness had never returned—her throne sat vacant.

Anxiety was also absent from her throne, but a quick glance into the ether revealed her frantically fluttering around her pocket, wrapped in tangled nets.

Then I noticed a new throne, one I hadn't seen until now. It was made of countless gilded coils and on it sat a woman made of gold.

Furious, I soared to her.

"Who are you?" I demanded.

Her gilded gaze greeted me. "I am the Face of Control."

"Control?" I asked, unsure what that entailed.

"You can call me Connie."

"No, that's okay. What is your purpose here?"

"To restore order."

My anger morphed into concern. "How bad is it out there?"

Control shook her head. "We fight the chaos every day."

I looked at Chaos's empty throne, then back to Control. "He's been in his pocket every day since arriving here."

She shook her head. "He is everywhere all at once."

"What can I do to help?"

"The dangerous sickness he nurtures cannot be fully absorbed by you or restrained by the Face of Fear—as we learned through Malsana. From now on, after you digest the nighttime fears, you must deliver those driven by emotion into my pocket. There, they will be weaved and caged."

"What about all the ones I've already delivered to Fear?"

"I have been working with the Face of Fear. Together, we have relocated the emotion-driven fears into my pocket."

"How long have you been here?" I asked, suddenly concerned that I had missed much during my daily sabbaticals in the Pocket of Trust.

"Since the seventeenth cycle."

I gasped. "Impossible."

"You ought to pay better attention." Control arched her golden brow. "My Pocket of Control is thriving. You'll see when you make your first delivery."

"There has to be more I can do to help."

"Do your job, and we will do ours. Only you can catch the poisonous sickness Chaos blasts into the night."

"Is that what he's doing in his pocket?" I clenched my fists. "Creating new fears and emotions that revolve around the sickness?"

"Inside our pockets is where our greatest influence over the Host exists."

"No wonder he never comes out."

"And it is why the Face of Fear never goes into his pocket. His presence there would only make matters worse."

"And what about Joy? Shouldn't she be more proactive?"

The Face of Control's lips tightened before she spoke. "Joy is infected, too. Chaos saw to that before revealing himself. He contaminated every happiness our Host cherished with chaos. Now, those things only cause her sorrow and anger. Hence why Sorrow and Anger also stay out of their pockets."

"It might also explain why the Face of Day struggles to smile. She senses the lack of joy."

"I've been spending a lot of time with Day," Control revealed. "I'm trying to help her."

My heart skipped. I observed the golden Face of Control and her golden throne, then recalled the golden sutures spidering up Day's arms.

"You're breaking her," I blurted, clutching the sides of my head.

"No, we are giving the Host structure. I offer the opportunity to regain control."

"How?"

"In my pocket, we take the emotions and we own them. We become their master. They cannot define us if we define them first. Follow my guidance, and together, we will restore order."

Control floated above her throne, almost sitting, but not quite. She was a golden wisp, a gleaming zephyr—she was hardly there at all.

How could such a strong-willed intention have such a delicate Face? But then I reminded myself that she was made of gold. She might be small, but she was sturdy, and I suspected little could sway her resolve.

My wings pulverized the daylit sky as I tore back to the Lunar Spire.

I felt helpless. My purpose here was jeopardized. I was failing.

One error, and I subjected our perfect existence to damnation.

My mind raced with diseased thoughts, and as I noticed its presence, my doubts turned to fury.

The sickness still lived inside me, too.

I landed in the tower of my spire and dug my talons into my belly, ripping through my shadowy complexion and clawing my way to the source of this madness. My open wound leaked grains of sand and expelled a ghastly vapor, but I could not stop until I freed myself. Deep into my gut, dizzy from the stress of this open sore, my grains of sand turned red as they fell out of me. I had been infected; chaos had burrowed itself into me with a leeching illness.

As the last red sand grain vacated my body, I fell to the floor. Weak and wounded, but free. I tried to recall my bravery, but I was terrified. It wasn't supposed to work this way. I was unprepared for this war.

"Father Time," I shouted, growing sicker by the second. "Father Time!"

He did not materialize; he did not reply.

"You must intervene," I begged, hoping he might hear me from the cosmos, but my request remained unanswered.

Vapor leaked from my eyes as I cried.

The sensation was foreign—I had never felt anything other than fearlessness before today. My nerve was gone. My valor was compromised. For the first time in my life, I felt vulnerable.

I loathed the feeling.

Propped on my elbow, muscling through the agony of my potentially lethal wound, I examined the damage I had inflicted.

The hole gaped.

I inserted my talons into the shadowy flesh surrounding the wound and pulled the edges until the broken ends touched.

I bellowed in agony.

When the ends connected, shadow threads stitched the wound closed.

My body healed itself.

Grateful, I breathed easier and let my shadow work. By day fall, the wound had sewn shut. The pain lingered, but I was on the mend.

Day arrived with the setting sun, and after placing Solís to rest, she looked directly at the fresh, dark scar running from my sternum to my hips.

"What happened to you?" she asked.

"I had a rough day," I explained. "Chaos really pulled one over on us."

Her pinched brow softened and her shoulders sagged with exhaustion. "I'm trying to fix it."

"I heard."

"I think it's working."

"Do you trust Control?"

Day's big forest-green eyes held great hesitation. "She's the only option I have."

"Maybe we ought to team up," I suggested.

Day shook her head. "Your presence in the day will only frighten Jane."

"Why? I inspire courage."

"Not enough, it seems. She's traumatized by the terrors arriving at night."

"How does she even know about them? I carry them for her, so she doesn't have to."

"You're doing your best, but it isn't enough. Chaos has inundated her. Surely, you've noticed."

"Yes, I am beaten down and dispirited at the end of each night. It takes a full day to recover and prepare for another round."

"Well, as brave and strong as you are, she can feel your struggle, too. Don't stop doing what you're doing—it's holding her together, but more needs to be done, and that's what I'm trying to accomplish."

"If I need to work in my downtime, I can do that, too."

"Recovering is work. If you don't continue battling the night with a brave face, all will be lost." Day sighed, then reaffirmed, "You're doing a good job."

"Sounds like I'm not doing enough."

"You are. I just found an opportunity to do a little more. I worry if you tried the same, we'd lose our Host to the night."

I conceded; she wasn't wrong. Without my frequent escapades with the little clam, I'd likely buckle beneath the weight of the relentless, chaotic emotions terrorizing the night.

"I understand. I am here and willing to help if there is anything more I can do."

"It's appreciated. I'll let you know." She did not use the portal. Instead, she took flight into the night through the open window.

I turned to Luna, who waited calmly in her ethereal glow. She did not weep upon her arrival this evening.

"You're quiet tonight," I noted.

"I can be strong for you, too."

I took a deep, tired breath and lifted her into the sky.

The moon and I were linked, forever bound inside this mind, and while I did not want her sympathy, a small part of me appreciated her compassion. Her docile nature made it easier to catch the toxic emotions swimming alongside the usual nighttime fears. My tasks doubled, I now had two very different types of intruders to catch, each requiring special handling.

The fears continued to pass through me, disintegrating as my coarse shadow shredded them. I delivered their tattered pieces to the Face of Fear as I flew over his throne—they fell like magnets into his palm.

The emotion- and sickness-inspired fears were far more evasive. My magnetism did not work on them—I had to search for them. I had to lure them to me. From a distance, I speculated what each represented, then called out their name. Loneliness, rage, jealousy, regret—if I guessed correctly, they'd float toward me. If I guessed incorrectly, I had to deviate from my route to collect them.

It took all my strength and wits to reel in each nasty emotion without straying too from my nightly path with the moon. I swallowed them, keeping them confined in my belly until I had time to deliver them to the Pocket of Control.

After a long, exhausting night, I gently set Luna into the Solar Citadel.

"Thank you," I offered, grateful she hadn't cried all night.

For the first time since I had known her, she smiled.

A small change—one that actually felt good.

Disease-ridden emotions filled my gut. I had to expel what I had caught before they infected me. Day had already risen with the sun into the sky, so I raced the morning light toward the Pocket of Control.

"Stop!" Control shouted from her throne as she realized my flight was aimed at her pocket. "You cannot enter in daylight! You will contaminate our Host with irreversible fear."

"You told me to deliver the emotions I caught to your pocket."

"During the night! While the weaver sleeps," she explained.

"You should have told me that before. I have a belly full of poison that I need to expel."

"You will make things worse!"

"I will give her courage," I countered as I rocketed into the new and unfamiliar land.

Once the haze of the outer layer subsided, the most intricate land made of woven threads greeted me. All the threads connected, leading to a golden tower where the weaver lived. These threads controlled everything—one snapped cord, and the entire pocket would descend into chaos.

Giants lumbered across the terrain, stitched together by specific-colored threads. I thought the weaver was instructed to knit cages, but she had weaved herself friends instead. Each giant possessed a specific sickness-driven emotion, keeping it contained and controlled within their massive bodies. They controlled the more volatile feelings, and only with the weaver as a strong guide would they continue as steadfast cages for their assigned emotions.

The braided world dazzled me with its complexity, but I could not lose focus. I had to finish my job.

I circled the tower, releasing all that I carried. The digested emotions fell as glimmering dust and turned into colored threads. I swooped lower, gazing through the tower window to witness the magic. The threads wrapped around spools attached to the wall, neatly organized by color.

Perhaps this system would work after all.

I flew higher, circling the tower and delighting in this pocket's wonderous nature, when I felt Control's wrath pressing in on me.

Within her pocket, I was susceptible to her every whim. Her fragile hands clutched my neck and dragged me upward, away from the glorious threads of order. I lurched through the sky, constrained until she threw me out of the pocket and back into the sandclock's ether.

"I caused no harm," I protested, rubbing my neck where her marks still stung.

"I told you no," Control barked as she hurried back to her throne. "Too much is at stake."

"How can I help if I'm left in the dark?"

"You must make your deliveries at night."

"I cannot leave the sky, and there isn't much time between night and day. I don't know when you expect me to make this delivery."

"In the moments of dusk before dawn."

I grumbled.

"Do as I say," Control insisted.

Unwilling to argue, I soared away, agitated by her inconvenient rules.

I spent the day with my little clam, happily napping on the floor of my spire.

When Day arrived to set the sun, I noticed she was not well.

"You look sick," I said.

"I'm trying to save them both—the Face of Time and the weaver. They need to be healthy for the Host."

"Focus on yourself."

"If I can fix them, I can fix myself. If I fix myself, I can fix the Host."

"It's breaking you."

"The seconds are ticking away. You better start flying."

Unable to argue, as time was not on my side, I lifted the moon and ascended.

My aggravation worsened when time glitched again. A brief but powerful lapse, the glass soldier managed to correct his mistake without much delay. Arms sore, head throbbing, I performed my job with as much precision as I could muster. Luna set herself into the Solar Citadel while I raced to deliver the emotions I had caught to the Pocket of Control.

Successfully completing my job before dawn, I exited the land of threads prepared to surrender to sleep for the next twelve hours. But as I exited the pocket, I learned that the sun had not yet risen.

I raced to the Solar Citadel to find Day huddled on the floor, body doubled over and shaking.

Her open-back dress revealed new golden sutures spidering like unnatural veins down her spine.

"What happened?" I asked.

"It's all too much. I cannot be the friend Time needs when I'm consumed night in and night out with saving the weaver. She wants to disappear. Each time she unravels one of her coils, I receive a new break. The Face of Control stitches them shut with gold thread." She shook her head. "I am exhausted."

"It doesn't sound like what you're doing is working," I suggested cautiously. "If it's doing this to you, it cannot be right."

She began to cry. "It's all becoming a blur."

"Stop going there."

"I'm in too deep now," she protested.

"It's breaking you! And as the Face of Day, you embody the face and persona of our Host."

"I have to see it through," she stated, reeling in her emotions and hastily wiping the tears off her porcelain cheeks.

She stood, and I noticed how frail she had become. She not only wore dangerous cracks in her porcelain casing, but she was also half her normal size. She was a wisp of herself, and suddenly, I recalled the Face of Control—the frail golden whip of order.

Day lifted the sun into the sky before I could comment again.

I raced toward Control's throne.

"The Face of Day is deteriorating."

"She is stronger than you know."

"You are killing her," I spat. "You're just as rotten as Mr. Darclove."

"I am trying to fix his mess."

"Fix it by yourself. Stop burdening Day with your failures."

"How dare you—"

I flew away, ignoring Control's outrage.

I could not force Day to abandon her mission to save everyone but herself, nor could I get Control or Time to stop leaning on her. At a loss, I did not know how to help, and while the world within the Pocket of Control might have been in perfect order, chaos still plagued the more important world of the sandclock.

A note from the Fox

At this point in my journey, though I was halfway down my foxhole's long, dark corridor, I was far from discovering why I needed to see these memories. They were not mine; these sad stories were not my burden to carry.

Or so I thought.

I did not recognize the various Faces of Jane's personality. I did not see them as old friends that I once lived among. They were merely strangers telling me a wretched tale and I had forgotten I was one of them — that my every action directly influenced Jane and her choices. That's how far gone I was.

These mementos were an unwelcome gift.

You see, no one wants to reckon with the hurt they've caused, not after they've lived years in blissful denial.

I was no different.

I didn't want to know.

On the day of discovery, as the trail of mementos kept going, my patience waned. My ability to imagine that these uncomfortable tales were sent to me for my betterment dissipated — I recognized nothing and no one, and I wanted to go home.

Despite my growing disinterest, I had no choice but to participate. The mementos blocked my path, and in many cases, I had to pass through them to move forward.

An impassable net of shimmering gold threads appeared before me.

Paw atop the longest cord, I surrendered to the past.

Memento #6

When: The 18th – 20th Cycle
Where: Jane's mind — Pocket of Control
Who: Jane Doe through the Weaver

Spools of colored yarn lined my chamber walls.

My tower, made of stacked golden rocks, stood tall enough that I could see into the eyes of the giants I wove.

New threads greeted me each morning, and I never failed to empty each spool before nightfall. My duty was to weave these threads, ribbons, and yarns into inescapable knotted patterns. I had been told to knit cages—inanimate prisons to bind the threads—but I built giants instead. Friends to keep me company, friends to talk to. Connie, the head seamstress, fought me at first, saying I could not give the threads life, but once she saw the orderly fashion with which I controlled each giant, her objections ceased.

She trusted me.

To honor my choice, she sent me a trunk filled with buttons and coins to stitch into their eyes. These artifacts gave the giants life; they made them real.

Grateful, I honored her by obeying her rules.

I never let a thread go unstitched.

Each color represented a nighttime emotion that I was tasked to control, and as long as I kept them organized and sewn to their assigned giant, all was well.

On my wall today, three spools had replenished: red ribbon on the spool of rage and irritability, fuzzy yellow yarn on the spool of mischief, and slate gray silk threads on the spool of fatigue.

I had a long day ahead of me.

Before starting my work, I checked the golden coils that formed my little body, ensuring they were all twisted tight. Building giants was dangerous work; I had to be in tip-top shape before summoning them.

I scanned the threaded fields and distant hills outside my window. Late morning sunshine reflected off my yellow-green crystal eyeknobs, casting a glimmering haze on my threaded world. The glare debilitated my vision, so I waited an hour for the sun to lift a little higher into the sky and leave my direct line of sight.

Coils wound taut and haze cleared, it was time to get to work.

Perched on my windowsill, gripping the stone frame so I did not fall, my voice boomed into the land of giants.

"Raivo, Jinx, Aldis! Report to the weaving tower for new stitchings!"

My voice carried across the woven plains and over the sewn mountains. Everything here was woven together—even the giants had yarned feet that moved with the land. The threaded terrain bound their massive steps, stretching and reattaching, allowing the giants to move in any direction they chose while keeping them landlocked. They could not escape this place, not without a snip from my golden shears.

Raivo arrived first. His goliath form loomed high above the sewn mountain peaks. I could feel his rage from afar. I took a deep breath, preparing to soothe his irritability with words.

"No more stitches!" he boomed, grumbling and snarling as he fought the terrain. The yarns connecting his feet to the ground stretched to their limit as he trekked toward me.

"It's not my decision which spools are filled each night. We are both pawns in a greater game."

"I am no pawn!" he roared.

I grimaced—wrong choice of word.

"All I meant was that we need to work together. I am your friend, not your enemy."

Raivo reached my tower. He placed one of his red button eyes to my window and peered through.

"What did they send?" he asked.

"Red ribbon—"

"No!" His colossal yarn fingers gripped my tower, causing everything to shake unsteadily. "It is frilly."

"It belongs to you," I insisted, stepping closer with the ribbon threaded into my tapestry needle.

"It's dark red—it's crimson. It belongs to Aridam."

"It showed up on *your* spool, not his."

Raivo pulled away from the window, ready to run, but I clenched my fist, commanding the terrain threads to tighten. Every giant in the land was now bound in place, including Raivo.

"Let me go!" he demanded.

I leaped out of the window, threaded ribbon in tow, and landed on his shoulder. He squirmed violently, desperate to thwart my attempts.

"If you don't carry this ribbon of rage, who will?" I shouted, struggling to pierce the needle and knot the ribbon into his intricate form.

"I carry enough! Don't weigh me down with more."

"I'm sorry, but this is how it works."

My needle stabbed his collar, anchoring beneath a solid string of yarn, and I knotted this new ribbon of terror to his intricate web of threads.

Raivo fell to his knees, utterly irritated by my success, but unable to stop the inevitable stitching process. I scaled his body, working as I clambered from stitch to stitch. My coiled golden feet locked into his netted threads as I descended carefully.

I did my best to make this new stitch look nice. From the top of his shoulder running down along his arm, I weaved the ribbon in warrior knots. It was fierce, it was regal, and it matched his energy.

As I sewed the tail end of the ribbon into his wrist, he looked down at my work. The agitated expression on his face softened.

"You're quite good at what you do."

"Do you like it?"

"It's not nearly as bad as I thought it would be."

"We are allies. Try to remember that for next time."

I scrambled up his arm, using the newly created knots to ascend. When I reached his shoulder, he leaned toward my tower so I could dismount safely.

Beyond him, I could see Jinx and Aldis waiting their turn.

"I hope I don't see you again for a while," he grumbled.

"If that makes you happy, then I desire that, too."

I loosened the threads constraining him.

Raivo stormed away, moving as quickly as his threaded feet allowed. As he crossed between Jinx and Aldis, Jinx poked him in the ribcage. Raivo's calmed demeanor resumed its rage as he spun and punched Jinx in the face.

"It wasn't me," Jinx insisted as he massaged the spot of impact. "It was Aldis."

Aldis stood in place, swaying back and forth with his threaded eyelids closed.

"I'm not a fool," Raivo barked before smacking Jinx once more and continuing his angry departure.

Jinx walked toward me, his threaded expression alight with mischief.

"Why do you taunt him?" I asked.

"Because he takes the bait."

I shook my head. "You're a troublemaker."

"What thread of naughtiness do you have for me today?"

"I don't get to see the emotions or the moments that gave them life. Perhaps you can tell me once they're woven into you."

"No, I just feel them. There is no beginning or end. No source to explain why I am how I am."

"Step closer," I instructed. "This fuzzy yellow yarn will look best on your head."

Jinx obeyed. He did not fight me as Raivo always did. I weaved peacefully without endangering my life.

"Ouch," Jinx said.

"Oh, I'm sorry."

His stitched mouth smirked.

"Just kidding," he said with a chuckle.

"Good one," I said begrudgingly, aware that Jinx was most appeased when he believed his pranks were appreciated.

His stitching took less time to complete, and when I finished, he stood tall with glee.

"I'm no longer bald!"

"You look great," I agreed.

"I'm going to show Livius first," he said, his smile sly.

"No, that will only upset him. You know how jealous he gets."

"That's the point! It will be hilarious."

Jinx played with his yarn hair as he stomped away, threads pulling at the ground with each step.

The sun began to set.

"Aldis, you're up," I announced.

Aldis did not move, and his eyelids remained shut.

"Wake up!" I shouted.

My voice startled him out of his waking slumber. He looked around, confused.

"Over here," I guided him. He took slow, threaded steps toward me.

"How did I get here?" he asked.

"You must've sleepwalked. I have a new thread for you."

His eyelids fluttered, threatening to shut again.

"Stay with me," I demanded. "Give me your hand."

He extended his giant hand to the tower, reaching two fingers through the window and locking them to the sill. I climbed onto the back of his hand, determined to work fast in case he fell asleep and dropped his hand. I latched my feet into his woven knots for extra security, then began threading the satin threads of fatigue around his knuckles. He grew more tired with each stitch.

I worked quicker, resolved to finish my work before sundown put Aldis to sleep for the night.

His grip on the sill loosened and his hand began to drop.

One more stitch and I'd be done.

I lassoed the final bit of thread around his giant thumb, knotting its end to a solid thread in his palm.

As his hand slipped off my tower, I leaped and clung to the windowsill. Aldis fell and landed with a ground-trembling thud.

Elbows locked to the inside of the window, I used all my strength to pull my body over the golden stone sill. Aldis snored loudly outside, shaking my tower with each rumbling snort. Inches from safety, I clawed my fingers into the cobblestone floor and yanked my legs through the window.

I was safe again.

After a few moments curled up on the floor, regaining my composure and calming my adrenaline, I went to the window to observe the fall I had narrowly escaped.

The ground was made of soft yarn, and being made of golden coils, I suspected I might have survived, but at what cost?

Dented coils, bent limbs?

Though sleep had always healed my injuries in the past, it wasn't worth the risk. A mishap large enough could debilitate me from performing my job here, and I needed to attach each thread to its respective giant in an orderly fashion to prevent pandemonium.

Failure to stitch every thread would result in a loss of control. The head seamstress warned me that such a fiasco would cause our neatly knitted world to come undone.

Connie—I had not seen the head seamstress since I came into existence a year ago. With gentle care and stern authority, she had wrapped my golden coils together, twisting and weaving each singular strand until I became what I am now. The rules she gave me were clear: I was the weaver of nighttime emotions. Poisonous feelings plagued this place, and my job was to knot their existence with inescapable precision. Without me, these toxic sentiments would run free and wreak havoc.

To date, I was mother to ten woven giants, each of whom brought me more strife than joy. They were my friends; they kept me company, but with time, I found they took more than they gave. They wanted, they needed, they begged, they manipulated, forcing me to bend to their wills.

I created them, after all.

I was responsible for managing their outbursts.

My work completed for the day, I admired the ten empty spools hanging on my wall. No threads left to weave, I could rest easy.

I laid my wiry body between two golden boulders protruding from the stone floor. Soft cushions and blankets lined the recessed nook—the only comfort I had in this cold tower.

Head placed upon my pillow, I stared at the wall of spools as my eyelids shuttered. I secretly hoped that I awoke to empty spools—I dreamed of a single day free from my giants.

This was wishful thinking, though.

It seemed, with time, the arrival of nighttime emotions only increased.

I surrendered to sleep's pull, aware I could not control the threads that materialized while I slumbered.

As always, morning arrived without warning.

Light infiltrated my tower, illuminating my freshly polished and tightened coils. I always woke up like this. Did someone take care of me while I slept? Or was the act of sleeping rejuvenating on its own?

I might never know.

Yards of vibrant new threads had wrapped around their assigned spools. My work was greater today than yesterday. Yards of colored thread wound tightly around four spools: chartreuse for jealousy, powder blue for regret, lavender for loneliness, and crimson for destruction.

I did not wish to leave my bed.

Gaze fixated on the wall of work awaiting me, I noticed a brand-new spool in the bottom right corner. It had not been there yesterday. Wrapped with braided black silk, its ominous arrival worried my tired heart.

With this black thread, I'd have to create a new giant. I'd need to keep it in the tower until it grew large enough to leave—just like I had done with all the others. My energy wavered; I was not in the mood to make new friends.

I rose to face the day, deciding to tackle the threads I knew well before addressing the stranger in my home.

"Jane!" a voice shouted from outside.

I walked to my window to find Livius pacing outside my tower.

"What is it?" I asked.

"You gave Jinx hair?" he asked, genuinely distraught.

"Jinx was sent fuzzy yarn. It made sense to sew it to his head."

"It isn't fair! I want hair."

"You're in luck," I informed him. "You were sent threads last night."

His envy morphed into delight.

"Weave it to my head," he begged.

"Come closer."

Livius rushed to me, yanking the terrain yarn attached to his feet with each giant step. I went to my wall of spools and found the end of the yellow-green chartreuse thread. It was thin cotton—not the best for weaving hair.

"It's very thin," I warned.

"I don't care. Give me hair."

He rested his forehead against my windowsill.

"I will do my best," I promised, afraid this short strand of thin thread wouldn't have the desired look Livius hoped for.

"Don't disappoint me," he growled in reply.

"I don't have much thread here—it will look like patchwork."

"Please make me look good. I need the other giants to envy me."

"You need nothing of the sort from them," I said as I made my first chartreuse stitch into his woven scalp.

"It's better than me envying them."

"I understand that it's hard for you to let go of all your jealous tendencies—these threads keep you bound to such covetous affinities—but you must remember that you are amazing just as you are. What the other giants think of you changes nothing."

"Still, I want them to think highly of me."

"I'm sure they already do."

Livius grumbled.

I wove a wide track of light green thread from his forehead to the nape of his neck.

"All done," I announced as I knotted the final stitch and climbed the backside of his skull. Atop the crown of his head, I had to leap over his giant hand, narrowly getting swept to a crushing fall as he felt my finished work.

"It only covers the middle," he griped.

I leaped through my window as he pulled away.

"Think of it as a racing stripe," I replied breathlessly.

He considered this.

"Does it suit me?" he asked, eager for validation.

"Yes," I answered honestly. "I won't be surprised if all the giants come asking for their own after seeing you."

His stitched grin stretched wide.

"I must show them all."

"Fantastic. You do that, but please visit Rue, Aridam, and Isola first. Tell them I need to see them before nightfall."

"Aye, aye, captain," Livius said as he skipped away.

At the top of the sewn mountains, a second silhouette joined Livius. The giant of jealousy massaged his head as he showed off his new stitching, and the second giant came barreling toward me as he departed over the mountain.

"I thought you had forgotten about me," Isola bawled as she tripped over the yarn keeping her secured to the ground. She stumbled repeatedly, often falling to her knees, but never stopping.

"I would never," I swore.

"It's been so long since you called on me," she stammered. "I cannot describe my relief when Livius said you wanted to see me."

"I have new thread for you."

Her excitement vanished.

"No, I don't want more thread."

"Why not?"

"Every time you give me a new stitch it only intensifies the isolation I feel."

"Then stay with me after I weave this thread into you. We can be together while you process it."

Her lavender eyebrows furrowed.

"You mean it?"

"Of course, I do. You can stay outside my tower as long as you'd like."

"What kind of thread is it today?" she asked.

"Lavender pearl cotton."

"Oh, my favorite. Would you mind elongating my eyelashes?"

"Anything you want," I said.

She leaned in close and I got to work weaving the new thread into her beautiful lilac lashes. Up and down, across both of her lids, the enhancement took up the entire yard of thread.

"Step back. Let me see," I requested upon completion.

She opened her purple button eyes, which brimmed with wet sadness.

"Beautiful!" I offered.

Her head lowered. "It's not like I have anybody to impress."

"I am impressed."

"You're kind, but you don't count."

"Why don't I count?"

"Because you made me. Your opinions are biased."

"I see."

"I will go. I am a bummer to be around."

"You can stay," I insisted.

"I want to be alone."

Isola walked away slowly—a stark contrast to her impatient arrival.

Aridam and Rue were already waiting for me. They held hands, ignoring Isola's pitiful departure.

I called out to them, "Why is it that you two are always needed on the same days?"

"We are bound," Aridam replied, dragging Rue forward as he approached the tower.

"Destruction and regret," I pondered aloud. "I suppose that makes sense. Who's up first?"

Aridam pushed Rue forward. She fell, slamming her head against the stone wall.

"Be careful," I demanded of Aridam.

"She'll be fine."

"Are you okay?" I asked Rue.

"Yes," she replied hastily. "I deserve his cruelty."

"No, you don't."

"The regret I carry is massive. If I cannot punish myself, then someone else must."

"I wish I knew what ailed you. I wish I knew the source of your regrets."

"All that matters is their potency. I do not deserve kindness."

"I am sorry that I must sew new threads of shame into you."

"It's your job." She raised her hand and looked away. "Do your duty."

I stitched the powder blue thread around her wrist and up her forearm. The long stretch of yarn covered her with fresh regret. It sheathed her entire arm. A vambrace of apologies yet to be uttered.

As I finished, Rue's posture sagged as if invisible weights had been placed on her shoulders.

"Will you be okay?" I asked.

She nodded. "It is my burden to carry."

I glared at Aridam. "Why do I sense her regret has something to do with you?"

"With me? I merely carry the destruction caused elsewhere."

He was right.

I grumbled—he was my least favorite giant.

"Stay where you are," I demanded, clutching my fist to tighten the yarn around his feet.

Though he did not fight my command, he blatantly eyed my tower with devious intent. The last time he arrived to collect new threads of destruction, he almost toppled my tower with a single, intentional swipe of his hand.

I pulled the crimson thread from the spool and knotted a noose at its end. After three calculated swings above my head, the lasso flew toward Aridam, snagging him by the neck. He stood still, bored by my elaborate methods to keep him distanced from my home. I leaped out of my window, swinging wildly on the rope. When I came to a stop, I latched myself to Aridam's torso and began weaving the bottom end of the thread into his ribcage.

Stitch by stitch, I worked my way up the right side of his body to his neck. I untied the noose and finished my work. Invisible to the eye, whatever feeling of destruction I just delivered blended in with the rest.

"Are we done here?" he asked.

"We are," I confirmed, suddenly aware that I was stuck on his shoulder, unable to return to my tower.

"Didn't think this one through, did you?" he asked.

Panicked, I looked at Rue, who had her back turned to me. Wholly consumed by her remorse, she did not notice my predicament.

"Let's see how good my aim is," Aridam suggested with a scheming smirk.

Before I could object, he lifted his gigantic fingers and flicked me off his shoulder. I catapulted through the sky, somersaulting in the air toward my tower. Unable to do anything but hope for the best, I tucked my knees to my chest and made myself as small as possible. I closed my eyes, praying for a soft landing. When I crashed onto the golden cobblestone of my tower room and rolled to a rough stop, Aridam's cheers echoed through the land.

"Perfect aim," he congratulated himself.

Sore, but relatively unharmed, I hobbled to my feet.

"What if you had missed?" I barked in anger.

"I suspect you'd have some severely dented coils."

I fell to my knees, too tired to argue with him.

He took my silence as a request to leave, which he and Rue happily obliged.

You need a friend who demands less from you, a voice whispered.

I searched for the source—I was alone.

The spool of black braided silk beckoned in the fading light of day.

"I'll deal with you tomorrow," I said.

It was the first time I fell asleep with thread left on a spool.

Hours later, during the few moments that night and day shared, a mysterious feeling compelled me to rise. My coils had been freshly polished during my slumber, as usual, and I slid atop the smooth cobblestone as I raced to my window.

A winged silhouette tore across the silver sky, casting a shadow over the golden land of giants.

I watched in awe—I had never seen such a sight before. A creature with talons for toes and feathered wings on his back soared above me, dropping wisps of colored dust as he circled over my tower.

Not quite a man, not quite a shadow—he was a being from beyond. He soared with daring confidence and an air of invincibility. He did not belong here, he was not of this land, yet he arrived with unabashed authority.

Unbound to the yarn prison I had created, this creature flew free.

I stood tall, hoping he might see me and save me from this threaded prison, but he did not notice me. I was too small and concealed by the tower walls. He soared up and away, disappearing out of sight.

Though he had only stayed a moment, this memory would linger eternally.

My coiled golden heart reverberated with ominous thuds.

I no longer wished to be here.

You could be free, too, a voice whispered.

My attention snapped back to the small prison I called home.

I was alone.

New threads had arrived on the wall of spools: navy for misery and indigo for obsession. Two of my least favorite giants.

They don't deserve you.

I could not escape the imaginary voice.

The black thread remained on its spool, waiting to be knotted into a tiny giant. I wasn't ready to discover what horrors it held. I had enough to manage with the giants already dependent upon me.

I hobbled to the window.

"Kenah! Desdemona!" My voice echoed for all to hear. "You are summoned!"

I knelt and rested my face against the hard windowsill. I could hear the stomping approach of the giants I had beckoned, but I did not lift my gaze to greet them.

"Why are we here?" Desdemona asked, her brooding energy potent.

"I've received new threads for you both."

Kenah perked up, stepping closer and poking my tired head where it rested.

"Where's mine?" she inquired.

Though she thought she'd been gentle, her rough touch left a slight dent in my skull. I massaged the spot.

Sleep would remedy my newest injury.

I lifted my tired body and retrieved her dark purple thread.

"Threads of indigo satin, made especially for you," I said.

Her silver coin eyes lit up with possessive desire; she was the only giant who enjoyed receiving new threads. She pressed her forearm to the side of my tower so I could climb on.

"Why don't you fight me like all the other giants?" I asked.

"These threads are the only thing in this world that I can call mine. They belong to me, and me alone."

I suspected this answer—she was the giant of possessive obsession, after all. Each thread was a trophy, and she collected them with zealous passion.

The moment I knotted the final stitch, Kenah flicked me off her arm and through my window, then pulled away to admire her new thread.

"Mine," she cooed, completely fixated on the fresh stitch.

I lifted myself back to my feet.

"Your turn," I informed Desdemona, who sat huddled with her knees to her chest.

"I cannot stand."

"Why not?"

"I am too sad."

"You need to be brave, for me."

"Why? What's the point?" she sulked.

"If I do not stitch these new threads into you, everything around us will begin to unravel."

Her interest piqued. "Are you saying that the responsibility of saving you and all the other giants lands on me?"

"Yes." My patience was wearing thin—we had this exact discussion every time she needed a new stitch.

She nodded wearily, as if the weight of the world was hers to carry. "I can do it. I can be strong to save you."

"Thank you," I said, assuaging her desire to play the hero.

Desdemona stood slowly, dawdling as she made her way toward me. Her navy yarn was already knotted to my tapestry needle. I had to work fast—the moment these new sorrowful threads entwined into her, her despondence would return.

She extended the inner side of her wrist to me. The threads lining this delicate spot were thin and frayed.

"Have you been sawing at your threads again?"

"I thought it might make me feel better if I cut a few loose."

"Only I can cut your threads."

"I wish you would."

"I don't want you to unravel."

Desdemona wore a sullen frown.

I continued, "I will strengthen these threads. Do not saw at them again. You're only torturing yourself."

She nodded half-heartedly as I reinforced the tattered threads. Stitch by stitch, I felt Desdemona's resolve weakening.

"Please stop," she begged.

"I'm almost done," I assured her as I neared the end of the new thread.

"These threads are poison. They are killing me."

"These threads give you life. Without them, you'd be nothing."

"I'd rather be dead."

"If you don't carry them, who will?" I had three stitches left.

"I don't care!"

I was losing her. She tugged and pulled as I raced to weave the last two stitches to her wrist.

"Please stay still," I pleaded.

Desdemona sobbed, falling to her knees in surrender while keeping her arm raised to my window. I knotted the final stitch.

"All done!" I announced.

Her arm dropped and she collapsed onto her side, curling up on the ground.

"You can stay there as long as you like," I shouted down to her. "You are always welcome here."

My words offered no comfort—her sobs echoed like thunder.

I retreated into my tower, wishing I could block out the sound of her sorrow, but it was impossible. The only way to help Desdemona was to let her cry herself to sleep. Patient tolerance was the only assistance I could offer.

You deserve better.

These whispers were devious.

"Who are you?" I demanded.

Your newest friend.

My gaze darted to the spool of black thread—it was time to discover what mysterious giant begged for life.

To the sounds of Desdemona's sobs, I slowly unraveled the black thread from its spool. Course to the touch, the thick, braided strands of silk were semi-rigid in my grip.

"What will you be?" I wondered aloud.

The thread fit tightly into my weaver's loom. Specifically designed for my purposes, this loom stood in the form of a small body. I began by lining the bodice with the black silk, zigzagging it through every notch. Then, I wove each of the lines together. Starting at the toes and working my way clockwise up the torso, I stitched the bottom half of my newest friend. Before crafting the upper part of the body, I reached my needle into the hollow space of the legs and hips, crisscrossing the thread and making this hollow body whole. Strong in stature, this giant would have solid legs to stand on. I finished the chest, neck, and head, carefully filling these spaces with enough thread to fill this creature's cavernous voids before using the last of the thread to bind the skull closed. With care, I gently removed the loom and revealed a tiny person made of threaded black silk. One day, they would become a havoc-wrecking giant like all the others, but for now, they were still small enough to call a friend.

It stood immobile, waiting for the last piece of its creation.

In my trunk of buttons, coins, and stones, I found none that matched the sleek, shimmering darkness of the black silk.

"I couldn't possibly give you purple buttons or pink stones for eyes," I grumbled, searching for something that would match this creature's aesthetic.

Wrist deep into the trunk, eyes fixated on the various trinkets I rummaged through, I did not notice the gleaming black marbles until they rolled into my foot. They hit my golden coils with a clang.

My eyes followed their path and landed on a shadowed corner of my chamber.

"Where did these come from?" I asked the empty darkness.

I received no reply.

They were flawless—a perfect set of eyes for my new friend. I placed the marbles into the hollow sockets, stretching some of the silk to hold the marbles in place. As they settled into their new home, the creature came to life. Animated for the first time, it stretched and fidgeted as it became acquainted with its body.

"My name is Jane," I offered. "It is nice to meet you."

The piercing marble eyes held vast depths.

I asked, "Do you have a name?"

"Malsana," she replied, her voice the same hoarse whisper I had heard in my head.

"Do you know which fear or emotion you carry?"

She shook her head. "I only know what I've seen from my spool."

"I'm sorry I took so long to weave you."

"It's okay. It gave me time to understand the way this world works. It also allowed me to see how undervalued you are. I will be a better friend to you than the other giants."

I never expected such an offer. I wasn't sure how to respond.

Malsana's woven mouth twisted into a smile.

"It's okay," she continued. "I know you're not used to kindness."

"I call them my friends, but I often find that their friendship is a burden."

"I'll show you true friendship," she promised. Her cavernous eyes bore into me, touching my soul with covetous kindness. Energy potent, I wished only to see the benevolence in her devious stare.

I retrieved one of the many pillows in my sleeping nook and gave it to Malsana. She accepted it gratefully and positioned it next to where I slept. I fell asleep, feeling hopeful for the first time since my creation.

When I awoke the following day, Malsana stared at me from atop her pillow.

"Did you know you have a nighttime visitor?" she asked me.

I glanced down at my polished and tightened coils, then asked, "Is it Connie?"

"It's a girl made of porcelain."

My brow furrowed; I knew no one made of porcelain. "I suppose she was sent by Connie then."

"Perhaps."

"It's a bit odd," I considered, "but it is nice to wake up without the dents and grime I collected the day before."

I looked at the wall of spools—powder blue threads of regret had arrived for Rue.

An easy task, as Rue was among the easier giants to manage, I'd have a full day to get to know Malsana better. She had received new threads, too—more black braided silk to add to her tiny frame.

"Who does it belong to?" Malsana asked as she rose from her pillow, pointing at the spool wound with light blue yarn.

"Rue. She carries the threads of regret."

Malsana seemed intrigued, but asked no further questions. I went to my window and shouted Rue's name. My booming voice startled Desdemona awake.

"I was sleeping," she said with a groan.

"You can stay, but you'll need to move so Rue can come to my window. New thread arrived for her."

Desdemona grumbled under her breath. "Better her than me."

She rolled out of the way once Rue arrived.

"What have I done now?" Rue asked.

"Your guess is as good as mine," I replied.

She placed her hand on my windowsill and her arm served as a bridge. Thread in hand, I crossed, making my way onto her shoulder. With care, I stitched the yarn along the rim of her ear. She winced and lamented that whatever vague memory she was acquiring weighed more heavily than those she'd received in the past.

I could do nothing to help and continued weaving, thoroughly securing this latest regret into her.

As I finished the final stitch, I glanced at her face. Her silver coin eyes coated in blue were fixated on the ground. Spots where the paint had chipped revealed her gleaming shame.

I hurried along her arm, back to my tower, before she lowered the bridge, forgetting I was there.

I hopped off her fingers and onto the golden cobblestone. My departure recaptured her attention.

"Do you think I could cut some of these older threads from my body?" she asked, peering through my window.

Before I could answer, she caught sight of Malsana and gasped.

"Who is that?"

"A future giant. Her first set of threads arrived two days ago."

"She is not one of us," Rue insisted.

"Not yet, no. But she will be after she grows."

"Don't feed her threads."

"Excuse me?"

"Don't let her become a giant," Rue begged.

"What am I supposed to do with the black thread that shows up on her spool?"

"Weave a blanket, knit a hat—anything else. Just don't give that monster life."

Malsana listened, but did not intervene. She sat patiently on her pillow, observing Rue's panic with calm amusement.

"Tell me why," I insisted of Rue.

"It's just a feeling I have."

"Well, I cannot forsake my duties for a feeling. Quite frankly, you're being mean. Malsana is new here and you're not being very welcoming."

"Because she is a terror! I can sense it in my threads."

"Okay, well, your concerns have been noted. Please leave."

Rue's coin eyes shimmered with disappointment as if my dismissal was betrayal.

I turned my attention to Malsana. "Do you know what she was going on about?"

"I have no clue." Her reply was confident.

I sighed. "Let's weave these new threads into you."

Malsana remained still, obediently allowing me to stitch netted cages around her eye sockets. This design better held her marble eyes in place.

"How do you feel?" I asked.

"Much better."

It felt strange to have such a docile friend. I tried to recall if the other giants had started off tame and dutiful, but the distant memories eluded me. I could not remember.

"I hope you stay this way," I expressed.

"I will set you free," she replied.

My golden brow furrowed—what an odd reply.

I let it go.

We fell asleep in our designated spots and I dreamed of the winged man in the sky. He twirled in swooping patterns over my tower, calling out my name as he rained wisps of sparkling, colored dust over me. I stood atop my tower with my coiled arms stretched outward, ready to embrace the winged man's gift. But as the glittering flecks touched me, they turned into threads and viciously entangled me.

The winged man felt no pity that I was bound in place.

"Only you can free yourself," he shouted before flying away.

Precariously perched atop the slanted roof of my tower, I struggled to stay upright. Ankles knotted together, arms fastened to my sides, I teetered. One wobble too many—I fell, tumbling down the golden shingles and plummeting toward the ground of knitted threads.

I awoke with a start.

The porcelain girl who cared for me in my sleep had wound my coils too tight.

Panting, out of breath, the restrictive nature of my golden coils made it hard to release my fear.

It sat trapped in my chest, clawing at my wire cage.

"What's wrong?" Malsana asked.

"I had a nightmare."

"Let it go."

"I'm trying, but the fear is trapped inside me."

"Where?"

"Here." I clutched my chest. Panic consumed me. In a whisper, I confessed, "I want to be free."

"Then be free," Malsana replied.

"How?" I asked, grimacing through my anxiety.

"Unravel one of your golden coils. See how it feels."

179

My eyes widened, unsure if this was wise. As the residual agony from my nightmare lingered, refusing to abate, I tried her suggestion.

My fingers dug into the narrow spaces between the coils, bending and reshaping their rigid form until there was enough room to firmly seize the first end I could find. I slowly unwound the tightly twisted wires. In and out, over and under—each careful shuffle created additional space for the panic within me to escape.

When I reached the coil's end, I untwisted it from the coil it was attached to. I refastened that coil to another, then slowly pulled the freed coil out of my body.

Tension released, I was liberated. The rigid cord transformed into a soft golden thread.

"How do you feel?" Malsana asked.

"Free." The word escaped my mouth as a whispered breath.

"You work so hard with no rewards. You deserve to be happy."

I nodded. She was right. I had undervalued myself for too long.

The golden thread lay limp in my grip. As I considered what to do with it, a jingling whirlwind swirled around my tower.

"What have you done?" a furious voice shouted at me.

Connie—I recognized her scathing tone.

Malsana retreated into the shadows, shrinking out of sight.

"Nothing," I answered.

"You cannot fool me. I know all that happens here."

The jangling cyclone did not cease when Connie gracefully hopped through my window. Her feet never touched the ground—she hovered weightlessly as she rocketed toward me.

"How do you do that?" I asked, enamored by her ability to levitate.

"Do what?"

I pointed at her feet.

She quickly lowered herself, planting her bare feet firmly on the golden cobblestone.

"Never mind that. Tell me what's wrong."

Up close, Connie was divine. Her few stitchings appeared to be decorative instead of functional.

"Nothing," I grumbled in reply.

"I am connected to every thread in this land. I know what you did."

I refused to admit my misdeed.

She continued, pointing at the golden thread in my hand as she spoke. "Why did you tear out this piece of yourself?"

"You have your porcelain associate to blame."

"Excuse me?"

"The girl who visits while I sleep. You know, the one who polishes and tightens my coils … she twisted them too tight last night. I couldn't breathe. I couldn't release my fear, but I feel better now."

She clicked her tongue. "Hand it here," she demanded as she took the thread from me. She examined it closely before announcing, "It is salvageable. I can fix you."

"I don't need to be fixed."

"I am tasked with maintaining order and control. Without you, the giants have no weaver."

"I'm not going anywhere."

"That's not the point. You need to be whole if you wish to control the giants. Any inkling of weakness and the giants will take advantage."

"Teach the porcelain girl how to control them."

"She visits to take care of you and inspire confidence, not to take on your responsibilities. She has enough of her own."

"Why does it all land on me? *You* can control the giants, too," I argued.

"No, I can't. I control you, and you control the giants."

I did not like this admission.

"I don't need a babysitter."

"Clearly, you do. Let me stitch this thread back into you."

"I don't want that thread. It's yours to keep."

Connie's frown tightened. "What has changed?"

"Nothing," I lied.

Stubborn, but willing to concede, Connie wrapped the long thread around her wrist.

"Just this once," she said. "Do not make this a habit."

"I won't," I promised, though it felt like a fib.

Connie floated away, disappearing in the fading breeze of bells.

How could I possibly keep such a terrible promise? I wanted to be free, like her, like the winged man in the sky. Unbound and weightless, I wished to fly away.

"Do you plan to keep that promise?" Malsana asked from the shadows.

"No."

"Then you will need to be clever."

She was right. I would need to hide my threads so that Connie or the porcelain girl could not detect their removal.

My wall of spools was decorated with color. Crimson, red, powder blue, and yellow—perhaps the giants could serve *me* for a change.

"Aridam, Raivo, Livius, and Jinx! Report to the tower immediately."

Thundering footsteps shook the land as my most volatile giants heeded my call. Threaded strides slowed their furious charge.

I watched from afar—Aridam and Livius led the pack, eager to claim more of their precious threads, while Raivo and Jinx lagged behind.

When they reached my tower, I was ready to try my scheme.

"Welcome, boys. You know why you're here. Line up," I ordered.

"Someone's feeling bossy today," Jinx teased.

"I'm tired," I replied.

"How is that our problem?" Raivo argued.

"Yeah," Livius chimed in. "Your bad mood shouldn't be our burden to bear."

I laughed. "The hypocrisy."

"Are you laughing at me?" Livius asked, offended by my refusal to accommodate their infuriating personalities.

"I'm laughing at the irony."

"Irony of what?" Raivo demanded.

"It doesn't matter. You're up first."

Aware that I needed to fulfill my duty and assuage their capricious temperaments, I mustered the strength to play pretend.

Raivo stepped closer to my window, eyeing me with suspicion.

"I'm still enraged by the last threads you gave me," he warned.

"I have an idea, something we can try that might make this process more bearable for you."

"What's that?"

I cautiously unraveled a gilded coil from my wrist. As it left my body, I twisted my golden thread and Raivo's red thread together.

"Let's see if this helps," I said, weaving both threads into Raivo's thumb knuckle.

His expression tightened, preparing to feel blinding rage, but the anger was muted. My golden thread subdued the fury.

"This is so much better," he expressed. A foreign serenity soothed the furious lines on his stitched face.

"Excellent."

I knotted the final stretch of thread, and Raivo walked away in a daze. My gaze searched beyond the giants who awaited their turn. Would Connie come for me?

Livius stepped forward, eager to receive the same gift I had given Raivo.

Connie was nowhere in sight.

"You'll give me the same thing you gave him, right?"

"Yes, of course," I assured him.

I unraveled a coil from my left elbow, and once it turned into a thread, I entwined it with his. He leaned in close, letting me stitch the threads to the tip of his nose. Each suture relaxed him further, and by the time I finished, his perpetual jealous sneer had morphed into a radiant smile.

Was I healing them? Was I alleviating their fatal flaws?

Connie did not sense the removal of my threads as they immediately found new life in another.

Jinx stepped forward, his smile devious.

"You're being sneaky," he said.

"Maybe I am."

"I like it."

He moved closer and turned his back to me so I could stitch our combined threads into his shoulder blades.

"It feels nice," he revealed once I completed the weaving. "Your threads reduce the potency of my own."

"Happy to help."

Last up was Aridam, the giant of destruction.

"What will you do when you have no threads left?" he asked.

"I'll be free."

He considered this. "I'd like to be free, too."

His docile nature was foreign. Perhaps my own self-destruction dwarfed his and he didn't know how to handle someone with less care for their well-being than he held for his own.

"Help me first," I commanded.

He leaned in and let me weave our combined threads to his lips. No fight, no contention, he let me apply the stitches without the usual battle.

When I finished, he took a step back. His giant fingers traced the lines of his lips.

"Maybe your unraveling will set me free," he said.

"How so?"

"Your golden thread weighs less than the destruction I carry. With enough of your threads sewn into mine, maybe I'll change. Maybe I'll be different."

"I can only give as much as I have."

"I will behave. I will comply if it means you will gift me with golden threads."

For the first time since my giants had reached towering heights, I was in control. I had found a way to sway their irritable, hostile demeanors.

My task done for the day, I was shocked to see that the sun was only halfway through the sky. I had time to myself, time free from my giants.

Malsana sat on her pillow, observing my astonishment.

"They did not fight me. They did not test my patience," I said. "It usually takes all day to weave four giants, but today, it took half the time."

"You gave them something invaluable—a gift they can only receive from you. They will be obedient moving forward in order to receive your threads."

My glee surged. "It won't take long to rid myself of these coils. Soon, I will be free."

Malsana stood. "I was thinking … who will tame the giants when you aren't around?"

This forced me to pause. "I hadn't thought that far ahead."

"Perhaps you ought to lend me some of your golden threads, too; I can wear them as a disguise. This way, once you're gone, I can take over your duties and Control will never notice your absence."

"Who?" I asked.

"Connie," she replied hastily. "That's what I said. Let me take over, and she'll never notice."

"You would do that for me?"

"Of course. That's what friends are for."

"The giants will deplete you," I warned.

Malsana looked unconcerned. "They can try."

This little giant before me offered a path to freedom, selflessly sacrificing herself so that I could escape my predetermined fate.

"Why are you being so generous?" I asked.

"I've witnessed your suffering. I am happy to step in so you can save yourself."

My heart swelled within its coiled cage.

This gift was more than I fathomed possible.

"I don't know what I did to deserve you, but I am grateful you are here."

Malsana's stitched smile curled upward. "Let's get started then."

Countless layers of golden coils comprised my existence—it would take many nights to unravel them all—but we began the long journey. I started with my chest, loosening the coils around my defeated spirit, hoping this release might liberate my soul.

It worked.

By sundown, I was five coils lighter and my energy had lifted. I sewed each of my liberated threads into Malsana, safely hiding them within her.

Connie never arrived to chastise me.

The porcelain girl did not notice my gradual decrease of coils.

My secret was contained.

I carried on this way, unstitching bits of myself and offering my loose threads to the giants who now adored me. They didn't understand my sacrifice—they blindly idolized me, showering me with compliments as I withered away. They knew not what they did—they only took what I offered freely. Their words of admiration lifted me to great heights while they unconsciously took what was left of me.

Their empty love filled my hollow heart.

Through them, I could disappear.

I could become one with my nothingness.

Through destruction, I would find freedom.

Malsana stayed with me every step of the way.

We began waking up before dawn to watch the winged man shower my home with glittering dust. After a few nights of observation, I realized his purpose. The colored particles he delivered always matched the threads that arrived the following day. He distributed the threads to my spools; he was the collector of nighttime emotions.

His flight had once invigorated my desire to be free. Now, I saw him as the catalyst of my imprisonment. He discarded terrors here, leaving me to clean up the mess. I was enraged, I felt like a fool, and I was more determined than ever to escape this place.

More threads arrived in larger batches. I now emptied five or six spools a day. Though it took up all my time, it also provided the perfect setup to release my coils more quickly. The giants I once fought daily now eagerly lined up to receive a bit of me with their assigned threads. What once was a chore was now an easy task. My suffering grew lighter with each layer I shed.

Each morning, I gave some of my golden threads to my devoted giants, and each afternoon, I gave some to Malsana. I crafted her a golden suit of armor, one that would disguise her as me. I taught her about the giants, explaining each of their quirks. I showed her how to weave so she could replace me without causing suspicion.

All was falling into place. My plans were unfolding without a hitch until Connie returned unexpectedly.

A whirlwind of bells encircled my tower, jangling with dire alarm.

"You are too thin," Connie declared as she majestically materialized.

Her sudden appearance gave Malsana no time to hide.

"What is she doing here?" the head seamstress demanded.

"Her name is Malsana."

"I know who she is," Connie seethed.

"She is a new giant," I continued, my heart pounding wildly.

"Why are her black threads entwined with gold?"

"That's how they arrive on the spool," I lied.

"Do you take me for a fool? This little monster is ruining you."

"No, she is my friend."

"She is sickness sent by Chaos. Look at her marble eyes."

"Your flying henchman delivered her threads, just like he delivers all the others."

Connie's frail, golden expression tightened. "Her threads are not like the others."

"You're right. She is kind. She is selfless. She is my friend."

"You must cut her threads."

"No!"

"You must. She is a devil sent to destroy order. She will ruin you and everything that exists beyond."

I ran to Malsana, wrapping my arms around her. "I will never forsake her."

"You are the only one who can save this land from her chaos!"

"She exists here with my protection. I will cut my own threads before I allow you to harm her."

Connie's glare narrowed. "I cannot harm her. Only you have the power to unstitch the monsters you've created."

"Good. Then she stays."

"What do you hope to achieve?"

"I am doing my job; everything is in order. Why are you so agitated to learn that I'm a little bit different today than I was yesterday?"

"Because you are behaving erratically and risking this world's stability."

"Sometimes change is good," I argued.

Connie vanished without warning. The clanging bells ceased and silence resumed.

I raced to my window to see where she went, but she was long gone. All I found were ten giants sitting patiently beneath my tower, waiting for their next fix of gold.

We weren't so different. Like me, their cords kept them bound. Souls entrapped within a knotted web of threads.

"Only you can set them free," Malsana said, repeating Connie's revelation. "Only you can unstitch that which you've weaved."

Her words shed light on a truth I had wished to avoid. Leaving meant forsaking the giants I had created. Though they were a burden, they were still mine. My conception had designed them. How could I leave without taking them with me?

"I can't take them with me," I said.

"I will watch over them," Malsana replied.

I shook my head. "Perhaps when I reach my end, when my last coil is unbound, I will relieve you of these giant burdens I created."

"That day is not too far away."

I looked down at my hands and saw my changing destiny. Where my golden coils were once bound tightly, gaping holes now existed in my design. A few more days of thinning myself, and I'd embrace true freedom.

"I will free you from the burden of my giants before I go," I promised.

Malsana smiled. "And if you do not, I will befriend them."

I fell asleep, resting easier than usual. Visions of eternal flight in a peaceful ether laced my dreams. Unbound and limitless, I flew with unrestricted freedom.

My serenity faltered when Malsana's screams echoed through the chamber of my mind. I could not wake or return to reality. My tranquil dreams shifted into an uncomfortable nightmare of my friend begging me to wake up.

When the sun rose over my tower, my eyes finally opened.

"Were you calling my name?" I asked, still groggy.

"Yes! Look at your hands."

I did as she asked.

All my discarded golden coils had been replaced. All the hard work I had accomplished was undone.

It took all my might not to cry.

"How?" I asked.

"Connie came in the middle of the night with the porcelain girl. Together, they wove new coils into you. The girl trapped you in slumber while Connie stitched you back together."

"No." The tears I held back fell. "I was so close."

"I tried to wake you."

I shook my head. "I will not sleep until I am free of this place."

Ignoring the new threads on the wall, I spent the entire day unloading my new coils into Malsana. When the sun crossed the center of the sky, I turned to my giants outside.

"Who wants golden threads?"

They all jumped to their feet and formed a line. One by one, I unraveled my gold coils and sewed the resulting threads into my giants. I left their assigned threads on the wall, no longer interested in performing my delegated duty.

When night arrived, I refused to sleep.

Connie's arrival came with the erratic clambering of bells.

"Why aren't you asleep?" she asked.

"I will never sleep again." Next to Connie stood the porcelain girl. Fine golden sutures covered her body. "Who are you?"

"My name is Day. I am here to help."

"Your help only hurts. I never asked to be put back together."

"You are being irrational, and the fault lies with that little monster you protect," Connie spat, glaring at Malsana, then back at me. "You must end her before she ends you."

"She is the truest friend I've ever known."

"She is manipulating you. She wants you gone so that she can take over."

"It wasn't her idea," I argued. "It was mine."

"Are you sure?"

I hesitated. "Yes."

"Do you know what emotion she represents?"

"No."

"She is sickness of the mind. She is dangerous. She has infected you."

Malsana interjected, "I have done no such thing!"

"Do not speak!" Connie bellowed, causing the tower to quake.

Malsana stepped back.

Connie glared at me. "Be sure of your actions. Disappearing will destroy everything you have built."

She disappeared into her ringing vortex. Day followed her out the window, spreading her giant wings and soaring away gracefully.

Another being who was free, unlike me.

I despised her without truly knowing her.

Night in and night out, we carried on like this. I refused to sleep, and they arrived enraged. Connie yelled while Day attempted to soothe my desire to disappear. It made no difference. I was determined to seize my freedom.

During the day, when Connie and Day were away, I sometimes wondered about Malsana. I wondered if her friendship was a lie, as Connie had implied. Was she sickness? Had she infected me?

"I saw the man in the sky before I created you," I rationalized aloud. "My desire to fly away arrived before I gave you life."

"Don't let Connie infect your mind."

I nodded. "You're right. She's the one poisoning me with sickening doubt."

"She doesn't want to weave another you. But once you're gone, I'll prove to her that I can handle the job. She won't need to replace you."

"So you *want* my job?"

"No, I want *you* to be happy. There's a difference. I'm taking on your responsibilities as a favor, as your friend."

I accepted her explanation. My desire to escape was too strong. It tore at my insides, demanding to be released.

I was nearing the end.

Afraid, but determined, I selected a single cord stretched tightly across my chest and pulled. A long gold thread lay limp in my grip.

I gave it to Malsana, who swiftly hemmed it to her hips.

193

I felt lighter.

"Today is the day," I revealed.

Only my frame remained—two golden coils that defined my silhouette.

"Are you ready for what exists beyond?" Malsana asked.

"I'm nervous. I don't know what to expect."

"Greatness," Malsana revealed. "Liberated weightlessness in a vast eternity of possibility. You will be tied to no one—not even yourself."

"No coils, no threads. Nothing to keep me bound."

"True freedom."

I thought of my giants. "I cannot bring them with me."

"Your giants are safe with me. I will care for them, and all their forsaken threads will find their way home."

I glanced at the wall of spools—I'd been ignoring the arrival of new threads for days. Malsana would be busy for a while.

"Thank you," I expressed.

"You deserve this," she reminded me. "You've served these giants long enough. It is time to serve yourself."

I was ready.

I whispered farewell to my giants, unwilling to face them directly. I feared they might fight my departure. They would be okay, though. Malsana would carry on in my stead.

With meditative care, I untwisted the last two remaining coils.

This was it—the start of something new. Liberated, I would ascend to great heights.

My coils turned to thread, falling to a heap on the floor, followed by my crystal eyeknobs, which landed with a clank.

My silhouette vanished.

I was unraveled.

Darkness consumed me.

Nothing waited on the other side—just another inescapable prison.

Consciousness bound to the emptiness, I was forced to witness the life I had surrendered.

Malsana greedily consumed my final threads, then called my giants to her window. The spool of black silk held yards of fabric, all of which Malsana weaved into the giants.

As they accepted her black threads, their individualized emotions intensified. She was making them worse.

Connie was right—Malsana was a sickness. She infected them all. Thread by thread, the giants turned violent. Worse than I'd ever seen them. Their nastiest traits rose to the surface, and they wreaked havoc across the land. Tearing apart the carefully stitched mountains, ripping their feet from their yarned confines, the giants were free to be their most chaotic selves.

"Stop!" I begged. "Your threads aren't meant for them!"

But it was too late—I had forsaken my life for false freedom.

I wanted to be nothing, and now I was.

No one could hear me.

I had lost all control.

A note from the Fox

I imagine you're feeling quite concerned at this point — I was, too.

Around this point in my discovery, I realized the worst was yet to come.

I didn't know how much more I could take.

Agitated and confused, I did not want to see Jane crumble beneath the terror Malsana inflicted. I did not want to see the monster win.

Why did I have to witness Jane's unraveling?

My heart pounded against my ribcage each time I wondered if I had played some part in this nightmare. My awareness grew, but my memories were still a blur.

What I recognized, despite my hazy recollection, was this harrowing fact:

New pockets manifested in Jane, ones meant to battle her sickness, and Malsana found ways to infiltrate and infect those parts of her mind, too.

Nothing was safe from the monster.

I had no glimpse of Jane on the outside, but the state of her mind was worrisome.

Our last hope was the Face of Night.

I returned to his black feather memento lodged behind my ear, praying that he had found the strength to carry on despite his growing infatuation with locating perfection in our imperfect mind.

Revisiting Memento #3

Time stopped.

The Face of Time had neglected his greatest responsibility.

For an entire day, the moon and sun did not leave their celestial keeps. I tried tugging Luna into the sky but failed.

The Face of Day was too weak to even try. The creatures of time went dark, their energy source depleted.

The following night, I managed to drag the moon across the sky, but the world remained dark without the sun.

I flew to the Tower of Time during the darkness of day.

"What happened?" he shouted at me, desperate to learn Day's fate.

"Seems I was wrong. I thought she'd break you, but it appears you broke her."

"I didn't mean to let so many seconds slip away."

"But you did."

"How do I fix her?"

"You can't," I answered. "You can only fix yourself."

I left the Tower of Time content with our exchange. Tough, but encouraging, I anticipated change.

I flew to the Ring of Thrones.

"You must wrangle Chaos," I demanded of Fear.

"Why?" the Face of Fear asked, his expression jaded.

"Day won't rise and time is glitching. These dangerous new Faces are manipulating our Host and transforming the Face of Day and the Face of Time."

"It's called coping. Let the Host sort it out on her own."

"What if it kills her?"

"Then that is our fate."

Outraged, I left the Ring of Thrones and the useless Faces. I couldn't sit by idly and let everything in our once-perfect mind rot. The Face of Control had arrived to create order, but only instigated more chaos.

I carried Luna through the sky, entirely absorbed by crisscrossing thoughts on how to heal the damage before it became irreversible. But every idea was implausible and I set the moon to rest with no solution.

"She has unraveled," Day revealed from the shadow she huddled within—it was the only dark corner in the Solar Citadel.

The little sun rose, awaiting its chariot into the sky and illuminating the Face of Day's grave state.

New cracks covered her arms that weren't stitched with gold.

"How could Control let you leave like this?" I demanded. "You'll burn!"

"We thought we were helping the Host, but Connie and I were deceived. Chaos infiltrated. He snuck his monster of sickness into the pocket. She lost herself in the illusion of control."

"Who is lost?"

"The weaver—our Host." Tears dripped from her eyes. "Our dear Jane."

"I knew Control was no good."

"Her pocket has unraveled," Day wept. "Giants carrying terrible truths run free, no longer bound to the threaded landscape. The marble-eyed monster who took the weaver's place has been stitching her black threads of sickness into the giants, making them reckless. Jane might never recover from this."

"She will, and so will you." I turned to the sun and spoke to Solís. The boy within was reluctant to look at me, and kept his charred body huddled in the center, gazing down as I spoke. "The sun needs to rise, but the Face of Day is injured. What can we do to seal her wounds?"

Solís slouched further forward, as if a giant weight had been placed on his back.

He replied, "I can subdue the sun's appetite for a few days, but not forever."

"Okay, great." I turned to Day. "Solís will protect you and I will find a way to mend your wounds."

Day nodded, standing slowly and turning to face the sun. She placed her hands on the fiery orb and screamed the moment she made contact.

"It hurts," she sobbed.

"You must be strong," I encouraged her.

Tears streamed down her porcelain cheeks as she lifted her wings and took off into the sky.

I raced down the tower staircase into the Solar Citadel's grand hall, where the Lumineers rested.

"How do I fix a break in the Face of Day?" I shouted.

All the petite figures of fire turned to me simultaneously. The swirling flames in their eyes held deep concern.

"She is up there with the sun and has cracks in her porcelain?" one of the Lumineers asked.

"Yes. Solís said he could protect her for a few days."

"I'll be amazed if she survives *one* day," the Lumineer said, astounded.

"How do I help her if she *does* survive the day?"

"You can't."

"There must be a way."

The Lumineers stood from their scattered resting places, huddled in small groups around the giant hole in the floor through which the sun rose each morning—it was adjacent to the room with a hole in the floor where the moon set each night.

The little Lumineers mumbled inaudible ideas that echoed down the bottomless hole and faded into the Southern Abyss.

When they finally turned back to me, the lead Lumineer announced an idea.

"This entire hall is made of kaolinite—clay comprised of glass and bone ash. Theoretically, you could chisel pieces out of this structure, melt them down to a putty, and then seal her wounds. We would need the sun's heat to melt the kaolinite, and it might not dry in time, but this is the only option."

"Then that is what we will try."

I carved small chunks of kaolinite out of the walls with my talons, and then we traveled through the portal to the Lunar Spire, where the sun would set.

When the sun arrived through the foyer ceiling at waning size, we prepared the materials.

"Solís, please give us a solar flare," the Lumineer requested, then caught a blast of fire from the sun.

The scalding hot flame melted the hardened kaolinite into putty in mere seconds. I raced up the tower with the concoction in a glass vial while the Lumineers latched onto the setting sun. They disappeared with Solís as he began his nightly journey through the Southern Abyss.

The Face of Day was still in the Lunar Spire tower; she hadn't taken the portal home yet.

"Fill your cracks with this," I insisted.

Day looked at me, confused.

"It's softened kaolinite. Fill your cracks with it and you will mend."

Her beautiful eyes welled with tears as she took my offering.

"Thank you," she expressed. "Except I've already missed so many days."

"It's okay. You picked up where you left off. We're back on track now."

She reached into her pocket and then handed me her most recent piece of broken porcelain.

"I want to let it go," she explained. "It reminds me of my failure to save the weaver. It reminds me of the fiery pain I now feel while holding the sun."

I took her broken piece. "Don't you need this bit of porcelain to fix your wound?"

"I have enough putty to fill the crack. I want to start anew."

I nodded. "I can drop this off in the memory receptacle for you."

Day smiled in appreciation as I lifted the moon into the sky, watching as we soared away.

For the first time in years, I felt hopeful, like I might improve things. I enjoyed the blissful night, careful to catch every fear that materialized.

At midnight, as I crossed directly over the Tower of Time, I dropped the broken piece of porcelain into the memory receptacle. From there, the Face of Time would deliver the memory to the Face of Awareness in the Southern Abyss, and she would process the loss.

Three a.m.

Time stopped.

Frozen in the sky, fighting with all my strength not to fall, my talons dug deep into the moon.

The village went dark.

The creatures of time left their assigned huts and surrounded the Tower of Time.

I did not know what caused this commotion, I just needed it to stop.

A moment later, time resumed.

Everything would be okay.

I finished carrying Luna across the sky and set her into the Southern Abyss, then waited in the Solar Citadel for Day.

Minutes passed.

Day never showed.

The sound of jeering turned my attention back to the village.

The sun was already halfway through the sky.

Day had pulled the sun out of slumber too early, and morning turned into afternoon. Time was skewed. Pure exhaustion ravished her body as she dragged the massive ball of fire through the sky.

Everything was *not* okay.

A note from the Fox

Utterly devastated at this point in my discovery, I wondered how it came to this.

In the trail of mementos, beyond the web of golden threads, stretched a barrier of broken glass. The shattered pieces lay strewn in my way.

"What a mess," I complained at the time. "Must I carry on?"

Within a large piece of glass on top of the pile, I saw my reflection.

Staring back at myself, my expression was unfamiliar.

Tired, defeated, weary—I hardly looked like myself.

Regret ravaged me, and though I fought to replace it with determination, sorrow maintained an unrelenting grip on my heart.

What had I done?

I lifted the glass to better look at myself, and as I stared at my faint reflection, my mind entered the bleak existence of the Soldier of Time.

What had started as a singular illness expanded to include other ailments and disorders.

Through Time, I discovered how Jane's sickness had worsened.

Memento #7

When: The 18th - 20th Cycle
Where: Jane's mind—Tower of Time, Northern Abyss
Who: The Face of Time

My glass fingers lifted the rustleweed branch from my inbox.

I never received letters, only discarded items from the world outside my tower.

Holding the thorned weed, I closed my celadon-green eyes and watched the memory it represented: a great love ruined by chaos.

Time was not on their side.

Time.

I was the Face of Time.

In another life, in another universe, time might have favored them.

My heart broke—I would never know a love like this.

I dropped the rustleweed into the outbox. The weed tumbled down the chute and dropped into the Southern Abyss. There, the Face of Awareness would process the memory.

It was best for everyone that I did not get involved.

The rustleweed felt familiar, though I could not recall why. It felt like home when I touched it, but like the memories of my origin, the tiny branch was no longer in reach.

The influx of discarded memories had recently grown overwhelming. Unwanted mementos from the pockets inundated me daily. I tried not to watch, but my will was weak. I was lonely, I wanted to live a full life, yet I was confined to this glass prison.

Each discarded memory from beyond reminded me that I lived this silent life alone. I would never experience connections like the ones so carelessly thrown away.

Father Time told me I was lucky. He said my fate was well-designed. But I often found myself wallowing in the sands of time, watching hundreds of grains sift back and forth as they waited to reach their end.

A quick drop and it was over. I wondered if I, too, could leave this way—a quick leap to stop the time that defined my life.

You could, said the voice inside my head. I had named her Malsana—the bad lady, my only friend.

Her arrival was recent; she came to me 1,440 hours, 30 minutes, and 13 seconds ago, to be exact.

Sixty full days since she took root in my head.

I had tried to bury her many times, but she always found a way back to the surface.

"Be quiet," I insisted, but Malsana was too loud.

I looked around—complete isolation.

"You aren't real," I asserted.

I am your only friend, Malsana reminded me.

I remembered Luna. "I also have the moon."

Malsana laughed. *A fickle friend indeed. She can't give you what you need.*

Too much time alone had me spinning.

I needed to see her.

Wading into the sand pools of tomorrow, I shushed Malsana as best I could and waited for my favorite time of day: three a.m.—when the world became quiet and I could be alone with the moon.

I lifted my glass body out of the sinking sand and raced up the spiraling stairs of my prison. The steps twisted around the enormous hourglass my tower encased. My tinkering glass toes created a familiar rhythm as I climbed; it was the only song I knew.

I reached the wall of gears on the clock tower's northern side. From here, I could see out into the world beyond.

Behind the clock's case, I stood as the Face of Time.

I used to let them see me—the creatures of time. I used to let them love me. But once I realized their adoration was hollow, I preferred the peace I found in isolation.

Now, I only came out at night.

They don't miss you, Malsana whispered. *They never did and never will.*

My demon was right—time ran smoothly without them seeing my face.

Hands aligned, the seconds ticked closer to three a.m.

I reached for the door to the outside—a forbidden exit, but I was not afraid. I turned the knob, as I had done many times before, and crisp air ran like rain down my glass flesh. Revitalized, I felt alive.

The hour hand pointed to three, and I walked the line until I reached its end.

A familiar place, a familiar feeling.

I looked over the edge.

This could be my end.

This could be your end, Malsana repeated inside my head.

I wanted to be free.

I closed my eyes, took a deep breath, and imagined I could fly. Lighter than air, I raised my arms, imagining a life much different from the one I'd known. A privilege and a curse—my life was not my own. I created order for this mortal mind, counting the seconds that defined this mortal life. I lived in solitude to prevent distractions that could disrupt the hands of time. But when the moon was full and I fitfully slept, my imagination dug up the secrets I kept.

I saw the love I never got to hold.

I saw the years I lost to my burdened fate.

I saw Malsana.

Alone on this ledge, I glanced down.

No alarms, no warning bells.

I could leave without making a sound.

Countless stories above an easy end, with countless stories left untold.

If I fell, time would halt momentarily until Father Time replaced me, and he would do so without shedding a tear—Father Time only held affection for the clocks. An ancient, eternal patriarch with one job: protect the fate of time. And he did so by selecting soldiers to guard his towers.

He had chosen me from the creatures of time bustling below, just like he chose all the others who guarded towers within different mortal minds. Trapped and unable to leave, carrying out a fate of his design. The life of a time soldier was presented as an honor, a life path deemed noble by society.

I once believed I was lucky.

Now, I realized I was cursed.

After bearing the crushing saddle of time for so long, I found myself ready to let go.

Let go, Malsana whispered.

I shook my head—this choice was mine to make.

Luna hovered above, glowing tears streaking down her cheeks as the Face of Night carried her through the sky.

I often wondered when it would end. How many more times would I see the same sun rise? How many times would I kiss the moon goodbye? The same heartbreak lived repeatedly in countless ways—a dizzying cycle I could not escape.

Day in, day out, nothing ever changed.

I closed my eyes and hovered my glass toes past the hour hand's edge.

"You could live forever," a gentle voice shouted up to me.

This time the voice was real—it did not belong to Malsana.

Startled, I opened my eyes and stepped back. Stories below was a porcelain girl covered in cracks. Her long glowing hair fell between her giant white wings.

"Not really," I countered.

"Well, as long as Jane, at least."

"I don't want to," I replied.

"I could live forever, too," she went on, swaying with her arms behind her back.

"Do you want to?" I asked, intrigued.

"Sometimes, yes. Sometimes, no."

"Who are you?"

"The Face of Day."

"I've heard about you," I said, interest piqued. "You're perfect in every way."

"That's what they say," she replied, though she did not sound convinced. "What are you doing outside of your clock?"

I was stunned that someone cared to ask.

"How high up do you think I am?" I countered.

"High enough that you'll break if you fall. You are made of glass, after all."

"I won't fall," I objected.

"Sometimes it looks like you want to."

"How many times have you entered the night?" I asked, doubtful that the Face of Day had a mischievous side.

"Some secrets are better kept," she answered.

I jumped over the swift second hand for the tenth time since exiting the clock tower and noticed that the minute hand hovered right above my head.

"I should go," I stated. "Will you come back?"

"I'm always here," she replied.

"Why didn't you say hello until tonight?"

"I thought you might actually do it this time."

I hesitated. "Do what?"

"Jump."

I didn't want to talk about it.

"Well," I carried on, "I hope to see you again."

I found the knob to the forbidden door and walked back into the safety of my prison.

Inside the glass tower, staring at the wall of gears, I fell to my knees.

A moment with the Face of Day—one tiny interaction changed everything.

I spent the night performing my monotonous routine: oiling the gears, tightening the bolts behind all four clockfaces, monitoring the second hand's rhythm—but I thought of her throughout. Her cracked porcelain smile and kind, shimmering eyes staring up at me, letting me know I was not alone. She cared, to some degree, and I lost myself in daydreams of her. My thoughts were so vivid and consuming that Malsana stayed away.

The following day, I sat behind the clock's case, hidden behind the gears, but able to see the inner world beyond my tower.

A sprawling village of ceramic huts separated my Tower of Time from the celestial keeps. On the west side, I could see the Lunar Spire. A crescent moon glowed silver atop the steeple. Seven p.m. to seven a.m. marked the hours of night, and during this time, the ceramics huts of time shined in neon shades of violet, indigo, and blue.

On the east side stood the Solar Citadel. A sun made of gold sat atop the fortress.

Seven a.m. to seven p.m. marked the hours of day, and during this time, the ceramic huts glowed red, orange, and yellow.

I looked for her there.

Within the sun sculpture atop the Solar Citadel sat a throne made of light. Too bright to see the beauty hidden within the blinding orb, I shielded my eyes and paused.

A pause held too long—the whole world hiccupped during my hesitation. Terrified, I looked away and quickly greased the gears so they continued their rotation. I waited for Father Time to arrive and ask what had caused my glitch, but a full cycle passed and he never showed.

At three a.m. the following day, I stood behind the clockface and stared toward the Solar Citadel. Blues and purples blanketed the village, and the ornate sculpture sitting atop the fortress had dimmed. I could see that side of the world more clearly in the shield of night. Within the pillar of day sat an illuminated throne—the only light within the shade.

I found her there, asleep on a luminescent cushion. Too far away to reach. Too far away to hear me whisper her name. I wondered if she'd visit me again.

The Face of Night tore over my tower.

The moon wept in its master's wake.

He was strong and brave; I was fragile and meek.

The Face of Day will never love you, Malsana taunted.

A glass tear rolled down my cheek; I feared this was the truth. I regulated her freedom—both she and the Face of Night could only thrive in their assigned timeframes. I was their oppressor.

This revelation was new, and while I felt like a prisoner all these years, I realized they were far more confined. My prison was this clock tower, and theirs were their polarities—the sun and the moon.

Father Time never came to check on me. Still, I could not find the courage to leave the safety of my tower. I peered through the glass wall every night, but never saw her there.

I kept time in order, but suffered many hiccups along the way. The seconds blended into minutes, which became hours too quick to count. I lost days to my sudden fears and had not tasted fresh air in months. I lost track of how many moons I watched come and go from the safety of the sandclock, but I sank a little deeper into the sand each time Luna passed overhead. Lost again to the numbing weight of nothingness, I prepared to suffocate beneath the sands of time.

At three a.m., I walked to the edge of the minute hand, hopeful that Day might be waiting for me in the shadows.

A full minute passed—she wasn't there.

Overhead, the Face of Night flew.

"Stop worrying about Day."

"I don't need advice from you," I shouted back.

"She cannot help you," he squawked as he carried the moon through the sky.

I wondered why.

"You know nothing," I challenged.

Night laughed. "I know more than you ever will."

"Then tell me."

"I'm too busy fixing your mess."

Furious, I clenched my fists and forced the world to stop. The Face of Night jerked in the sky, rendered immobile where he hovered. Each second I held hostage, he fell a little closer to the ground.

"Stop!" he insisted. "The moon is too heavy."

"Tell me why she won't come back."

Night grimaced as the moon's weight slowly dragged him out of the sky.

"You'll ruin everything," he urged. "Let me go."

"Tell me why!"

"I'm trying to help you—to save you and me and everyone else."

"I don't understand."

"She is obsessed with broken things. They make her feel better—they make her feel less broken." Night scoffed at my blank expression. "She *will* come back for you, but you must reject her."

"She is my only friend," I objected, fists still clenched and halting the progress of time.

The Face of Night's large, feathered wings quivered as he fought to stay airbound. "She will try to fix you to make herself feel whole. She is selfish. Let her go."

My fists released and time resumed.

"You were designed to be alone," Night reminded me as he battled the moon's weight and worked hard to make up the lost time.

I hardly heard Night's departing remark—I was too fixated on his harrowing revelations about Day. I sat with his words for the remainder of the night, trying to make sense of them. Even if Night was right, even if she had only befriended me to make herself feel better, I could not see how it was a bad thing. Her selfishness healed us both.

I watched the Face of Night struggle to fix what I had done, but I felt no remorse. I would not fall victim to his ambiguous threats and insults. I would not let him make me feel worse, nor would I let him sully my friendship with the Face of Day.

She was all I had.

She was my only reason to stay.

The moon shone a little brighter, and the Bitlings hustled, helping Night recollect the seconds lost.

Months passed without a visit from my friend.

This could be the end, Malsana suggested.

I wondered if she was right.

I saw Day through the glass ceiling of my tower. She often smiled at me and waved, but it felt hollow. An emptiness plagued our friendship. Was this all she could give? Or was she avoiding me?

I saw Night, too, but after our first interaction, which went terribly, he never stopped to check on me again.

Fine by me.

I didn't like him anyway.

Luna was the only one who still seemed to care—she sang sweet songs each night that only I could hear.

Always there, but out of reach.

Just like the Face of Day.

Let them go, Malsana insisted, but I refused.

At three a.m., I forced myself out of my ever-deepening sand tomb and up to the wall of gears. A look from behind the eastern clockface revealed dark isolation.

I twisted the forbidden knob, pushed open the door, and fresh air slapped my face. Painful relief—I coughed up the sand lodged in my throat.

The grains rained down as shards of diamonds.

I walked to the edge, daring fate to stop time and take me.

Another cough, another batch of diamond rain enacting the fall I dreamed about.

"Stop doing that," a familiar voice called up to me.

I looked over and saw Day brushing sharp shards out of her long, luminescent hair.

"I thought I'd never see you again."

"I have a lot of responsibilities, too," she reminded me. "And each time you hiccup, it gets a little harder to pull the sun through the sky."

"I noticed the sun rose late the other day. I'm sorry."

"That was my fault, not yours. I was injured."

"Are you okay?"

"I'm fine now. Are *you* okay?"

I shrugged, jumping over the quick-moving second hand. "It's nice to see your face."

"Would you like to go on a walk?" she asked.

My brow furrowed. "I can't leave the Tower of Time."

"Of course. How silly of me." Day shook her head. "Is there a way for me to climb up to you?"

My heart skipped and time hiccupped, halting the world for half a second.

"I'm a terrible influence," Day stated with a giggle. "Night is surely cursing you for that."

"Why?"

"The moon is much heavier than the sun."

"Oh, I see."

"So, can I come up?" she asked.

"Yes. You can use this door." I pointed to the only door I knew. "I've never had a visitor before," I further confessed, jumping over the second hand as it passed.

She spread her wings and lifted into the sky, but as she ascended to my height, she slammed into an invisible wall.

"Something is blocking me from flying closer." She felt her way around the barrier, but it surrounded the top half of my tower like a bubble.

"A trap set by Father Time, I'm sure," I griped.

"It's okay," she expressed with a smile. "My feet work, too."

"I'm not sure if there are stairs, or even a door down there."

Day took it upon herself to examine the bottom of the tower, porcelain hand dragging across the glass facade as she looked for a door. After checking the entire wall, she lifted her chin toward me.

"You better watch out. The minute hand is getting close to the top of your head."

I looked up to find she was right. It already blocked the top half of the door, so I grabbed the thick needle and climbed atop, patiently riding out the minutes until it no longer barricaded my escape.

Day continued her search.

I lifted my soft celadon gaze toward the village below — the most organized chaos, time thrived here.

The wild Bitlings, who represented the seconds, lived in tiny huts that glowed red during daytime hours and violet during nighttime hours. Thirty rings — each made up of Bitling huts — outlined the tower, starting small around the base and growing larger at the outer edge of the village. The rings glowed as their second was counted, pulsating in and out like a heartbeat.

Jiffies rested in the larger huts that glowed orange during the day and indigo at night. They embodied every minute of every day and also lived within thirty rings circling the Tower of Time—their rings were situated between each Bitling ring. Each minute ring pulsated in and out more gradually than the seconds. Though manic, the living minutes were never as rushed as the Bitlings.

Twelve Circlettes represented the hours and resided in cabins along the village's outer edge. During the day hours, they glowed yellow, and at night, they glowed bright blue. Not only did they manage their underlings, but they also kept strict reports of each yearly cycle and submitted their reports to the Face of Day. She kept track of the months and years, as the length of our existence would always remain undefined. We could cease to exist tomorrow if the fates decreed.

I used to be one of the creatures of time, or so I was told. I could not recall anything prior to my arrival in this tower.

I suppose I was lucky to a degree, as I didn't wish to live down there. It was chaotic and overwhelming. I saw the world as a whole; I understood the gravity of time, whereas the Bitlings, Jiffies, and Circlettes only knew the short timeframes they managed. Awareness versus oblivion—I wondered which was the more oppressive burden to carry.

"I found it!" Day shouted.

I looked down at my new friend, who traced her fissured hands along a hidden cutout in the wall. Concentration focused, she pressed at the corners and pushed along the edges until an internal latch lifted. The sound of gears turning and levers clicking brought a smile to her face.

Seeing the complexity of the door, I understood the true nature of my prison—I wasn't meant to get out, and no one was meant to get in, except Father Time.

Day walked through the clandestine door, letting it lock behind her. The minute hand no longer barricaded my own secret door, so I raced back into the tower.

"Are there stairs?" I shouted, hoping she could hear me.

"No," she replied, her voice muffled and distant. "I'm at the neck of the sandclock. It's completely unfinished down here. I'm going to climb the scaffolding lining the walls."

"Be careful," I insisted. I had no idea what obstacles she would face, nor did I know how to let her in once she reached me.

I started looking for loose floorboards or a hidden trapdoor. I could hear her climbing higher—her porcelain fingers against the glass scaffolding generated the most unpleasant noise. Each screeching scratch announced her approach. Still, I hadn't found a way to let her in.

"I'm nearing the ceiling," she announced, her voice clearer than before. I could see her silhouette through the thick glass floorboards.

On my hands and knees, I searched for a door.

Desperate, I clawed at the floor. I needed to feel connected to another person. A handshake or a hug—the simplest connection would brighten my heart.

But there was no door.

There was no way to let her in.

This tower entombed me, with death as my only escape.

I could see her, but the thick, foggy glass blurred her image.

"I don't know how to let you in," I finally confessed aloud.

"There must be a way." Day banged on the ceiling she crouched beneath.

"Be careful," I insisted.

"Why? It's glass. We can make our own door."

"Damage to the tower is damage to time. I cannot even scratch the surface of these walls without risking cataclysmic dents to the clock's workings."

Day stopped slamming her fist against the glass.

"So, I guess this is it then," she conceded.

"It's nice to hear your voice up close."

"Place your hand against the floor."

I did as she requested and she lifted her hand to mirror mine.

"Can you feel me?" she asked.

My eyes filled with glassy tears.

"No," I answered honestly. "But I want to."

"I can stay awhile."

I rested my body against the floor, pressing the side of my face against where her hand remained on the glass. I imagined I could feel her warmth through the unbreakable barrier separating us.

"I just wanted a friend," I confessed.

"I am your friend."

I closed my eyes. "Where do you go in the night?"

"Here," she stated, revealing what I already knew.

"Where else?" I probed.

She paused before revealing more. "I spend a lot of time by myself."

"Me too."

"And sometimes I travel to the edge."

My eyes opened in shock. "Near the Ring of Thrones?"

She nodded, her smile mischievous. "From there, I can see the pockets beyond. Lately, I've been needed inside the Pocket of Control. I've been spending a lot of time there, which is why I haven't been able to visit you."

"I see."

"I'm sorry about that."

"It's okay. I'm happy you're here now."

"I wish I could show you that pocket. Colorful giants weaved from yarn voyage across knitted mountains and sewn valleys, all while threaded to the terrain!"

"Sounds incredible. I can't see any of the pockets from here."

"It seems unfair that you can't, considering one of them belongs to you."

"I have a pocket?"

She nodded, then frowned. "Well, you used to. Chaos took over the Pocket of Time."

"How'd that happen?"

"No one could stop him. He couldn't override time, though—he just blanketed it in red fog. The beings who still live there are descendants of Father Time. It's where you came from, where you were born."

"I thought I was a creature of time," I said, gesturing to the village of time below my tower.

"You are, but not like the Bitlings, Jiffies, or Circlettes. You were born as a shadow in the Pocket of Time. Father Time chose you at birth and gave you glass armor so you could exist here."

"Does that mean I have a family somewhere out there?"

"I suppose so."

This notion filled me with joy, but as I remembered that I'd never get to know them, my melancholy returned.

"I'm not sure if this information is helping or hurting."

The Face of Day frowned. "Everyone is grateful for your measure of time."

"Is our Host grateful for the work we do?" I asked, unsure how to navigate my intensifying thoughts.

"Of course. I am the Face of Day; I am she, and she is me. I appreciate you, and so does our Host."

I smiled.

Day continued, "The pockets are spectacular. There are many, and they are all unique. They each represent different defining moments in our Host's life. Emotions, experiences, different parts of her identity—they have shaped our Host into the person she is and who she is becoming."

"Have you ever entered the other pockets?" I asked.

"Yes," she revealed. "I used to visit all the pockets often—it was fun to live a double life, one free from my responsibilities as the Face of Day—but recently, I've been needed more in the Pocket of Control. I don't have time to visit the others." She pointed at the fine, surface-level cracks on her face, then lifted her wrist. "That's where I got these breaks." A long golden stitch stemmed from her palm to her elbow.

"That looks painful."

"I am healing."

"How'd it happen?"

"Every time the weaver uncoils one of her golden threads, I get a new crack."

"I don't understand."

"The Host embodies creatures within each pocket—the weaver *is* the Host, and she is sick. Chaos unleashed a monster that infected every facet of her identity."

"That's horrible!"

"Yes. I am doing my best to help."

"Is there anything I can do?"

"Keep managing time. And don't let the monster in."

"What does it look like?"

"It takes many forms, but always has the same black marble eyes."

"I'll be on the lookout," I promised. "But if you couldn't reach me, I doubt this monster could either."

"You never know. The monster is sneaky."

"Father Time has ensured that I'll be alone forever."

"Just be careful."

I didn't like thinking about my solitude, so I changed the topic. "What has the Face of Night said about the pockets he visits?"

"He doesn't tell me much about anything," she explained.

"Why not?"

"He only likes perfect things."

I lifted my head and examined her hand. Like the rest of her porcelain body, thin fissures filled with gold lined her palm.

"I like you as you are."

She smiled. "Most can't see my cracks—the sun blinds them from my imperfections, so they think I'm perfect. But you and Night can see me as I truly am. You're the only ones."

"Night is a fool."

Day wasn't bothered by Night's rejection. "He's got problems of his own."

I examined my hand pressed firmly against the glass. Hers, on the other side, was half the size of mine.

"I have always been alone here," I confessed, "but I now realize the extent of my isolation."

"I'll visit you often."

"That climb was dangerous."

"I'll visit you outside the clock."

I nodded. "Thank you."

I felt the neglected seconds squeezing my heart, demanding I return my love to them.

Another hiccup—I had let them go unattended for too long.

Day giggled, surely imagining Night cursing at the stars whenever I let time glitch.

"I ought to go," I expressed as I lifted my hand off the foggy glass floor.

"No hiccups after sunrise," she insisted.

"I promise."

Day smiled and departed, carefully climbing down the glass scaffolding lining the empty cavity beneath my prison.

I worried the tiny smile on my face would not last long.

That was nice, Malsana sneered condescendingly. *Too bad it's all a lie.*

"What do you mean?"

She can never love you more than she loves the sun.

I shoved Malsana into the cage I made for her in my mind.

Alone again, but spirits lifted, I held on tight to the feeling of Day's kindness.

For a moment, I was happy.

For a moment, I felt compelled to carry on.

I wanted to feel this way every day.

I fought the sorrowful seconds as they chipped away at my mind. Every hour spent alone became harder to conquer, and the creeping hopelessness I knew too well began clawing its way out of its cage.

A delivery in my inbox—this time, it was three black marbles.

I had gotten these same marbles before, but now I wondered if they belonged to the monster.

I quickly dropped the black spheres into the outbox.

A full cycle of day came and went.

The Face of Day did not return.

The days turned into weeks, and when I finally stopped counting the days without seeing my friend, I wondered if I had made it all up in my head. Mental stability frayed, I questioned what was real and what stemmed from my lonely imagination.

Another year gone; the twentieth cycle arrived without fanfare.

Time was the truest prison, and as its conductor, I was forever trapped in its monotonous cycle with Malsana as my only companion.

I could not trust myself.

At three a.m., I found myself tiptoeing along the ledge of the eastern clockface toward the forbidden door. I exited the tower, balancing precariously along the hour hand. When I reached the edge, I glanced over to find the world below blanketed in deep tranquility. The Bitlings paced within their huts, their frantic energy more serene in the dark. The Jiffies sat atop their roofs, quietly illuminating their ring a brilliant shade of indigo during their active minute within the hour. The Circlettes absorbed the hourly energy orb once it reached them and transported it to their neighboring Circlette so it could complete another rotation and the day could move forward an hour.

Everything was in order; the creatures of time had their roles and knew what to do.

I scanned the ground directly beneath where I stood.

The Face of Day wasn't there.

Nor was she in her tower; her throne atop the Solar Citadel sat vacant.

She must be in the Pocket of Control.

Frustrated, I returned to my prison, closing the forbidden door with a slam.

Malsana clawed at the inside of my skull, but I refused to let her speak. My anger surpassed the sorrow she thrived within.

I searched for Day's face in the bright sunlight every morning, listening for her voice in the daylit sky, hoping she might say hello as she flew by.

At night, I scanned the streets, wondering if she might appear while the Lumineers guided the sun through the Southern Abyss.

I counted the days, growing wearier as another month passed. I retreated into the top orb of the sandclock, watching each day and night pass through the glass ceiling.

Like clockwork, the moon cast its mournful light upon me as Night dragged it through the sky.

Luna knew my pain.

When the clock's creaking grew too loud, I left my sandy sanctuary to grease the gears—one of the many responsibilities I had neglected.

Without regular upkeep, my work became harder. I had to stop the clock many times to scrape off all the grime that had collected between the gears. By the time I reached the western side of the tower, I felt the lagging pull from the celestial keeps. Both Night and Day struggled to resume their posts in an orderly fashion—I had stolen too many seconds from their shifts.

When the sun remained in the sky through the night, and the moon never arrived, I realized I had made a terrible mistake. I manually turned the gears, trying to help the sun set, but the Bitlings and Jiffies panicked, and the village descended into chaos.

After twelve long hours of manually turning the clock, time resumed its rightful state.

Relieved, but exhausted, I returned to the top orb of the sandclock to sink into the recesses of time.

The Face of Night came and went with the moon, but when the hour of daylight arrived, the sun never rose.

Night arrived in the darkness of day.

"What happened?" I shouted to Night as I exited onto the minute hand.

It was 12:15 p.m.

"Seems I was wrong," he replied, looking bone tired. "I thought she'd break you, but it appears you broke her."

"I didn't mean to let so many seconds slip away."

"But you did."

"How do I fix her?"

"You can't. You can only fix yourself."

I released a heavy sigh as he departed.

The Face of Night was right—I had to do better.

For her.

For me.

For them.

I reentered my tower, prepared to evolve. If I wanted to save her, I had to fix myself. But before I could organize my thoughts, a familiar voice boomed through the glass hall.

"What have you done?"

I did not want to turn around.

"I am sorry."

"Face me," the ancient voice insisted.

Gaze lowered, chin down, I turned to face Father Time. His hollow cheeks and strong brow created menacing shadows—I could hardly see his face, just a skull with a gray beard that stretched the lengths of time.

"You look a lot like Death," I commented.

"Have you met Death?" Father Time asked.

I looked down at my hands and wriggled my fingers—confirming that I was still very much alive.

"No," I answered.

"Good. He sometimes visits places he shouldn't."

"I just imagine he'd look like *that*." I pointed to Father Time's peculiar choice for a face.

"I wear many faces. This one felt fitting today. I heard it might be time to replace you."

I shook my head.

"You've made a mess," he chastised. Deep within the voids concealing his eyes glowed a shimmering gray light of disappointment. "Time is ruined here."

"I can fix it."

"Why did you let it break?"

"I was lost inside my head."

"Inexcusable. The Face of Day suffers from your blunders."

My heart skipped. "Will she be okay?"

"She has enough problems as it is … this setback will be costly."

"But is she okay?" I repeated.

"Her porcelain armor saves her from the scorching heat, but her breaks let some of the fire in." Father Time shook his head. "Without her, this mortal mind is doomed."

"She will be better with someone else as the Soldier of Time."

"As I assess you now, I see there is no need to replace you. You appear fit to perform your job."

"You're wrong."

"I'm never wrong."

"Sometimes sickness can't be seen."

Father Time narrowed his gaze. As he considered my request, the shadows consuming his face lifted and his appearance shifted. He once again looked like the ancient man I had come to know. "I have been the master of time since the dawn of creation," he revealed. "And in all that time, I have never had to replace a capable soldier because they wanted to quit."

"I don't want to quit, but I am also not well, and I think it's in everyone's best interest if I was replaced."

"This is not your time."

"Then how does it end?" I asked, my tone pleading.

"For you? When this mind dies. Swapping guards is not a choice; it comes from necessity."

"I think my mind has rotted in isolation."

Father Time scoffed. "Impossible."

He wasn't listening to me.

"Time would be better cared for by someone else," I urged.

"And what of you? You cannot join the underlings outside this tower. You already grasp the greater concept of time."

"I could leave forever. I could go back to the Pocket of Time."

Father Time frowned. "You were chosen to be a Soldier of Time. An untimely return would cast shame upon your family."

"But at least I'd get to experience love," I pled.

"Love? Do not test my patience."

"Don't I deserve love?"

"Love is a mortal desire. Though you are bound to this human—she is you, and you are her—you certainly are not mortal. Let go of these trivial ideas and perform your duty," Father Time warned. "I have not readied a replacement for you."

I understood. Still, my everlasting desire to disappear had heightened.

Belittled and disregarded—my noble request was ignored.

Father Time departed, disappearing in a burst of dust. His smell lingered—it reeked of wars past.

I raced to the eastern side of the time tower and pressed my hands against the backside of the clockface. In the distance, I saw the darkened citadel. The absence of the sun left it black.

If I could not leave, then I had to make things right. I climbed to the top orb of the sandclock, unlatched the hatch, threw down a rope, and jumped. The sands of time softened my fall.

I had to save the Face of Day.

I had to relocate the seconds lost.

Fingers sifting through the grains, I rummaged, collecting every minuscule piece that had turned gray. No longer living, no longer in the correct place, these grains had lost their luster among the sands of tomorrow. Bit by bit, I seized the defective granules and placed them into my pocket. A glance toward the sky revealed a glimpse of light. My strategy was working—the sun was lifting.

I continued until the darkness covering the day vanished. The Solar Citadel reignited with sun fire and the day resumed its expected glow.

I climbed out of the sandclock and returned the lost seconds to the past by swallowing them. They fell into the bottom orb of the sandclock. Landing among the grains of yesterday, their luster resumed. Dimmed, but revitalized, as were all the grains of the past.

It won't be enough, Malsana said. *You broke her.*

When the sun did not rise, I worried Malsana might be right.

Later that night, something heavy landed with a clunk in my inbox. I turned my attention from the village to my mail, afraid to see what it might be. What sacred memory had they discarded now?

I opened the door to the tiny box and found a broken piece of porcelain sitting inside.

"No," I said with a gasp. "It can't be."

I snatched the porcelain, held it tight, and closed my eyes. This piece belonged to the Face of Day. Her face was stamped all over this memory. I felt her fear. I felt the heat—she was burning alive. Buried within the swirling flames of the sun, fire consumed my mind.

I opened my eyes, horrified by what I saw.

My friend was gone.

It was only a matter of time, Malsana commented.

"Stop."

You only made her suffering worse.

"No," I objected. "We were friends. We made each other better."

Then why is her memento marred by fire?

I had no rational explanation.

I dropped her discarded piece into the outbox, passing this tragedy to the Face of Awareness. It was her job to process this, not mine. Though I wanted to understand, the message was clear: our friendship wasn't enough to save her from herself.

More vibrant than ever, Malsana took true shape—a sight I'd never seen before. A shadow monster with black marble eyes—no wonder I could never rid myself of her; she was the monster Day had warned me about.

229

"It's you," I said with a gasp.

Suddenly, the truth was clear. She was not only a danger to me, but also to everyone I loved.

Look at what happened to Day.

No one would be safe until Malsana was out of my head.

"It's time to be brave," I said confidently, prepared to summon Father Time. He needed to replace me before Malsana's influence caused more damage.

Your greatest error was placing your contentment in the hands of others. Especially someone as malleable as Day, Malsana revealed.

I narrowed my gaze. "Go away."

Make me.

"Once I leave this place, the new Soldier of Time will do better. He won't have a monster plaguing his every move."

I will befriend him, too.

"You live inside *my* head."

Once I cut my tether to you, I can nestle someplace new. A change of scenery sounds nice.

"No, you are leaving with me."

I think I'll stay, Malsana threatened.

Eyes shut, I finally understood what I had to do. I could not wait for Father Time to name my replacement. I needed to act now.

This was my chance to save everyone from this monster.

I took a step closer to the edge.

Wait, Malsana begged, desperately gnawing at the tether keeping us bound.

I lifted my gaze and looked my demon in the eyes. No longer afraid of the terrors she planted in my mind, I took a deep breath and shoved my monster off the ledge. She plummeted—a freefall only I could see—her tether to me still intact. It yanked me off the edge with her.

I was set free.

For her.

For them.

For me.

This was the bravest surrender.

A note from the Fox

To my dismay, and I imagine yours, too, I solemnly report that Malsana survived.

This terrible news was delivered to me later, but for the sake of transparency, I felt it prudent to tell you now.

The Soldier of Time acted nobly, though his actions were misguided.

He saw Malsana for what she was—a devious monster corrupting his ability to perform his job, and in an attempt to save everyone from her, he killed the part of her that lived inside him.

Sadly, that killed him, too.

But he is only one small part of the Host, as are all the Faces, and Malsana could not perish while she continued living elsewhere in Jane's mind.

When I learned of this, I worried that the monster would live with us forever, and if that was our fate, how would we survive?

I am getting ahead of myself—let's rewind a bit:

Initially, after Time's freefall, I thought he had saved Jane from the monster. I thought his sacrifice would be the turning point in this story. From here, things must change for the better, right?

No.

I discovered his sacrifice was for nothing when I returned to the story through the black feather. Through the Face of Night, I saw Jane's ultimate surrender. I saw her final attempt to save herself and discovered that she had chosen the wrong Face to find courage through.

Revisiting Memento #3

When: The 20th – 21st Cycle
Where: Jane's mind—Lunar Spire, Northern Unknown
Who: The Face of Night

Crowds of Bitlings, Jiffies, and Circlettes chattered relentlessly, hovering around the broken soldier.

The creatures of time turned their attention to the Face of Day and shouted their accusations into the sky.

"Where were you?"

"He loved you."

"How could you let this happen to him?"

Day looked down at the back of her hands, wounds still fresh.

I rocketed into the sky, terrified that she might drop the sun.

"It's not your fault," I assured her from a safe distance. Heat radiated from the sun.

"I can't carry the sun anymore," she revealed, ravished with guilt.

"Be strong."

"Everything I touch breaks."

"We aren't so different. I can help you."

"Leave me alone," she demanded.

I raced ahead, landing in the Lunar Spire to wait for Day. In the few moments we shared between day and night, I hoped to soothe her sorrow.

When she set the sun, she glared at me with bereaved energy.

"I want to be alone."

"Did the putty work?" I asked.

"Does it matter?"

"Of course, it matters."

"I lose everyone I love."

"He was troubled. Perhaps our Host needed a new Face of Time. Maybe this soldier will be able to manage the chaos."

"You are part of the problem."

"How so?" My anger rose. "I helped you heal!"

"All you care about is yourself and your perfect little treasures."

"I'm trying to care about you now, but you're making it difficult."

"Life is difficult. People are complicated. You have to love them through it all, not just during the easy times."

"Teach me."

"It cannot be taught. Either you can or you can't."

She marched to the sun portal and vanished.

Her anger rattled me; it made me uncomfortable. I turned to my chest of treasures and retrieved the little clam.

"I would love you even if you weren't perfect."

She did not reply.

I wondered if she believed me—I wasn't sure if I believed myself.

Night came and went, and after setting Luna in the Solar Citadel, I retired to my spire and spent the day sleeping with the little clam clutched to my heart.

The Face of Day continued arriving in the Lunar Spire with new cracks. When I asked where they came from, she hung her head in shame.

"He's gone, yet I'm still here. I don't deserve to live without pain."

"Are you making these new cracks yourself?"

"It's only fair."

I returned to the ground floor of the Solar Citadel the following morning to carve more putty and create an ointment for her newest wounds. That evening, before I lifted the moon into the night sky, I offered her the cure.

"Please heal."

She took the vial of putty and smiled weakly at me.

"Thank you," she offered.

"Will you use it?"

She nodded.

I could ask no more of her.

The stress of all we had lost, and all we continued losing, was defeating—I no longer had the energy to explore during my downtime. Instead, I took naps during the day to recharge for the night.

When the moon arrived, her glow coaxed me out of my slumber.

"You look so peaceful when you sleep," Luna said.

"Reality can't reach me in my dreams."

"I understand. Just don't forget about me."

"I would never."

I returned the little clam to her bowl before lifting the moon into the sky.

I'm not sure when the shift happened, but everything had changed. Time ran smoothly and the evening sky was calm. Even the poisonous emotions infiltrating the night had stopped—I hadn't needed to visit the Pocket of Control since Time shattered.

When we landed in the Solar Citadel, the Face of Day stood proud with her forest-green eyes closed and arms extended as she waited for the sun to rise.

Her porcelain-coated flesh was so smooth it looked as though the cracks had never been there at all.

"Your fissures are completely gone," I stated in amazement.

She nodded.

"How are you feeling?"

She did not answer.

The sun emerged, aligning perfectly with her outstretched hands. They took off, illuminating the sky with daylight.

I was relieved, but also confused. The Lumineers never said that all traces of the cracks would vanish. In fact, they said the wounds would take time to heal. I shielded my eyes as I stared into the sun. Day flew with strength, grace, and beauty.

Too tired to dispute her success, I returned to the Lunar Spire to rest. I retrieved the little clam from her bowl and held her tightly to my chest as I fell into a deep slumber. She sang to me throughout, her voice transforming my worried thoughts into sweet dreams.

Luna's voice woke me.

"Have you forsaken me?" she asked, her voice sad, but calm.

"I would never," I promised, hastily shaking myself from the grip of my dreams. With care, I returned the little clam to her saltwater bowl and gave all my attention to the moon. We rose into the sky, giving life to the night.

Something peculiar was afoot. I could feel it in the air.

When we lowered into the Solar Citadel, Day waited stoically for her turn.

"I'm so happy the putty worked," I expressed, hoping to understand how she got it to dry so fast.

She kept her back to me as she spoke. "It's a miracle. Thank you. Without your help, we would have perished."

"And you've stopped assisting in the Pocket of Control?"

"I will never go back there," she said, focus intent on catching the rising sun. "I learned my lesson."

"There hasn't been a single poisonous emotion to catch in ages. It feels like everything is going back to normal."

"Finally," she agreed.

Solís arrived and Day snatched him in a bear hug before I could greet him. They lifted into the sky and began the new day.

I left, content with our new order, even if it felt strange. We had regained control and eliminated chaos, which was all that mattered in the end. Satisfied that all was back to normal, I dedicated my free time to rest and healing. Night in and night out, I performed my duties but spent my days within the Pocket of Trust with the little clam.

Alone together, we were happy. I didn't have to fight anymore. I didn't have to save or worry about anyone here, and the little clam's songs healed me from the long-held battle I once fought.

I hadn't realized how beat up I was until given the chance to heal.

A year passed before I was finally well enough to notice the darkening sun. It rose through the sky like a backlit shadow, an ominous, ailing threat.

I left the false haven I had found within the Pocket of Trust a few hours before sunset and discovered a world I did not recognize.

The sandclock had transformed; in daylight, it was unrecognizable. Dark shadow tendrils tethered all the Faces to their thrones—a detail I had not noticed during the night. Held captive, they could not access their pockets.

"What happened?" I asked as I flew toward them.

"Where have you been?" Control demanded.

"I thought we had restored order. I thought our Host was safe."

"You were wrong—another fatal mistake." She laughed. "And you thought *I* was a menace to the Host."

"Who did this to you?" I asked.

"Chaos," Sorrow explained. "We have been trapped like this for an entire year."

"The only Face he left alone besides you was Time," the Face of Anger added.

"What about Day?" I asked.

"He wears her Face," Joy revealed, her bright emerald eyes vacant of hope. "Chaos rules the day."

"We don't know where Day is," Sorrow added.

"I will kill Chaos myself once I'm freed," Anger seethed, face red with fury.

"Then let's set you free," I stated as I slashed at the dark shadowy tendrils trapping the Face of Anger. But as I severed one, two more formed, imprisoning him further.

"Stop!" the Face of Anger insisted. "You'll only make it worse."

Control scoffed. "You think we didn't already try to break free?"

"Chaos seized our pockets," Sorrow informed me. "He controls everything now."

I flew higher to assess the damage from afar.

Grave devastation greeted me.

Darkness blanketed the village of time, and the light it cast to indicate the seconds, minutes, and hours glowed dimly.

"I need to stop him," I announced.

"Will you fight him?" Anger asked.

238

"I see no other way," I replied, my resolve wavering.

Control cut in, "If you want to win, you'll need to keep the element of surprise on your side. Don't let him know that you're on to him."

I nodded.

"I will fix this," I promised before rocketing to the Lunar Spire.

I had thought the battle was over.

I had wasted so much time recovering from a hard-earned victory I had never truly won. I had let myself succumb to the illusion of peace while the war raged on.

A coward's move—I should have known better.

I paced the Lunar Spire as I waited for the sun to set. The little clam sat on the windowsill, humming a soft, soothing melody to calm my mind. While she set my thoughts at ease, the fury in my heart grew, strengthening by the minute.

Right on time, Chaos arrived disguised as the Face of Day. He looked just like her, and as usual, he refused to make eye contact with me.

"It's nice to have everything working so smoothly," I stated, coaxing him to converse.

"I told you everything would be fine."

I seethed—he even stole her voice.

"Although," I said, "I feel like we don't talk much anymore."

Chaos kept his back to me as he inched toward the portal.

I continued, "Where do you go during the night?"

Chaos lunged to touch the sun etching, but I caught his wrist and threw him to the ground. Still cloaked in Day's body, he appeared tiny and fragile. He shielded his face as I held him down by his throat.

"What are you doing?" he asked in Day's voice, feigning horror.

"You cannot fool me anymore," I seethed.

He lowered his arm and his red gaze met mine—his grin was sinister as he struggled to breathe beneath my grip.

"Took you long enough," he sneered, his deep voice no longer disguised.

"I will kill you."

"You know you cannot do that."

I growled and pressed harder against his neck.

"Where is Day?" I demanded.

"Right where you left her." His red eyes darted toward a dark corner of the Lunar Spire, casting a crimson glow on her curled-up body.

"No," I gasped.

"You offered her the remedy to her wounds, but she never used it. I offered her a way out instead, and she took it," Chaos revealed.

My grip loosened around his neck as my attention turned to my oldest friend. For an entire year, she lay crippled by defeat in my home and I never noticed her there. I had been so consumed by my own needs that I missed her silent, solitary struggle. She needed me, and I failed her.

Furious with myself, I glared at Chaos, the mastermind of this disaster.

"You are to blame," I growled.

"Am I? You're the Face of Night; you are supposed to protect this world. If Father Time was here, I suspect he'd blame you."

My rage boiled over. I bared my teeth, ready to rip Chaos in half, but he fought me and wriggled free.

Unbound, he punched me in the throat.

The strike came as a surprise and sent me stumbling backward. Still wearing the disguise of Day, his arms turned into long blades and he wielded them like swords.

"Take off her Face." I dodged his swinging arms.

"The day is mine," he cackled. "And soon, so will be the night!"

"Never," I swore as he hurtled toward me. The fight was unmatched—I was defenseless against his arm-length blades.

He pushed me into the corner, pinning me to the wall with his swords crossed around my neck. One move and my life would end.

"All I need is your Face," he bartered. "Give it to me willingly and you can live."

"You can't kill me," I corrected him.

"Are you sure?" Chaos countered, his playful tone sinister. "I killed the Face of Time."

"*You* did that?"

"Well, technically, Malsana did it, but she was only there because of me. I sent a version of her to him through the memory receptacle. He thought that by killing himself, he would also kill Malsana and protect everyone else, but he didn't understand how the monster works. She exists in many places at all times. Eliminating one version of her doesn't eliminate the rest."

"You've infected the Host with this monster. If you kill her, you kill us all."

"She isn't going to die. Just as I have done with Day, I planned to do with Time, but Father Time intervened before I could take the soldier's Face." Chaos smirked. "It's what I plan to do with you, too."

"If you kill me, you'll destroy the Host."

"I only wish to wear your Face."

My anger intensified—Chaos was reckless and held no concern for the greater good.

He smiled, still wearing Day's Face. His swords pressed into my neck, drawing sand and vapor. He cut into me slowly, letting each second of pain resonate.

I swung my talons, but I could not reach him. Each slash through the air was energy wasted.

Angry for all I had lost and remorseful for those I had let down, I resigned my fight and surrendered to the delivery of this cruel destiny.

The distant fingertips of death reached toward me, growing closer as the blades cut deeper into my neck.

This was the end.

My anguish intensified as granules of sand fell faster from my neck, my vapor sizzling with a whistle as it left my body—I would lose this fight.

As the light began to fade and defeat was mine to hold, a horrifying scream tore me from my forced surrender. It resonated through the tower, echoing across the land like an alarm. Piercing in volume, it rattled every living creature to the bone—including Chaos. The sound crippled the nefarious Face and sent him shaking to his knees.

Set free, but impaired, I clutched the wounds on both sides of my neck to stop the spill of life and stumbled away from my executor. Steam and sand crept through the cracks between my fingers. The wound throbbed, but I still had fight in me. If forced to surrender, I would do so defiantly.

I pressed the edges of my new wounds together until my shadow stitched itself shut, then turned to the culprit of this travesty.

The earsplitting shriek did not cease, and though the sound weakened me, too, I muscled through the agonizing noise toward the traitorous Face of Chaos. He seized on the ground, paralyzed by the bone-shattering screech, and an opportunity to reverse my fate arose. I placed my palm over the mask he wore, dug my talons into the edges, and tore Day's Face off his wretched skull. The moment I freed her Face, his body morphed back into the shadow figure of Chaos. His red eyes bore into me, a murderous stare that would have been worrisome if he wasn't still crippled by the deafening scream.

I raced to Day and gently positioned her Face back where it belonged. Her porcelain-coated flesh did not mend itself like my shadow flesh did, so I added some of the still-soft ceramic putty from the sealed vial I gave her many moons ago. After a moment of waiting to see if it worked, Day opened her pretty forest-green eyes.

Sorrow brimmed her gaze.

"You'll be okay," I promised, noticing all the scars covering her body from old wounds.

"What happened?" she asked.

"You let Chaos wear your Face."

Tears fell down her cheeks. "I remember."

"It's okay. I am fixing everything."

"What's that horrible noise?"

For the first time, I questioned the source of the screaming as well.

On the open windowsill sat the little clam, her shells wide open and producing the most horrific screech. I had never seen her this way before. While grateful she had saved me, I couldn't stop the repulsion that had entered my heart. My perfect little singing clam was now broken open and echoing a nightmarish siren for all to hear. My

243

weakness against the Face of Chaos had ruined her—I broke her just like I broke every perfect thing I loved.

I shook the guilt from my mind—I still had work to do.

"I will make everything better," I promised Day.

She sniffled. "Thank you."

With a sturdy grip, I clutched Chaos by his shadowy shoulders and tore into the sky. Luna waited for me in the Lunar Spire, but the start of night would have to wait.

I flew into the ether and threw Chaos into his pocket. He plummeted out of sight and into the Fringe. Then I touched the haze engulfing his pocket and reconfigured the border so an alarm would sound whenever he tried to leave.

Chaos eradicated, for now, the little clam stopped screaming and our world resumed its natural, tranquil state. The shadow tendrils constraining the Faces along the Ring of Thrones evaporated, setting them free.

I raced back to the Lunar Spire.

"I thought you forgot about me," Luna wept.

"Never," I reassured her.

We lifted into the sky, traveling fast to make up for lost time. The Tower of Time had a newly assigned glass soldier—he stared at me intently from behind the glass clockface. When the moon finally reached its proper place in the night sky, the Face of Time retreated into the depths of his tower.

My concern revolved around Day. She had to heal. Morning quickly approached, and she needed to be strong to carry the sun through the sky.

When I arrived at the Solar Citadel and set the moon to rest, Day sat on her golden sun throne, expression blank.

"Are you okay?" I asked, stepping close to examine her healing scars.

She shook her head. "I am unworthy."

"We all make mistakes. Now is the time to do better."

Her expression tightened and her lip quivered. "I can't remember how to smile."

"It isn't hard," I promised, forcing a grin. My lips curled upward awkwardly—I didn't show happiness often—and the uncomfortable sight coaxed a small smile out of Day. "There you go! The memory of happiness will return, and so will your smile."

She nodded, smile already fading. "I want to believe you."

"For now, be brave. Be strong. The rest will follow."

"I can do that."

Solís arrived and Day raced to him.

"I missed you," she confessed through the tears.

Solís hesitated to emerge from the fiery center of the sun.

"Is it really you?" he asked.

"Yes," Day sobbed.

Solís inched forward, and eventually, his charred flesh and burnt eyes became visible through the thin outer layer of solar flares.

"You abandoned me," he stated.

"I didn't mean to. It all happened so quickly."

"I had to be strong for the both of us in your absence," he revealed. "For a year, I had to do both of our jobs because the impostor was useless. He just flew next to me, pretending to carry my weight."

"I am so sorry. I will make it up to you."

Solís looked utterly fatigued. "I am so tired."

"Rest," Day begged. "I will take care of you."

Solís retreated to his spot in the center of the sun.

Guilt ravaged Day's demeanor, and though I felt sorry for her, this was not within my power to repair.

"I'll be waiting for you in the Lunar Spire. Be brave," I reminded her.

Day uncrossed her arms and straightened her shoulders. She inhaled deeply, then released her fear as she took Solís into her hands and flew into the sky.

I could hear her crying as she lifted the sun higher.

"Be strong," I whispered, unable to take my eyes off her.

But as the words left my mouth, she burst into flames. My heart lurched in horror—the Face of Day was burning alive. She released a bloodcurdling scream as the sun swallowed her whole.

There was nothing I could do to save her.

Nothing I could do to reverse this tragic turn of fate.

I had helped her heal just to lose her again.

Nothing I ever did was enough.

I slammed my wings against the morning air, incensed by the unfairness of it all.

"Solís!" I shouted. "How could you let this happen?"

"It's what she wanted," he replied, his voice a whisper swallowed by the sizzling sun flares. "Sometimes surrender allows us to start over again."

This stopped me in my tracks.

I hovered in place while the sun soared farther away.

She wanted this.

After all I had done for her, all I had sacrificed, she chose to give up.

I almost died for her.

The Lunar Spire no longer felt like home—the stain of Day's weakness lingered, reminding me of my futile fight to save her life. Upon my arrival, the little clam was closed and humming a pretty melody, but her voice no longer soothed me. It no longer gave me comfort. I could only see the version of her with cracked-open shells and the tormented creature living inside. All I could hear was her monstrous scream that rattled the bones of every living being within earshot. The sight of her now turned my stomach. She was no longer perfect, no longer my beloved.

"Everything is ruined," I confessed, lifting her into my palm.

She stopped singing.

My heart hurt. "I am no good. You are better off without me."

I wrapped my fist around her and flew toward the Pocket of Trust. Through the haze and into the beautiful world within, I let her go.

The little clam fell from my grip, plummeting hundreds of feet into the ocean below.

I turned and left without looking back—I did not want to know where she landed for fear that I might return one day to find her.

Solís finished the day on his own, and I fulfilled my duties for the night. When I set the moon in the Solar Citadel, I found the Face of Day there, fresh-faced and clear of scars.

"How are you here?" I demanded, afraid the Face of Chaos might have escaped and stolen her Face again.

She recoiled, afraid. "Who are you?"

Her fear was genuine.

"You don't remember me?" I asked, noticing her missing wings.

"How could I? I just got here."

A rustling noise came from the ceiling. I looked up— Father Time hovered above.

247

Let her start over, he said into my mind. *Let her forget.*

She gets to forget while I am forced to remember? I questioned in thought.

Your purpose here is not to save Day. You must let her find her own salvation.

Father Time disappeared, but his orders were clear: only she could save herself.

A note from the Fox

As you can see, our faith in Night was misplaced. He was just as broken as the rest of us.

Later, after the day of discovery and my meeting with Awareness, I came to understand that Malsana's initial infection had caused his increasing obsession with perfection — though he saw through the lies, he never truly recovered from her touch.

His fixation with perfection had worsened Jane's condition. She was obsessed, just like him.

On that day of discovery, witnessing his flippant disregard for the clam ignited my rage. He thought he broke her and labeled her brave vulnerability as shameful when, in reality, his love gave her the strength to save everyone.

She wasn't broken — she was heroic.

I yanked the feather from behind my ear and threw it to the ground. A scoundrel, a traitor — the Face of Night thought he was helping, but his selfish love had ruined another.

The little clam.

A voice within me spoke, one I did not recognize, one kinder than Malsana's: We are her, and she is us. We are all interconnected parts of the Host, various parts of her identity that must work together to remain whole.

This blast of awareness forced my anger to turn inward — I was no better than Night; I was guilty of being selfish, too.

I was remembering, though the full spectrum of my identity still eluded me. All I knew was that when Jane needed me, I wasn't there.

This brush with fleeting self-importance left me humbled as I recalled my reflection in the pond. A little fox who ran away to save herself.

A terrible decision that saved no one, not even me.

I never managed to escape the thoughts Malsana had planted in my mind. Her mantra of unworthiness spun like a broken record every day. It shaped every decision I made, and I suspected that black marble was still nestled in my belly, thwarting my ability to heal.

I had to become fully aware.

Once I understood who I was, perhaps I could find a way to help silence the monster.

The shimmering black pearl reappeared in the trail of mementos. It radiated with lost innocence.

I worried what it might show me.

Pearl lifted in my paws, I closed my eyes and saw Jane's struggles through the little clam—an attempt to hide within herself while the world around her felt unworthy of her trust.

Revisiting Memento #2

When: The 21ˢᵗ – 23ʳᵈ Cycle
Where: Jane's mind — Pocket of Trust
Who: Jane Doe through the Little Clam

Discarded yet again.

Pushed by the tides, fluttering downward in somersaults, I fell through the water into my underwater garden. Glimmering sunlight spotlighted my fall. Shining from above, illuminating the betrayal plaguing this place.

Broken when he met me, broken when he left.

For a brief moment, his love gave me courage. It gave me the strength to sing again. And when I finally felt secure enough to fully open up, I realized his love was a farce.

He only liked my pretty songs — the sad ones made him cringe.

He only liked my outer shell, not the creature existing within.

My darkness scared him, and though it had saved his life, he no longer loved me. Without remorse, he tossed me back into this underwater junkyard where he'd never have to see me again.

Long ago, my home was a beautiful coral and sea flora garden. Now, I lived atop a trash pile of rubble and bones. I sat on a mile-high throne of ruined attempts to love.

I wasn't a queen by any means, just a lonely soul in a broken world, building castles out of bones.

Every fear, every heartbreak, every moment of weakness formed the pillars of my throne. And all around me, introverted creatures like me took the discarded hope that sunk to the depths of this sea and turned them into homes.

I desired no disturbances during my attempt to resume my sequestered surrender—a grand request, I quickly learned.

Wishes for quiet always led to noise. Dreams for peace often led to war.

I was not immune to such cruelly fated jokes.

An explosive current tore through the ocean's underbelly, demolishing every boneyard throne in its path and sending the passive sea creatures into disarray. We tumbled in the rushing undertow and were catapulted far from our homes. I somersaulted, disoriented and unable to fight the stream.

When the current finally let me go, I tumbled into a shallow wave that carried me ashore.

I cracked my shells open ever so slightly to learn that I had landed on a foreign beach. I was still within of the Pocket of Trust—I recognized the sky—but I had never been on this side of the ocean before.

I closed my shells and hummed a comforting tune as I debated what to do. It was unwise to open wide outside the safety of the sea. The birds in the sky and land-bound creatures might see me as food. If I wanted to, I could extend my arms outside my shell and drag myself back to sea, but I sensed that I wasn't alone.

I hummed a sad song to ease my nerves.

Within my closed shells, I rocked back and forth until my momentum rolled me forward.

One inch closer to freedom.

Another exhausting bout of exertion and I flipped again.

It was a slow roll, but it was progress. I continued singing as I worked to save myself.

Inch by inch, the ocean grew nearer. I could smell its salty shelter beckoning me home.

One more somersault and I'd escape whatever unknown terror had dragged me here.

One more roll and I'd be safe.

One swift snatch and I was taken.

"Your song is so sad," the stranger stated, "and it has grown so loud. It echoes across time and space; it's been keeping everyone awake."

I thought I sang in whispers.

"Let me go," I demanded.

He placed me back onto the sand.

"I can bring you home," he offered.

I opened my shells and peeked through. A furry little creature scurried around me in circles.

"What are you?" I asked in awe.

"I'm an otter."

"I've never met an otter before."

"We are warm-blooded, like the whales and dolphins."

"What am I?" I asked.

"Your blood is cold."

"Does that make me less alive?"

"Some might argue so, but I think you are vibrant with life, even if that life is a bit sad."

"I'm not sad," I argued.

"Then stop singing sad songs."

"I can try." I thought of my night songs. "But I can't control what comes out of me when I'm asleep."

He smiled. "That's when the truth is revealed."

I wondered if he was right.

"What's your name?" I asked, unwilling to admit that my long-held apathy stemmed from sorrow.

"Davy. What's yours?"

I paused, shocked that I could not remember.

"I don't know," I answered honestly.

"No wonder you're so sad!"

My shells clamped together tightly.

"I'm sorry," he offered. "Let's give you a name."

"I don't want one."

"Well, if we're going to be friends, I need to know what to call you." He paused for a moment, deep in thought. When he spoke again, I could hear his smile. "How about Jane?"

The name struck a chord in the void that once held my pearl heart—it felt familiar. It was a perfect fit. My shells cracked open and I peered out at Davy.

"I don't mind that name," I said, concealing my true excitement.

"Excellent. From now on, you are Jane."

A heavy weight in the depths of my being lifted. Something inside of me changed. Davy was an exuberant ray of light in my otherwise murky world.

Davy took me home to my underwater garden of bones.

He visited often, keeping me company whenever he could. The deep darkness holding me down began to lift, and I found it easier to face each day.

Though he could only stay for a few minutes each time, he visited frequently.

I told him about my first love and my missing pearl.

He listened with empathy.

Together, we relocated my smile. He brought a joy into my life that I had never known before, and I clung to him for happiness. I found myself leeching his infectious energy for renewed purpose.

He became my everything.

Through him, I became whole.

"I have a gift for you," he announced one day.

He extended his furry hand. Something hidden remained clutched in his grip.

"What is it?"

His little fingers uncurled.

Atop his paw sat a magnificent black pearl.

"I know it can't ever replace the pearl you lost," he said, "but I thought it might help."

"I think that *is* my lost pearl!"

My shells opened wide and he dropped the black pearl inside. Smooth and pristine, it sat perfectly on my tongue.

"Where did you find it?"

"At the bottom of the sea. I had to dive pretty deep to retrieve it." He paused. "It called to me—singing a song as sad as yours—and I felt compelled to investigate. I was shocked to discover a pearl."

"Malsana must've discarded it after ruining it."

"Who?"

"The octopus who stole my pearl so many years ago. That's why it's black now—it's stained with her ink."

"I'm sorry," he offered.

"Don't be. I feel whole again, thanks to you."

"I am happy to help."

His time was up.

In a flash, he swam away, leaving me alone with my new and cherished gift.

My blackened pearl filled the void left so many years ago.

I tried to scrub the ink off my pearl, tirelessly muscling the stains. A few hours of futile attempts revealed that the discoloration was permanent.

I would need to learn to love this imperfection.

"Can you take me above the sea?" I asked Davy after weeks of brief visits in my dark corner of the ocean.

"I like seeing you here," he replied, dodging my request.

"But I want to see where you go when you're not with me."

"Why?"

"It seems so much more exciting than my quiet isolation."

"I spend most of my time at the surface," he informed me. "I fear you'll die if you come with me."

"I can last two hours in the open air. Just a quick trip, and then you can bring me back," I pled.

He was reluctant—I could feel his hesitance to include me in the other parts of his life.

"Fine," he eventually conceded. "I'll show you where I go."

He lifted me with his furry hands and cradled me close to his heart as he swam. The steady rhythm of his heartbeat reverberated against my blackened pearl, giving temporary life to my pulseless heart.

When his swift pace slowed, I cracked my shells open to watch our ascent through a kelp forest toward a floating huddle of furry bodies.

"Are those your friends?" I asked, partly in awe, but mostly terrified.

"Yeah, that's my raft."

"There are so many of them."

"Fifty-seven."

I clamped my shells shut.

We surfaced, but I refused to open.

"Hey, Davy," one of the other otters greeted. "How was your swim?"

Another otter cut in before Davy could answer. "I thought we were eating urchin tonight."

"We are," an older otter insisted. "Davy, don't ruin your appetite with snacks."

Davy looked down at me and cringed, his embarrassment abundant. "I'm not eating this clam. She is my friend."

"Friends with a clam?" one of his fellow otters scoffed. "Why?"

"She sings pretty songs and I enjoy her company," Davy replied.

A younger otter chimed in, "Boring. Clams are meant for eating."

Davy scowled. "Don't be rude."

The raft assaulted him with questions, talking over each other and shouting to be heard.

"How long can she stay before her insides shrivel?"

"She has no face, no arms—is she even alive?"

"You want her to join our pod? Without arms, how will she join our resting raft?"

Davy groaned. "It's just a visit. She wanted to see the world above."

"Well, take her back. Before one of us eats her."

I trembled in Davy's grip—he could feel me shaking within my shell.

"It's okay," he whispered, diving below the sea's surface where we could be alone again. "I won't let anyone hurt you," he promised.

Removed from the hostile group, I peeked out of my shell again. "I am not welcome among your friends."

"They will come around," he swore, but his voice held uncertainty.

His raft never came around.

Davy's visits became shorter and less frequent, and I became more desperate to keep him close.

"Where have you been?" I asked after not seeing him for two days. My black pearl felt heavier than usual.

"With my raft, mostly. I did a lot of swimming along the shores, too."

"Why didn't you visit me?"

"I was busy."

"Feels like you don't want to see me anymore."

"I'm not so sure I'm good for you," he stated cautiously.

"How could you say that?" My voice quivered. "You are the best thing that's ever happened to me."

"You love me too much."

"I don't understand."

"I can't be what you need," he explained, his tone gentle and sympathetic.

"Why not?"

"I live up there, and you live down here."

"We made it work before. Why can't it work now?" I asked.

"It never really worked," he revealed. "I was so tired all the time, and my lungs often hurt from pushing their limits."

"You never told me that."

"I didn't want to make you feel bad."

I had no heart, yet I felt the ache as if I did. "I just want to be with you. You make me happy."

"I will still visit," he promised.

His time was up—he needed air. He swam away, disappearing as quickly as he had arrived.

Months went by without him.

I clung to my pearl, leaning on it for strength during my loneliest hours, but it never offered the reprieve I so desperately sought. Contaminated, infected—Malsana's mark forever drained all comfort I once found in my pearl.

My frenzied desire to have Davy nearby turned into a disease that caused me to swell in size. I grew into a giant clam, and there was nothing I could do to calm my mind and reverse the transformation.

When he returned to see me after a year-long absence, I was no longer a little clam. I was a behemoth, a freak of nature.

"What happened?" he asked, horrified by my mutation.

"You abandoned me."

"I'm here now."

"Why did you take so long to come back?" I asked.

"I can't be expected to spend all my time going back and forth between the surface and the bottom. I can only be underwater for so long."

"I'll build a new throne closer to your kelp forest so it's easier for you."

"No," he objected. "You are smothering me."

"Admit it—you'd rather be with your raft than with me."

"I do enjoy being with them, yes. I was trying to be a friend to you, too," he paused to assess my current state, "but this is too much. I thought I was helping, but I'm making you worse."

"Don't pretend to know what I need," I shouted.

"Clearly, it's not me."

"Your love was a lie." I spat my black pearl at him.

"I never called it love."

Infuriated by his rejection, I clamped my giant shells together, which launched me through the water. I opened my shells and closed them again, this time trapping Davy by his tail.

"Let me go!" he demanded, but I refused to budge.

If he would not stay by choice, then I'd decide for him. With me, he would stay, and together forever we would be.

He struggled to break free, fighting my firm grip futilely. Venomous threats spat from his mouth as he cursed me, declaring that I wasn't worth the time and energy he gave.

My grip became tighter.

"No wonder you're alone," he seethed, oxygen running low. "You are a cancer—your love is a disease."

This accusation halted my resolve. I paused, realizing what I was doing. I was killing that which I claimed to love the most.

Horrified with myself, I let him go.

Davy swam away, frantic to reach the air before his lungs gave out.

I sat with myself and the crime I had almost committed. Who had I become?

While I could not see my reflection, I felt the grotesque enormity of my metamorphosis. I thought I was healing, but I had simply turned into an unrecognizable monster. I never fixed my problems; I never filled the void. I simply distracted myself with another hollow love that wasn't meant to last. My trust placed into another who never promised to stay, and even if he had, there was nothing stopping him from changing his mind and leaving one day.

Nothing that brought me joy ever stayed.

Alone again, with no love and no pearl, I greeted the swelling darkness like a friend. I welcomed it, praying silently for it to end my suffering. But something inside of me revolted, begging that I fight off the tempting nothingness.

But how?

I thought of my first love, I thought of my worst love, and I thought of my lost pearl. None of which I could replace.

In the aftermath of every heartbreak, I was the only one left standing.

Regardless of what came and went, I remained.

I closed my eyes and, for the first time in years, noticed the faint etching of a saying I had carved there back when I still trusted myself.

It read: *I am me with you. I am me without you. I am all I need.*

Self-trust was the answer; the solution existed within me.

Instead of letting outside entities define my happiness, I had to find joy and purpose within myself. I had to dig deeper. I had to trust my choices.

Only I could save me from myself.

I thought again of all I had lost, then recalled the strength it had taken to survive.

"I am me with you. I am me without you. I am all I need," I whispered to myself.

I repeated this over and over until the words held weight.

"I am me with you. I am me without you. I am all I need."

The darkness threatened to seep into my shell and consume me. Then I realized I had created this darkness. It came from me; I was its master.

I could lift myself and swim higher. I could relocate and find sunlight.

Only I could save me from myself.

My whisper turned into a shout as I repeated, "I am me with you. I am me without you. I am all I need."

A glimmering light from the depths of the sea caught my attention. My black pearl sat there, beckoning me to return. I could retrieve it; I could make it mine again.

Swim to new heights? Or revisit old depths?

The black pearl shimmered, tempting me to claim what was mine.

If I could control the past, I could control the future.

I took a quick detour to retrieve my discarded heartache. My shells pumped open and closed, propelling me out of the shadows and away from my throne of trash. I dove deeper than I had ever gone before until the black pearl lay within reach.

Save me, it hissed.

I opened my shells and scooped the pearl into my mouth.

Its return filled me with warmth. The loneliness I once felt disappeared.

The dark depths of the sea surrounded me.

I thought of my first love, I thought of my worst love, and I thought of my ruined pearl.

Darkness now filled the void.

Enveloped by the massive emptiness, I forgot everything except the pain.

The black pearl's weight kept me in place. Too heavy to move, too content with staying put, we existed in idyllic isolation. The fleeting bravery I had felt vanished, gone with the rushing tides. The mantra I had carved inside my shell was now illegible—the words that once gave me courage were forgotten.

Though it took me some time to realize it, choosing the past prevented me from having a future.

I had made the wrong choice, yet again.

A year passed in quiet nothingness, and though I wanted to leave, I feared change. I did not trust my ability to handle any new choices change might bring.

When another clam swam next to me, I recoiled in the light, afraid to engage.

"You ought to let it go," he advised.

"Let what go?"

"The darkness that keeps you here."

"But I like it here," I lied.

"There is greater beauty above."

"I don't trust what's above."

"I understand," he said before swimming away.

He returned the following day.

"I thought you understood my desire to be alone," I said.

"We don't need to talk. I like to be alone, too."

His rationale baffled me, but I let him stay, and we spent the day together in silence.

He left as the sun set.

"Will you come back?" I blurted.

"Do you want me to?"

My sudden desire to have a friend came as a shock.

"We can be alone together," I suggested.

"I would like that."

He returned every day to sit by my side in comfortable silence.

Weeks after our first encounter, the black pearl grew heavier.

"I used to lack trust in myself, too," he said, noticing my struggle. "I thought I needed something outside of myself to be whole."

"You didn't?"

"Nope."

"How did you discover that?"

"I heard a voice in the darkness. It shouted, 'I am me with you. I am me without you. I am all I need.'"

It sounded so familiar.

"I've heard those words before," I said.

"That's because they are yours."

"I said that?"

"You did. When I heard you, I dropped the golden trash I clung to and followed the sound of your voice. Your declaration of trust and worth did not last long before you went silent again, so it took some time to find you here. It seems the freedom you found vanished as swiftly as it was discovered."

"You felt better after letting go of your weight?"

"Very much so. It wasn't mine to carry."

I hesitated. "Who will I be when I have nothing?"

"You will be you, and that is enough. Your instincts are good—trust yourself."

"I am me with you. I am me without you. I am all I need." The words felt natural as I said them.

I opened my shells.

You need me, the black pearl jeered.

"I don't think I do."

My tongue lifted and pushed the pearl out of my mouth. It toppled over the side of my bottom shell and plummeted over the side of my cliff dwelling.

"Do you feel better?" my new friend asked.

"I do, but I think it will take time."

"Time is a friend you can count on," he promised.

I smiled.

Learning to trust myself again would be a wonderous adventure.

A note from the Fox

So many moments, so many experiences plagued by Malsana's overarching presence.

Who we were, who we are, defined by the ailment we coveted.

At this point in my discovery, I had lost all sense of beginning and end. I knew how we got here and that I was somehow connected to the Host, but I could not pinpoint the exact moment we lost our way. I certainly had no idea where we were going or if it would result in a new beginning or a tragic end.

I held on anyway, terrified of what I might find next, but aware that I needed to see it, no matter how grim the outcome.

On that day of discovery, black marbles separated me from the end of the foxhole.

I did not like the nightmare land, so I tried to walk around them, but with each sidestep, the black marbles rolled toward me like metal to magnets. I began to trot, and the marbles rolled faster.

"I don't want to go back there!" I shouted—in hindsight, this was where our healing truly began. If I had known that then, I would have embraced these marbles with delight. But at that time, I was not yet fully aware of the journey I was on.

The marbles bowled past me and barricaded the corridor.

"I just want to go home," I pled.

The marbles did not budge.

"Am I almost done?" I asked.

A marble at the center of the line broke formation and rolled toward me.

I groaned.

This nightmare would not cease until I saw its end.

Revisiting Memento #1

When: The 23rd Cycle
Where: Jane's mind—Pocket of Fear
Who: Jane Doe through the Warden

I opened my eyes, squinting against the blinding orange glow.

Home again—I was back in the fight.

Everything was in order. The world had not changed. It was the same horrific utopia I had left when I surrendered my mind to sleep.

I glanced at my legs—I was healed. Malsana had not lied; rest had restored my health.

Where was Malsana? Without standing, I searched the area. She was nowhere to be found. I scanned again, this time noticing a familiar face.

Cressie walked along the sidewalk, chin lifted and gaze determined.

Why was she here?

"Cressie, you're back!" I shouted. "But why? I thought you found freedom."

She did not answer me.

"You need to finish what you started," she advised, pointing to the sewer grate near her feet.

"What do you mean?"

She paused to scrutinize me. A quick examination of my condition rendered a scowl.

"How long until you fall asleep again?" she asked.

"I am healed. I no longer need rest."

"You said that the last time, too."

"Last time?"

"Don't you remember?" Her expression softened as I shook my head. She hopped the fence and knelt a safe distance from me. "You let your monster win."

"I would never."

"But you did."

"Come closer," I beseeched.

"I cannot."

I did not understand.

"Please," I begged.

"The cage she built around you is impenetrable," Cressie revealed.

"What cage?" I saw no bounds, no bars, no barricade.

Her head hung low. "Your monster has taken over everything. It runs this mind now."

"Malsana promised she wouldn't do anything reckless while she was healing me," I countered, struggling to recall what happened before I fell asleep.

"She did not heal you. She drained you dry. Look harder—beyond the imaginary reality Malsana designed for you."

I did as she suggested, focusing on shattering the blockade illusion.

"You are not free," Cressie repeated, fueling my strength with the truth. "Do you remember the red eyes in the sky?"

I remembered.

Malsana had befriended the nefarious invader and volunteered as tribute, forming an alliance with the enemy.

Recalling this truth demolished the façade Malsana had built around me. I looked down at my skeletal body, horrified by what I had become. I was a corpse, hardly alive. My soul was just a sliver of its former self.

I was a fool.

Enraged, I was determined to locate Malsana, but struggled to move. I was weak, I was debilitated—the simple act of turning my head took all my energy.

"Where are you?" I shouted, voice scratchy and raw. I gasped for breath—even speaking was a challenge. My eyes focused on Cressie, who was leaving the yard.

"Don't leave me!" I pled.

Cressie glanced over her shoulder. Her face flickered, glitching as it revealed her true nature: an ancient man with a hollowed face. Her green eyes turned gray as she glared at me.

"I return here time and time again in the image of your friend to teach you, to guide you," she said, her voice a deep growl. "But you've yet to escape that cage."

"Who are you?"

"Fix this mess," she warned before turning away. Her image sputtered in and out as she walked away.

Nothing was as it seemed.

My panic heightened—was I hallucinating?

My neck creaked upward, slowly facing the wall I leaned against. I read the numbers on the door: 875.

This was the home I actively avoided—how did I get here? And when?

Reality returned. The true horror of my situation unveiled. Not only was I emaciated and rendered immobile, but I was also constrained by wax-covered webs. Wrists and ankles bound together—I was trapped. An intricate net of meticulously woven threads encased where I sat.

Malsana hovered at the top of it all.

No longer disguised as a puppy or an ogre, I saw her for what she was—a giant spider with eight marble eyes.

"What have you done?" I screeched.

I am keeping you safe.

"You are killing me."

I would never. I need you.

"Set me free! We had an agreement."

Yes, but you never truly trusted me.

"I wonder why," I spat sarcastically.

I am in control now.

"How long have I been imprisoned here?"

Malsana laughed. *Your entire life.*

"I meant here, in this web."

Hush, hush. You won't heal if you don't rest.

My memories jumbled together. I could no longer separate reality from deception. Was I ever truly free? Did I ever roam this world as a Walker? Or had Malsana's projected façade always entwined me?

Black marbles rained down, bouncing off my webbed shelter. I was safe, but what of that which existed beyond? I used my remaining energy to scan the world outside my threaded prison—the perfect world I once knew was demolished. For the first time since my creation, this place truly exemplified the nightmare it was. Monsters ran rampant, harassing wardens that weren't their own. Walkers ran, never breaking their pace. Sleepers slept, unwilling to wake. Screams, cries, and agonized howls echoed through the land, deafening the world with nonstop horror.

The perfect utopia was gone.

Everything was out of order.

"I have ruined this place."

Malsana scuttled closer. Her long, hairy legs navigated the thin, waxed webs with ease.

It is better this way. I will keep you safe, and you will keep me fed.

"I don't need your protection," I growled, fighting my constraints.

I set the monsters free. They now feed on anyone they want, except you. If you leave this shelter I built for you, they will hunt you, too.

"Let them! I'd rather die with honor than wither away with you."

You belong to me.

"I should have never called you a friend," I said, my remorse a giant knot in my stomach.

Malsana's marble eyes blinked. She studied me, scrutinized me.

Go back to dreamland. You are happier there.

A gossamer thread snaked up my back and wrapped itself around my neck. The tip of the fiber entered my ear and slithered into my brain.

Seeing my prison as it truly was, I did not want to fall back asleep. I wanted to fight; I wanted to prove I was worthy of my place here. I was a fear warden. I would prevail.

I squirmed, battling the overpowering force holding me down, wiggling until all my energy was spent.

The spider thread won.

I slipped into Malsana's memories of the inside world.

It looked different from before. Darkness covered the sandclock, shadowing the colorful counters of time. I rocketed toward the Pocket of Fear. Instead of a spherical steel cage churning with orange and gray smoke, the pocket appeared as a solid black marble.

My heart twisted into a knot.

What had I done?

A red glow pulsated from the pocket next door. I turned, aware that I had seen this red light before.

The pocket was a flat piece of jagged charcoal encased in a menacing red orb. I flew closer. Dancing flares separated me from the world below. Unlike the last time I was in this recollection, I could see into this world. Shadow figures covered the large rock; those with red eyes existed near the edge. Those with green lived in a large metropolis in the center. It was a functioning society, unlike the treadmill loop of horror I once walked every day.

A winged shadow with red eyes lifted into the sky, rocketing toward me. I tried to back away, pounding the enormous white wings attached to my back, but as I pumped them against the hollow sky, I noticed they were damaged. Singed and broken, these wings had lost their grace.

The intimidating shadow soared higher, aiming directly at me. I shielded my face, preparing for impact.

He flew through me.

I wasn't truly there—I was just a figment, an imaginary presence.

This was wrong; I felt real despite my appearance as the porcelain girl. Maybe my mind was the only real thing in this illusion.

I did not belong here. I had to escape.

You like it here, Malsana objected, her voice slithering into my mind.

"I want to be free!"

None of us are free. We do not belong to ourselves—we belong to her.

"Who?"

The one we live inside.

Without warning, my surroundings changed. Everything became bigger. Each item in sight had a crisp outline—this place was vivid, it was raw, it was real.

I observed my surroundings: a porcelain sink streaked with black raindrops, two hands pressed against the tiled wall. Fingers tense, wishing to break something, but unable. I could feel the cool pressure against the smooth wall pacify the fiery battle being fought within.

My remaining senses came to life: the scent of evergreen and honey, the sound of water dripping from the faucet, the bitter taste of failure.

My sight lifted to a mirror.

A young woman stared back at me. She was ravaged. Ink leaked from her eyes, staining her cheeks with black-veined streaks. Green eyes glassy, she held an anger so deep I dared to wonder the cause. She took her hands off the wall, dug her nails into her forehead, and sobbed. Her suffering was silent. She never made a sound.

Hands over her eyes, my vision went black. I saw nothing except the faint light filtering through her shaking fingers.

Her breathing was frantic and unsteady. Her heartbeat thudded so violently that my own heart threatened to break.

"What are you doing, Jane?" a voice shouted from outside the bathroom door.

Eyes wide with panic, her hands cupped her nose and mouth. She stared at her reflection, desperate to remain silent.

"Are you okay?" the outsider asked.

She squeezed her eyes shut, took a deep breath, then replied.

"I'm fine. Just going to the bathroom."

"Well, hurry up. You left the table ten minutes ago."

"I'm almost done," she promised.

At the sound of feet walking away, she dropped her hands from her face. She stared at her reflection—her green gaze unforgiving.

I suddenly realized where I was—I sat in our Host's eye. This was the outside world. Everything I saw was Jane's reality.

Her hands clutched the edge of the sink.

Glaring at herself, fury leaving her body through her tight grip on the porcelain. As the anger transferred elsewhere, her expression softened. Rage to defeat, this battle was lost.

What was she fighting? What did I miss? Could I save her? Could I help?

I thought of Malsana—had she caused this suffering?

The Host wiped her mouth, removing a strange grime I hadn't noticed before. She washed her hands, cleaned the ink off her face, stepped back, and assessed her appearance.

She wasn't happy, yet she smiled. She smiled until her happiness appeared true. She was a good actress—I almost believed her, too.

Something wasn't right; I felt a strange pull to dig deeper. I looked closer at her reflection and saw myself in the mirror.

She was me, and I was her.

We were one and the same.

I was part of Jane.

That's enough, Malsana said, ripping me from her recollection of the outside world and returning me to her dreamland recollection of the inner world's sandclock.

"Why is she so sad? What did you do to her?"

All her choices are her own. I merely influence and feed off the repercussions.

"Help her be happy instead!"

Malsana laughed. *Happiness gives me nothing. I need fear. I need weakness.*

Determined more than ever to escape, I pounded my charred wings against the hollow sky. I had to help Jane; I had to help myself. My actions directly affected my home. Every time I failed myself, I also failed our Host.

Wings spread and hovering in this dreamland version of the inside world, I screamed. A guttural cry ripped from my gut and echoed through the weightless sky.

No one heard me.

No one came to help.

Determined to escape, desperate to find something real, I pinched my wings together and plummeted. I fell through the Northern Unknown, leaving the village of time behind as I dipped into the Southern Abyss.

It was darker here—there was no neon light from the time counters, nor any glow from the pockets. All life existed above.

With the sun to the north, shrouded by the haze separating the horizon, the only light to be found came from the waning moon. It was dull, and tiny creatures orbited the massive satellite, preparing the moon for its next trip above. A soft cry came from inside. I couldn't see the girl within the moon, but I heard her sorrow.

We were all prisoners here.

If I could fix the inside of my pocket, perhaps the layered worlds beyond would change for the better, too.

I continued falling.

Deep within the Southern Abyss, near the bottom of the sandclock, I came across an unexpected sight: a graveyard tended by a lonely caretaker. Black circles encased her empty eye sockets and bone peeked out from under her rotting flesh. Skeletal cheeks gaunt, this woman looked as dead as those she had buried.

Each fresh mound of dirt had a memento drawn onto the tombstone marking the plot. Feathers, shards of glass, rustleweeds, golden threads, a black pearl—strange bits of garbage that clearly held great meaning. The caretaker combed the soil methodically, humming an eerie melody as she tended to the dead.

I looked beyond her workspace to find freshly dug plots, empty but ready to be filled. A pile of scorched porcelain lay beside the grave.

My heart ached—I wondered if my ability to wrangle Malsana might save a few souls.

Wings squeezed together and pressed to my back, my fall quickened. The sandclock, leagues above me, grew smaller every second.

The drop was never-ending; there was no bottom to this abyss.

I extended my scorched wings, hoping to slow my momentum, but the force of my fall ripped the remaining feathers off my bones. Only the skeleton of my wings remained.

Useless.

I surrendered to the freefall.

The longer I fell, the less I felt the lurching sensation in my gut.

My grasp of time vanished as I entered total darkness.

I prepared to live like this forever when a streak of gray infiltrated the black space.

"Who's there?" I asked, my voice raw from lack of use.

"You have a choice," a familiar voice replied. "Stay here or fight."

"I will fight."

"Then why did you give up?" he asked, his face concealed.

"I couldn't find my way out of this place."

"All you have to do is wake up."

All I had to do was wake up.

His gray light covered me, and I realized I wasn't falling at all—I was lying on the pavement.

"Where am I?" I asked.

"The rustleweed is the key—it holds the answers you seek. Only you can rip it from its roots."

"Rustleweed? Who are you?"

He ignored my questions.

"Her time will run out if she continues living like this."

He offered his skeletal hand, which I accepted, and he helped me to my feet. The gray light began to fade.

I never saw his face.

He disappeared as quickly as he had arrived, leaving behind the stench of old wars.

I was alone in darkness again.

"Wake up," I murmured to myself.

The black space shook, trembling beneath my determination. I focused on my life within the Pocket of Fear. I pictured where I wanted to be. Manifesting transportation out of this nightmare, the illusion around me disintegrated. Orange strips of light strobed through the darkness. The dreamland sandclock above reappeared, flickering in and out. It fought to exist while I battled to break free.

While the inside world dissipated into the orange light, one thing remained: a rustleweed that had grown through a crack in the pavement. Prickly and dried out from the sun, it stood strong in the orange light. Never wavering, never faltering—it was real.

I reached for it, desperate to touch something true.

As the thin branches scratched my fingertips, I drifted home. The darkness lifted and reality resumed.

The Pocket of Fear was still volatile—nothing had changed during my slumber. In fact, it appeared to have worsened. Black clouds swirled, masking the orange sky that battled to shine through. Wardens' bodies were strewn all over: hanging from tree limbs, pierced on the picket fences, crushed in the street. A true death for many—no sliver of soul remained in their mangled bodies. Monsters ran free, feeding on whomever they pleased.

Groggy, but determined, I assessed my situation.

The webbed net Malsana had built around me still imprisoned me. My ankles were bound together, but my wrists had escaped their knotted constraints while I slept. Outside the gossamer cocoon, my right hand touched a very real rustleweed.

Hope lifted, I seized my chance. I clawed at the soil, digging for the roots. The man who had entered my dream said this was the way to fix things; this was how I would save myself.

This was how I would save Jane.

Dirt caked under my fingernails. I had to rip this terror up from the roots before Malsana returned.

What are you doing? Her voice was loud and clear.

I searched the sky but could not find her.

I dug faster.

Do not touch the rustleweed, she demanded.

"Where did it come from?" I demanded.

The Face of Chaos gifted it to me.

"It does not belong here." My words escaped with a gasp—my energy was depleting.

As I fought to catch my breath, my finger latched underneath one of its roots. I yanked the delicate tendril from the ground and Malsana screeched. The black clouds dissipated, allowing more orange light to shine through.

It was working.

The rustleweed—a powerful relic from the former Pocket of Time—was the key. While it was linked to Malsana, its strength and wisdom poured into her.

I could not let this continue.

My fingers scoured the soil for another tendril. As I located a lateral branch off the well-developed primary root, Malsana cried.

I thought we were friends.

I tugged the root from the ground. The swirling sky brightened. With each lateral root pulled, my strength returned.

"Try to stop me. I dare you!"

Malsana did not emerge, but her webbed prison constricted around me. The sticky, suffocating walls closed in. I had to work faster.

Reenergized, my left hand tore through the web to help rip up the primary root. I had to end this.

When I pulled the third lateral root, the slick clouds parted with a wail.

You're hurting me, Malsana whimpered.

"Where are you?" I demanded, unimpressed by her lack of fight. Defeating her was too easy; this didn't feel right.

Thunder cracked as I yanked a fourth lateral root from the ground. My attention turned upward as black marbles fell from the sky.

Malsana *was* the storm clouds—she reigned terror from above. Determined to finish her off before she reformed as something else, I stood and used all my weight to tear this rustleweed clean out of the soil. Malsana shifted her form as the root loosened.

Stop, she begged, unable to morph quick enough. *Let's talk.*

"You broke our agreement. There's nothing left to discuss."

Wait—

"You aren't welcome here anymore!"

With a final tug, I ripped the whole rustleweed out of the ground. The thick, primary root writhed in objection, shriveling the longer it was exposed to air.

The black clouds rapidly dissolved as the rustleweed reassigned its allegiance to me. This plant carried wisdom. It granted confidence and courage to its possessor. With it, I grew stronger.

Malsana's strong hold on this pocket deteriorated, and a tiny caterpillar with black marble eyes fell from the sky. It landed in the spider's nest I still stood within. Threads weakened, I used the sword still strapped to my back to slash my way out of this prison.

The heavy blade felt good to hold—it carried memories of my former bravery.

"This might help," a friendly voice offered.

I sheathed my sword and turned to find Cressie offering me a glass jar from the other side of the fence. I accepted the gift, unscrewed the lid, and walked to where Malsana struggled in the prison she had designed.

"Now you know how it feels," I said, carefully plucking her out of the webbing and dropping her into the jar. I screwed the lid shut.

"Glad to see you woke up," Cressie offered.

"Will she be able to bust out of this jar?"

"Not if you maintain control."

I nodded, unsure how I ever lost control in the first place. "I thought you left through the sewer."

"Yes—Cressie left a long time ago. Her work here was done."

My brow furrowed. "Then who are you?"

Her grayish-green eyes turned into dark hollow voids, gray light gleaming within, and her voice deepened. "I am Father Time."

My heart fluttered.

"It was you I heard in the darkness."

He nodded.

"Why do you appear as my friend?" I asked.

"I am not supposed to interfere, but you made such a mess, I had no other choice."

"I'm sorry."

"You have one thing left to do."

"What's that?" I asked.

"Stop carrying your monster with you."

I touched the side of my pocket and felt the remaining marble trophies. Understanding washed over me. Without delay, I emptied my pocket, letting the marbles fall down the sewer.

Cressie's grayish-green eyes reappeared and her normal voice resumed. "You've remedied your mistake. Don't let it happen again."

I examined Malsana in caterpillar form within the jar. "If I was allowed to kill this little monster, I could ensure she never wreaks havoc again."

"That's not how it works. The fear you were assigned is everlasting. Malsana will live for the duration of the Host's life. Your battle will rage until this mortal life ends."

"I'm exhausted thinking about it."

"Prepare, Warden Jane, for you are the only one who can keep this devil subdued."

Malsana was weakened temporarily, but this reprieve would not last forever.

Father Time, disguised as Cressie, gave me a solemn nod before shedding his skin and revealing his true form— an ancient man with a beard as long as time itself. His dark voids bore into me, holding my gaze as he disappeared, leaving behind the dust of ancient wars.

It was time to remedy my mistake. I examined my new surroundings—dead wardens were strewn everywhere. Those who slept slowly woke. Those who ran were finally safe to walk. Without Malsana to empower the other monsters, they retreated. This heightened nightmare would return to normal; the terror would be manageable once more.

I wondered how Jane was doing, though I suspected I'd never see our brave yet broken Host again.

Malsana stirred within the jar, awakening to defeat. She scuttled about, searching for an escape. Upon realizing there was none, she crafted a cocoon for herself.

"Do you plan to transform into a butterfly?"

I plan to resume what I started.

"I won't ever let you take control again."

We'll see.

She crawled into her cocoon, retreating out of sight.

I was in for the fight of my life.

Undeterred and determined to succeed, I would transform, too. From warden into victress, I would rise to the occasion.

This eternal battle was mine to win.

The Face of Worthiness

When: The 24th Cycle
Where: Jane's mind — The Foxhole
Who: The Fox

I had reached the end of my foxhole.

Fantastic ... except I still had no idea who I was or why I had been shown this tragic story. Not until I found a small girl huddled in the shadowy corner of my foxhole, rocking back and forth and singing to herself.

Perhaps you remember her from the beginning of this story and recall that she is the Face of Awareness, but on that day of discovery, I had no clue who she was. I did not recognize her. I was damaged. My memory had only partially healed, and I needed guidance.

Let me show you my awakening as it transpired.

I opened my eyes.

With a trail of mementos in my wake, I walked into the heart of my foxhole, hoping to forget about them, but a familiar scent froze me in place.

Evergreen and honey.

Was I trapped in another memory?

"Where am I?" I shouted to no one.

"You are home," a gentle voice replied.

I searched the darkness and located a girl sitting in a shadowy corner.

"Who are you?"

"I am you."

"Are all of those mementos yours?" I asked, ignoring her strange reply.

"Yes."

I looked over my shoulder at the trail of junk, then back to her. "You made a mess."

"I often do."

A shard of porcelain lay at my feet—more of her clutter. I picked it up and handed it to her, but she declined.

"I don't want it," she said.

"But it's yours."

"All of those mementos—I used to keep them buried. I used to keep them close. But I learned recently that the past is easier to carry when I let it go."

"Well, I don't want them either," I said.

"Do you know where we are?" she asked.

"We are in my foxhole."

"Yes, but *where* does your foxhole reside?"

"In the giant evergreen tree."

She shook her head. "I meant, which pocket of the mind?"

I didn't understand.

She continued, "I couldn't have run *that* far."

"Who are you?" I asked again.

"I am you."

"No, you're not."

"I am the Face of Awareness," she explained. "Every creature in this mortal mind is part of me, and I am part of them. Hold out your paw."

I did as she requested, and she stepped out of the shadow to reach me. In the faint light filtering through the cracks in the tree trunk, I could see her face. It was beautiful, yet tired, and appeared to be healing. Scarring wounds lined her cheekbones as she took my paw.

She closed her hunter-green eyes and smiled.

"You are the Face of Worthiness. No wonder I ended up here—those mementos are just as much yours as they are mine."

"Excuse me?"

"You were there, too. You were just wearing a different Face."

"I was *not* there."

"Well, you were supposed to be."

I was exhausted by her riddles and concerned about the gravity of her accusations if they were in fact true.

"None of it matters," I explained. "The past cannot be changed."

"You are right. The past is the past—but what about the future?"

"The future?"

"You are the key to healing, and I can show you how."

Heart pounding, my fear manifested as defiance. "I am fine as I am."

"It's not about you. It's about her."

"Who?"

"Jane. The girl we live inside."

"I live inside a tree—"

"—which resides within her mind."

"I don't like riddles."

"No one does," she said with a smile. "It's really quite simple—our Host lives in the outside world, and within the inner world of her mind exists pockets that contain unique parts of her identity. We are the Faces she wears when she controls each of those pockets. We help her manage every fear, thought, and feeling. If you abandon your job, you're abandoning her, too."

"And what is my job?"

"I already told you. You are the Face of Worthiness. How you value yourself is how she values herself."

This forced me to pause—my severe criticalness surely did not serve her well. No one was harder on me than myself.

"It's a shame she's stuck with me," I noted. "If my feelings of worth are reflected onto her, then she must not feel very good about herself."

"You are correct. Her lack of esteem sits at the root of those mementos."

"It's my fault things fell apart?" I asked.

"You and I are partially to blame—but Malsana and the Face of Chaos were the catalysts. The sickness that entered our Host's mind was the true cause, but her inability to see clearly and love herself anyway worsened her fall. She felt broken instead of imperfectly perfect."

"Imperfectly perfect?"

"Our brokenness is an asset. It makes us stronger." She smiled. "Take my hand again."

I did as she asked, and this time, she filled my entire being with awareness. Every fuzzy memory became clear—I knew who I was, and I remembered how I got here.

"Malsana came to me first," I realized with a gasp.

"Strategic," Awareness noted.

"She presented herself as a friend, and I fell for it."

"It's hard to fight back when you don't understand who or what you are fighting."

You'll never be enough.

The voice in my head belonged to Malsana.

I let go of Awareness's hand and clutched my belly.

"The black marble pill. It's still in me."

"She might live there forever."

"No! I want to be rid of her."

Awareness cupped the side of my furry fox face and said, "Remember: our broken bits make us stronger."

"So, I'm better because of what I've survived?" I asked.

"If you choose to be. You either wallow or you grow. It's a choice."

"I've chosen to wallow," I revealed, ashamed.

"Every day is a chance to do better."

"I can change?"

"Of course, you can! Once you learn to love yourself, she too will love herself again."

While it seemed simple, in reality, I wasn't sure if I could.

"It might take me some time."

"That's okay, as long as you're trying. I'm still working on me, too." She paused in thought. "There's a lot of healing to do … maybe we can be friends while we sort it all out. Awareness and Worth is a powerful duo."

Friends.

The concept rang like a symphony of bells inside my mind.

Friends.

"I suppose I should return home," I said.

"You have one more story left to see."

"Whose?"

She pointed at the shard of porcelain I still held.

"The Face of Day," she replied. "She needs you most of all."

I held the jagged piece of porcelain tighter and fire consumed my senses: the stench of scorched flesh, the searing agony of being burned alive repeatedly, a frantic inability to escape her own suffering. She was lost, forsaken, desperate, and only I could help her now.

This was my chance to save Jane.

Before I could enter the memory and witness Jane's story, a voice boomed from the ether.

"It's time to go."

Awareness looked into the darkness above.

"I only just got here," she argued.

"Do not force my hand," the voice commanded.

"Who is that?" I asked.

"Father Time," she answered.

She grabbed my paw, holding on tightly, but her willingness to stay was no match for the force of time. In a blink, she was swept away.

"I'm only a thought away," she shouted, her voice a fading echo.

I was alone once again.

The tease of friendship stung as the dust settled.

I looked around my home, which now felt empty for the first time since I had lived there. All that remained were the mementos Awareness had left behind. What I once viewed as garbage I now revered as treasure—perhaps there was something within me worth saving.

A burned-out fuse sat on the ground in place of the Face of Awareness. I recognized this foreign object—it belonged to me. In my pocket, in the part of Jane's mind that belonged to me, everyone who lived there had one of these fuses.

My fuse waited for me, patiently pleading to go home. I lifted it with my left paw while my right paw located the scar on the back of my neck. Claw pressed into the healed wound, I made a new incision and placed my fuse back in place.

Eyes closed, a tiny spark illuminated the darkness and a world of neon lights appeared in its place. I could see where I had lived before running away.

I saw the Host within my pocket—she manifested here as a girl addicted to black marble pills.

I had to help her.

I had love left to give.

I sent a burst of self-worth into the home I had forsaken. I gave all of myself to Jane within the Pocket of Worthiness, and the surge of love sent her to her knees. I watched from afar as she retrieved her stash of black marble pills and tossed them into a nearby sewer grate. Neon eyes filled with glimmering vapor, she turned her gaze toward the sky, gratitude beaming through her smile.

Confidence restored—my best was good enough—I was ready to fix my mistake.

I dashed down the corridor of my foxhole.

Remnants of the past littered the path. I leaped over broken glass, black marbles, and porcelain shards as I made my escape.

A slit of light beamed beyond. I ran toward the source, determined to right my wrongs.

I would be strong for Jane.

My appearance transformed as my fuse settled into place and reconnected to my wired nervous system. Four legs became two, my spine elongated upright, and the snout I wore shrank into a human-sized nose. My fur shed from my flesh and my burnt-honey glow resumed. All that remained of the fox were my large ears, bushy tail, and illuminated moss-green eyes. A hybrid of who I was and who I had become, I was ready to lead with love.

I leaped through the opening of the tree trunk. Intention set on home, a swirling breeze of stardust carried me out of the Southern Abyss and returned me to the Ring of Thrones.

My chair was no longer there.

I had been absent for so long, my place among the other Faces had vanished.

I looked into the ether to see my neon pocket floating securely next to the Pocket of Trust.

"You came back," the Face of Trust said with a gasp.

"I never should have left."

"My pocket suffered in your absence. All the worth you had sprinkled into my lonely sea disappeared upon your departure. We managed to relocate some of it, but it has been tough without you here."

"Well, I'm back. I won't ever abandon you again."

"Don't make promises you can't keep," she warned.

"Why would you say that?"

"We've got a long life left, and there's no telling what terrors the future holds."

"I will be strong."

"I hope so."

My resolve summoned the return of my throne.

Vines covered in neon foxglove and fluorescent honey blossoms decorated the backrest of my woven wicker splat.

The sun flew overhead, unsteady in Day's grip.

The Face of Trust sighed. "Looks like we'll lose her again."

"The Face of Day?"

"She never lasts long, not since Malsana arrived, not since you left."

My heart sank.

"Well, I'm back now. I will help her ... I just need to figure out how."

"You're too late to save this Face of Day. You'll have to help the next."

As the words left her mouth, Day burst into flames. Broken bits of charred porcelain rained down around us, followed by the screeching plummet of Day's marred body. A horrific end to witness; a heartbreaking fate to behold.

Though tragic, I recognized this as an opportunity for growth.

This moment would deliver healing.

It was here that I was needed most.

The Face of Day

When: The 24th – 25th Cycle
Where: Jane's mind—Solar Citadel, Northern Unknown
Who: The Face of Day

"Why does it always end this way?" I cried.

Father Time examined me; his hollow eyes were empty voids of darkness.

He stated plainly, "You choose this fate time and time again."

I stood naked and exposed, my scorched body shivering in the cool air. Covered in black streaks of char and boiling burns, I embodied the destruction I could not seem to escape.

"What happens next?" I asked.

"I fix you," Father Time replied, no emotion in his voice—he only held affection for the clocks.

"Why?"

"Because you are the Face of Day, and your time isn't done yet."

"When will this suffering end?"

His shadowed face turned toward the enormous sandclock this mind was built around.

"When the last grain of sand falls."

I began to sob—the top orb was full. I'd burn ten thousand times before it emptied.

Father Time held no sympathy for me. "How do you wish to proceed?"

"What do you mean?" I sniffled.

"We've done this many times before," he chastised. "Do you wish to remember or to forget?"

I hesitated. My brittle bones shook under the crippling agony of my burns.

"I don't want to suffer anymore."

"It's a simple answer: remember or forget."

I mumbled to myself, "Perhaps forgetting would be a kindness."

"What is your decision?" he demanded.

"I wish to forget." My eyes widened in terror as I looked at my maker.

Father Time shook his head, but honored my request. His skeletal hands hovered around my head as he spoke.

"You are the guardian of the sun. You are the director of daylight."

I nodded, aware that this continued burden carried great weight.

"You choose to forget the past and start anew."

I nodded.

Father Time held his bony hands against my blistered face and promptly replaced it. No warning, no tenderness; he tore the charred porcelain from my skull and slabbed on a fresh mask. The heaviness of my new Face sent me to my knees—it had no life, no memories, and its emptiness consumed me. Wet porcelain poured out of Father Time's palms, covering all of me until there wasn't a visible trace of my past. The cool clay soothed my scorched flesh. The more it covered me, the more I forgot the countless lives I had lived before this one, the choices that always led to my death—all of it was buried under the hardening cement. As it dried, I became paralyzed, trapped in place for my rebirth.

I stood still, letting the porcelain harden. It numbed my nerves until I felt brand new.

Reborn, I remembered nothing before this moment except my basic purpose here—both then and now: I am the guardian of the sun. I am the director of daylight.

I stared at Father Time, my eyes wide with renewed innocence.

He would not meet my gaze.

Instead, he placed his skeletal hand on my shoulder and fire expelled from his fingertips. It danced along my porcelain-coated flesh, dispersing a ceramic glaze strong enough to withstand the sun's flames.

I screamed.

"It will soon be done," Father Time promised, sending one hundred thousand flames down my back. They seared my skin, leaving deep trails as they reached my legs. I cried, but Father Time did not stop. An army of pirouetting flames engulfed me until I was utterly consumed.

I peered through the fire, wondering who I would be when I reemerged. Father Time held my gaze, his stern, hollow stare unmerciful.

My tears dried as they exited my eyes—the fire had no sympathy for me.

Neither did Father Time.

I surrendered as the flames raged on. This pain would make me strong.

As my eyes closed and my body buckled beneath the agony, Father Time lifted his hand.

All at once, I was released. The fire ceased and the world turned cold.

I looked down at my porcelain arms, now singed with black ash trails, then up at Father Time in horror.

"We aren't finished yet," he stated.

My eyes widened as he grabbed my neck and engulfed my body in another round of flames. This time they were blue and their heat caused me no pain.

I was confused, but grateful. The blue fire kissed my wounds, stitching the fresh ruts in my porcelain-coated skin until they were smooth.

I closed my eyes as the fire healed what it had previously harmed. When I opened them again, I was sitting on a throne made of light. A cautious glance in both directions revealed my new position.

"I am the Face of Day," I stated.

"You are," Father Time confirmed.

I looked down at my hands, pristine and smooth, but beneath my perfect casing, something clawed—a memory desperate to escape.

I looked up, confused. "Have I lived lives before this one?"

"All that matters is the now."

I stared at the ancient shadow of a man and panicked, suddenly aware of my lack of memory.

"I can't remember yesterday."

"Perhaps forgetting is a kindness," Father Time stated, his words familiar, then reminded me, "You are the Face of *today*."

Eyes glassy with sorrow, I solemnly nodded.

"I am the Face of Day."

"I must be on my way."

"How do I begin?" I asked frantically. "I am ill-prepared for my duties."

"The sun will explain everything."

Father Time vanished. I choked on the lingering stench of death, aware that I was in this alone.

You will burn again, warned a voice inside my head.

A deafening scream followed, and I woke up in a panic. Cold sweat beaded along my hairline.

The throne room in the Solar Citadel was empty; I was alone, just as I had been when I slipped into a deep slumber. My heart pounded inside my porcelain chest as I raced to the balcony, trying to forget and remember all at once.

Impossible.

My nerves were permanently rattled and all my yesterdays had been erased. I looked over the edge of my balcony, surprised to learn that my memory of time remained. I watched the creatures of time bustling in the village below—recalling how the sandclock worked settled my racing heart.

Thirty rings lined with Bitling huts counted the sixty seconds in each minute, each ring glowing twice before a new minute started. Thirty rings lined with Jiffie huts counted the sixty minutes in each hour, each ring glowing twice before a new hour started. The sixty rings circling the Tower of Time were small at the center of the village and grew larger as they extended to the outer edge. The main difference between the two groups was the colors and duration of their ring's glow.

Time here was visual. From above, it pulsated like a steady heartbeat.

I was running out of time.

Circlettes controlled the hours. Twelve of them lined the outer edge of the village. I kept an eye on the final Circlette before sunrise; once the first hour of daylight was upon the world, I'd already be too late.

I returned to my throne and examined the room. This was the Solar Citadel—home to the sun. My throne resided

297

within the sculpture perched atop this massive fortress, and the entire structure rested on the eastern side of the sandclock.

Directly below, I watched the last Circlette dance atop its shadowed yellow hut, ready to kiss the night farewell.

There wasn't time to waste.

"Where are you?" I shouted to the absent sun. "I'm ready."

The final Bitlings of night prepared to shift into the first second of day—their violet ring would soon glow red.

"Tell me what to do," I pleaded.

The final Circlette of night blew a kiss to the moon, raised its glowing blue orb overhead, and inserted it into a previously unseen slot at the base of the Solar Citadel. The orb bounced through a few different doors before the noise of its movement ceased and a new yellow orb projected out of the opposite side of the Solar Citadel to be caught by the first hour of day. The Bitlings and Jiffies in the ring nearest the edge of the village shifted to their daytime colors and began their in-and-out time count.

I prayed for the sun to appear.

One full minute into the day, I remained sunless. As the second Jiffie of day prepared to illuminate, a swelling heat emanated from the floor.

I looked down, amazed at the warmth caressing my feet.

The seat of my vacant throne came alive with light.

I rubbed my eyes as the sun peaked through.

Smaller than I ever dreamed possible, the sun was tiny enough to hold within my hands.

"Why are you so little?" I asked.

"It's the size of my glow that matters most," the sun replied, his morning voice soft and disappointed.

"I'm sorry. In my faint recollection, you seemed so big in the sky."

"I grow as the day grows."

"Will you be heavy to carry?"

"Very. But you will grow too."

"Bigger?"

"No. Stronger."

"I won't let you fall."

The tiny sun swirled with fire—red, yellow, and orange flares streaked across its surface, creating beautiful patterns as they danced.

It felt so familiar.

"Have we met before?"

"Maybe, in a different life," he replied.

"Do you have a name?" I asked.

"Solís."

"I'm Day," I said with a smile, then noticed the loud cheers from the creatures of time below. "I think it's time to begin."

Solís lowered his chin and raised his arms. "It has already begun."

My heart raced—I was already blundering my responsibilities.

"But we're still here," I expressed. "How do we cross the sky?"

"You carry me."

I looked at the blazing star Solís hid within, then down at my hands.

Solís sensed my hesitation. "I won't hurt you," he promised.

Fear suppressed, I extended my hands toward him. As my tiny fingers reached his glow, the swirling flares latched onto my hands and we were bound. Securely connected, Solís lifted us into the air.

As we rose higher, ever so slowly, he grew bigger. I felt his weight increase as we ascended.

"You must guide us," he explained. "You are the director of the day."

"Where?"

"West. To the Lunar Spire."

I looked across the sprawling village of time. "That tower over there?"

"Yes."

I understood and kept my intention directed due west. But as time passed, Solís became harder to hold. My body began to shake as his weight increased.

"Our first trip will be the hardest," he warned as we completed our first hour. The Circlette below cheered as it passed on the hour orb. The Jiffies and Bitlings also danced with excitement as I succeeded, though my success felt a bit premature to celebrate, and as Solís grew heavier, I wasn't sure how much longer I could endure.

"I'm not strong enough," I expressed through gritted teeth as we crossed the second hour—Solís was triple the size he had been at our journey's start.

"It will only get harder. Hold on."

Tears fell from my eyes as the pain consumed my senses. Blinded by the sun's fire, deafened by the ever-expanding star's crackling flames, I could no longer see or hear. My arms threatened to rip from their sockets as the hours passed, but I refused to let go. The wild Bitlings continued celebrating below, cheering loud enough for me to hear over the sizzling sun, and though I knew them not, their enthusiastic support fueled me with the energy to succeed.

The agony felt familiar—I had suffered like this before. Or worse. But the memory resided in the hidden pockets of my mind.

It will end in flames! a voice screamed inside my head.

My heart raced in panic.

"I don't want to burn!"

"You are designed to endure the sun's fire," Solís consoled.

The foreigner inside my mind screeched in protest.

"Who am I?"

"You are the Face of Day," Solís reminded me, his voice pained.

It wasn't the answer I sought. "But who was I before?"

Solís did not reply.

"Don't let me go," he pled. "We're almost there."

I squeezed my eyes shut, forcing the darkness away, and when I opened them again, I saw a blurry vision of the village below. I kept my sight locked on the steady minute rings, which pulsed in and out like a heartbeat every hour.

"How much farther?" I asked Solís.

"We just crossed the top axis of the Northern Abyss. I will start to shrink in size."

A surge of relief washed over me. Still, his weight decreased ever so slowly. It wasn't until our final hour in the sky that I felt the change.

"Can I let go?" I asked, breathless from the pain.

"No. You need to hold on a little longer."

"I can't," I sobbed.

"Close your eyes," Solís instructed. "I can guide the rest of our journey."

I did as he said and the sun's flares latched tightly to my loosening grip. Solís finished the day's work while I succumbed to a deep slumber.

When I awoke, Solís was gone and the world was dark. I sat up in a room of white. Moonlight reflected off the floor, and with a closer look, I realized the tiles were made of pearls. The walls, too—every surface reflected flawless beauty as the moon crossed overhead. Luna, I recalled; I retained vivid memories of the moon.

I exited the room through an arched doorway that led to a balcony with no railing. The fall from this spire was long. Still, I peered over the edge anyway.

"Be careful!" a voice shouted from above.

I looked up at the moon, but could not see past its glow.

"You sound like a boy," I replied.

"I am."

"I thought Luna was a girl."

"Luna stopped talking years ago."

"Why?"

"She is a glutton for sorrow."

Luna's light flickered slightly, indicating a long-held frustration.

"Then who are you?" I asked.

"You don't remember?"

"Should I?"

He groaned. "You chose to forget."

"Forget what?"

"I am the Face of Night."

I squinted my eyes, attempting to adjust them to the dark, and I eventually caught sight of a distant silhouette dragging the moon through the sky.

"You have wings," I said with a gasp.

"Of course, I do. How else would I drag the moon through the sky?"

"I carried the sun through the sky without wings."

"You didn't carry it—you guided it."

"Still … I had to hold its weight."

"You used to have wings," he revealed.

"I did?"

He ignored my question. "You have the night to do as you please. Enjoy it."

The Face of Night vanished in the moon's glow.

I examined the narrow set of black pearl stairs spiraling around the Lunar Spire. The height was great, as would be the fall, and there was no railing to hold. I took a deep breath, summoned my courage, and took the first step.

Mind over matter.

I descended with slow precision, determined to reach the ground without error, when a slight slip on the black pearl steps sent a familiar lurching sensation through my gut. My heart suffered a nostalgic kick.

I paused, clutching my chest.

What was I forgetting?

There was no time to wonder; I had to save myself from this precarious dilemma. I regained my composure, reignited my courage, and resumed my departure from the Lunar Spire. More careful now, I took slower steps and kept my gaze glued to my bare feet. Step by step, the ground grew closer. Salvation radiated from the ceramic cobblestone. One final lap around the spire and I was free. I was back on the ground with half the night to do as I pleased.

The ground was coarse against my feet, scratching their pristine porcelain soles. After a few minutes of walking, I sat on the ground to examine the damage.

The scuff marks were minuscule, but visible, and a tiny part of my heart rejoiced.

Odd.

I had been terrified to fall mere moments ago, and now the sight of these small cuts soothed my soul. They felt familiar; they made me feel whole.

"Why'd you take the long way down?" the Face of Night shouted at me.

I glanced up, brow furrowed. "That was the only exit I could find."

He grumbled. "I'll show you an easier way tomorrow. Just don't black out after sundown."

He spoke like I ought to know, like I had done this many times before. My frustration threatened to unleash, so I took a deep breath and focused on what I *could* control.

The Solar Citadel sat on the opposite end of the village; endless rows of minutes and seconds separated me from where I needed to be. I walked through the crowded huts of Jiffies and Bitlings lining each circular second and minute—a row of Bitling huts sat between each ring of Jiffie huts. They shouted support as I passed, but their words blended together into one solitary buzz. It droned on, making me dizzy as I marched forward. The closest landmark was the Tower of Time. I kept my attention focused there, hoping it might provide some relief.

I found none.

The giant glass tower radiated sad energy. I examined the doorless structure, scanning its western wall. Near the top, behind the western clockface, stood a melancholy boy. He pressed his glass hands against the confines of his glass prison, his expression blank. His energy radiated everything and nothing all at once.

The Face of Time.

Though I glowed in the moonlight, he did not see me. His attention was elsewhere, lost in the isolating loneliness of time.

I carried onward.

The Face of Night had crossed the top axis of the Northern Unknown, indicating I had less than six hours to make it back in time. I could not be late for sunrise.

I ran faster.

Racing into the eastern side of the village, I was almost home.

I zigzagged through the rows of time, absorbing their supportive buzz as they cheered me on. I would make it to see my second journey across the sky. I would be stronger this time.

At the base of the Solar Citadel, two Solards waited. They guarded the door with blazing ferocity.

"You're late," one growled. His glowing expression tightened into a scowl.

"No, I'm not. I have at least two hours before sunrise."

"You're supposed to report back to the citadel directly after setting the sun at the Lunar Spire."

"I was told I could spend the hours of night however I pleased," I countered.

"By who?" The Solards bore their orange gazes into mine. I wondered if they could read my mind.

"Father Time," I lied.

They leaned in close to whisper, their skulls of fire almost touching, but their voices echoed loud enough for me to eavesdrop.

"He would never have granted such a liberty," the taller of the two stated.

"We're supposed to play along," the other Solard cautioned.

They glanced at me. I looked away, pretending I could not hear.

"But we have to keep her safe," the taller Solard rationalized.

The taller Solard addressed me. "We will consult Father Time the next time he visits. Until then, we will honor your claims under the condition that you carry a sunstone with you."

The Solard reached his fiery fingers into his ear, retrieved a red stone, and extended it toward me.

"What does it do?" I asked.

"It tells us where you are."

I crossed my arms over my chest. "And if I refuse?"

"We will wait for you in the Lunar Spire and escort you back ourselves each night after sundown."

"Fine. I'll take the sunstone." I opened my palm and the Solard dropped the sizzling rock into my hand. I could not feel its heat.

I wrapped my fingers around it and the Solards moved aside.

Tiny creatures made of fire filled the grand entrance to the Solar Citadel. They stood huddled around a large hole in the floor that pulsed with orange light.

"Who are you?" I asked.

"Kelvin," a light creature standing closest to me replied.

I shook my head and extended an arm toward the lot of strange beings. "I meant, *what* are you?"

"Lumineers. We are the engineers of light."

"You create light?"

"No," Kelvin answered with a chuckle. "We merely maintain it. Without us, Solís would have burned out ages ago. And without a divine soul commanding this mind's sun, chaos would ensue."

"In what way?"

"This illusionary sun is a wild star that feeds on the fuel of life. It would consume everything in this mortal mind without the strict governance put into place by the gods."

I understood. "That includes me?"

Kelvin nodded. "Yes. You, Solís, and us—the Lumineers. We are the wranglers of this sun. Without us, the sun would consume all, leaving this mind in utter darkness. No mortal can survive without a daily, healthy dose of sunlight."

"I feel like I've been here before."

"This is your home."

"I mean, I feel like I'm reliving moments that have already happened."

"No two moments are exactly the same. That is the beauty of time."

His vague reply only strengthened my suspicion.

"What about Solís? What does he do inside the sun?"

"He keeps the sun tame; he wrangles its appetite." The Lumineer hesitated, concealing a thought he did not dare speak aloud, then added, "He does the best he can, given the circumstances."

"What do you mean?"

The Lumineer diverted. "Solís is a celestial being from the sun beyond the confines of this mortal Host—he, Luna, and Father Time are the only creatures within this mind who come from elsewhere, the only entities not directly connected to the mortal Host. Solís comes from the heavenly star that gives life to all."

"How did he end up here?"

"He was assigned to serve as a guide in this mortal's mind."

"And Luna, too?"

"Similar, yes. She is from the moon beyond, but instead of fire, she tames the tides. Without Luna, fear and emotion would flood the mortal's mind."

I looked closer at Kelvin's figure—a fiery silhouette.

"What are you made of?"

"Solar flares. A sheer coating of stardust keeps me contained in this form; without it, I'd be as vulnerable as any ordinary flame."

"I am contained, too," I said while looking down at my hands. "Something rotten lives inside me."

Kelvin's fire eyes swirled with confusion. "You are brand new—you are perfection."

"I hear a voice inside my head. Sometimes, she cries. Other times, she screams."

"That's worrisome," Kelvin speculated, unable to empathize with my predicament.

I felt embarrassed. "Aren't you different on the inside, too?"

"What you see is all of me. I am nothing more and nothing less."

He'd never understand.

"I need to prepare for sunrise," I concluded. "It was nice to meet you."

Kelvin's facial flames twisted into what looked like a smile.

He returned his attention to the hole in the ground, where all the Lumineers coaxed the orange glow to shine brighter. I ran up the grand staircase in the middle of the hall to get a better view.

The radiating light grew by the second, and the Lumineers swayed in unison, celebrating another successful light harvest. Their song started as a gaseous hiss and grew into the most beautiful melody I had ever heard. The song of day—a melancholic symphony of life and loss. The story of one soul bound as guardian to a vicious star so all others could live freely.

I thought of Solís; this song was about him.

The final Circlette of night dropped the hour orb through the slot in the side of the Solar Citadel. The glowing orb of time floated across the space, silencing the Lumineers as they watched it hover overhead in awe. When it reached the opposite side, it floated through the perfectly shaped hole in the wall. The Circlette waiting outside caught it, initiating the first hour of day.

Absorbed by the intricate workings of time, I was taken aback when the sun began to rise from the pit the Lumineers gathered around.

Brilliant in color, blinding with light, the sun rose.

The sudden realization that I would be late for the day sent me running up the rest of the staircase toward the top of my tower. As I raced into the open space of my throne room, the little sun emerged.

"You're tiny again," I stated, out of breath.

"I always start the day this way."

I stepped closer and admired the crossing solar flares rocketing through the star.

"You are lovely," I expressed.

"Not as lovely as you."

I looked down at my perfectly smooth porcelain hands, then thought of the voice inside my head.

"I'm not as lovely underneath."

"Neither am I," Solís confessed.

My brow furrowed, and I looked closer.

Beneath the twirling flames sat a withering boy, cross-legged and slouched, his image charred.

"How long have you lived this way?" I asked.

"Hard to say. I've lost track of the time."

"You come from elsewhere, as does the moon," I stated, confirming what Kelvin had said.

Solís nodded. "But Luna is always out of reach."

I understood the gravity of his woes—something out of reach slumbered inside of me.

"Well, at least we have each other now. I will be a good friend," I promised.

Behind the haze of solar flares, the charred boy perked. His posture lifted and his solemn expression cracked.

"You remind me of someone I know," he said. A flurry of ashy flesh fell from his cheeks as his brow furrowed.

"Who?"

Solís stood from his usual spot in the center of the sun and navigated through the gaseous flames toward me. His hand pressed against the wall of fire separating us, and for the first time, I could see him clearly. He wore the face of a sad boy—a boy wholly scorched and disfigured. Beneath layers of wounds and soot, his burnt eyes shimmered with tears too dry to spill.

"My sister," he said from his chamber.

"Really?" I asked, overwhelmed by the thoughts this revelation stirred.

"Something ailed her, causing her to choose ruin over love and destruction over happiness."

I took a step back, confused.

"I don't understand."

"It's nothing you need to worry about. Her problems are not yours. Just know I am learning a lot from you. Tell me, how are you feeling?"

"I think I'll be stronger today," I answered.

"Don't feel bad if you aren't."

His words were heavy.

Solís returned to his spot in the center of the sun. "If the Lumineers did not nourish the sun while we crossed through the Southern Abyss, I'd never be able to control its hunger." His expression slackened. He looked away. "You ought to be careful. It could eat you, too."

"I trust you."

He gave me a cracked smile. "If you stay this way, I can keep you safe."

I looked below to see that the second Jiffie of the day was now illuminated.

Solís sighed. "Yes, it is time."

I leaned forward and wrapped my arms around the tiny sun, allowing its tendrils of fire to entangle around my arms.

We flew across the sky like this—a knotted embrace of sparks and porcelain. I held the sun close, hoping Solís could feel me through the fire. He was the saddest boy I'd ever known.

As we crossed the peak of day, the sun grew to its largest size and my strength wavered.

Terrified that I might drop Solís, I turned my attention downward. From this height, I could see orbs of light hovering in the ether surrounding the sandclock.

The beauty served as a distraction and helped ease my aching arms.

"What are those orbs of light called?" I asked.

Solís took a moment to respond.

"They are pockets of the mind, each representing a different part of the mortal's identity. The Faces rule over them."

"Faces?"

"The Faces the mortal wears when she channels each pocket," he explained.

"Can the creatures who live in the pockets see us soaring overhead?"

"No, but they can feel us. You wear the Face my light shines through. Happy or sad or angry—whatever you feel, they'll feel it, too."

This forced me to think of my predecessors.

"Am I like the others who came before me?" I asked.

"I hope not."

I paused, afraid. "Why not?"

"I remember them all in a distant way—today feels a lot like yesterday, and the memories often mix and muddy until all the faces look the same. What I remember most is the pain. You have always known how to smile through pain, and I fear for you."

"Why?"

"Because you are they, and they are you."

"I want to do well."

"You could be different." Though he sounded hopeful, this grave realization was heavy. Solís sensed my dismay. "Just stay as you are."

The illuminated beat of time pulsated day in and day out—I enjoyed watching its glowing heartbeat in the village below my tower. A full month passed before I could deliver the sun to the Lunar Spire without passing out from the pain. As I set the sun on my thirtieth day, the Lunar Spire filled with shadows.

"Finally," a voice groaned.

I looked around, but saw no one.

"Who's there?" I asked.

"You don't remember me?"

I felt vulnerable and exposed. "I can't see you."

A whirring breeze spun me in a circle. I closed my eyes, unsure what devil toyed with me. I fought the whirlwind and steadied my stance, using all my might to stand sturdy in place.

"Open your eyes," the voice instructed.

I obeyed, and all at once, the world became still.

In front of me stood a winged creature. Not quite a shadow, not quite a man. The moonlight pierced through him and I could see him without seeing him at all.

"Better than ever, it seems." He scrutinized me, leaning in close to examine my head. "Unless you're still broken up there."

"Are you the Face of Night?" I chose to look past his intrusive first impression.

"Who else would I be?" he countered while carefully cradling the tiny moon.

"Why do you look different from me?"

He clenched his jaw, refusing to answer.

"What's wrong?" I asked.

He huffed. "We've done this so many times before."

"No, we haven't."

"Yes, we have. You're just wearing a new Face."

My aggravation read plainly. "I was not gifted the memories of she who came before."

"Right," Night resigned, his tone mocking. "I'm supposed to play along."

"Play along?" I asked, infuriated to hear this phrase again.

He ignored my inquiry and entertained my previous curiosity. "I am the possessor of nighttime fears," he revealed with a sarcastic bow and bored tone.

This revelation redirected my anger. "Explain."

"The thoughts and anxieties that only emerge when the mind starts to fall asleep—that is where I live. That is the burden I'm tasked to carry." He took one hand off the moon, lifted my hand, and admired my porcelain-coated skin. "It's why I love perfect things."

"Nothing is perfect." I snatched my hand from his grip.

"Perfection is a rare discovery," Night agreed. "I have found few flawless treasures in this mind—that's why it's so special when new ones emerge."

His dark green gaze bore into me.

"There is beauty in the broken," I argued.

"Everyone is broken," he scoffed. "There is no beauty in that."

"Including you?"

"I do my best to stay whole."

I took a step closer and Night flickered before my eyes.

"Are you translucent?" I asked.

"Partially. How else would the fears pass through me?"

I shrugged.

He continued, "If I am brave, they are brave."

I finally understood. "If I smile, they will smile."

He nodded, leaned in, and closed his eyes. He inhaled deeply, then exhaled with a smile.

"You smell of evergreen and honey."

My expression creased. "What is evergreen and honey?"

Night smirked and shook his head. "Of course, you wouldn't know. Those things don't exist here."

"Then how do *you* know?"

"I leave this place as often as I can."

"Where do you go?"

"Into the pockets."

"You've been inside them? How?"

He lifted his wings and pounded the air. "Out there, in my off-hours, I can be anyone I want to be. You could be, too."

"I don't have wings. I can't come and go."

"Stick around a little longer and maybe you'll grow a pair," he goaded with a wink.

His arrogance angered me. I sniffed my wrist, then asked, "How could I smell like things I have no access to?"

"It's strange indeed." His stare was mischievous. "Perhaps my memories are playing tricks on me."

"Show me an easier way to exit the tower," I demanded, desiring to leave this conversation.

Night pointed to a small sun etching on the eastern wall that I hadn't noticed before.

"Only you can open that door," he stated.

I touched the drawing and a surge of light swallowed me.

When my eyes readjusted, I found myself back in the Solar Citadel throne room.

It was a portal.

I cursed beneath my breath—I wanted to spend my free time exploring. Instead, I was trapped in the prettiest prison. On the western wall, I noticed a tiny etching of the moon.

I touched it.

Nothing happened.

A one-way portal—how inconvenient.

With a long sigh, I threw my body onto my throne, unconcerned by my own force. My head slammed against the armrest and searing pain shot down my neck. I lifted myself carefully and cradled the back of my head.

A newly formed crack snaked down my neck.

As I touched it, my thoughts were transported elsewhere.

Inside my head, I saw the girl I used to be. Though far away and blurry, I felt her more clearly than ever. The memories I longed for, the identity I craved—she was the key to it all. I ran toward her, desperate to hold her close, but as I reached out to touch her, I was stripped away. Suctioned out of my own mind by an unknown force.

I screamed.

"Oh, dear," a kind voice expressed.

I opened my eyes and found an unfamiliar face standing over me.

"Who are you?" I demanded.

"My name is Therma. I am your caretaker."

My long, luminescent hair was now knotted into a bun and my fear had left beaded condensation all over my body. I touched the back of my neck to find the crack I had made already welded shut.

"What have you done?" I demanded.

"I fixed you," Therma stated, her confidence wavering.

"I didn't need to be fixed."

"You had a gaping crack in your neck," she argued in a meek voice. "That type of injury could kill you in the sun's presence."

"It would make me stronger," I countered.

Therma shook her head. "The body beneath the porcelain would burn alive."

I lost my will to argue.

"I finally found her." I sunk into the plush throne cushion.

"Who?"

"The girl who lives inside my head. She can help me remember."

"There's not much worth remembering," Therma stated, no malintent in her voice.

"You know who I was?" My enthusiasm returned.

"All that matters is who you are today."

I shook my head. "Something awful happened to her; she cries in a corner of my mind. I need to help her."

"Why? She is then, and you are now."

I thought of what Solís told me. "I am she, and she is me. Without each other, we are no one." I groaned. "I don't like riddles."

Therma smiled. "No one does."

I rose from my throne and walked to the golden rails of my balcony. The creatures of time bustled below, carrying out their monotonous tasks without complaint. The Bitlings, Jiffies, and Circlettes happily counted time, moving the seconds, minutes, and hours forward. If they could conform, why couldn't I?

Because they weren't designed to have thinking minds.

The thought left me rattled.

"Can I leave?" I asked Therma, though I wasn't sure she held true power over me.

"You shouldn't. That patch will take hours to dry."

I returned my gaze to the hurried village circling the enormous sandclock.

In the center of it all, wrapped around the narrow neck of the giant sandclock, stood the Tower of Time. The boy in that tower surely had a mind that worked—he was the director of time, far outranking the creatures scurrying around below. I wondered if he might understand how I felt.

Too far away to ask him myself, I turned back to Therma. "I've been here a month ... why haven't I seen you before today?"

317

"You hadn't needed me until now."

"Will you be here again tomorrow?"

"Only if you need me."

"I won't."

Therma lowered her head. "Should I leave?"

"Yes, please."

She complied, leaving without saying another word.

I wondered who sent her and how she knew I had cracked my perfect porcelain casing, but she left before I could ask.

I'd need to be clever if I wanted to avoid her while rediscovering the past.

I let the night pass, resting and preparing my body for the strenuous day.

Solís arrived, looking as tired as I. He stayed slouched in his chamber within the sun, ribcage rising and falling methodically as if he were trying to contain immense pain.

"What's wrong?" I asked.

"The spot where my heart used to sit," he replied.

"It hurts?"

He shook his head. "It's the last piece of myself that feels alive."

"What happens if it dies?"

He glanced over at me, deep resentment in his burnt eyes. "I will have failed, and everything will end."

My problems suddenly felt small. "How can I help?"

"Stay the way you are."

I could do that; I could be strong. I had to stay focused. If not for me, then for him—I was his only friend, and together, we protected the day.

We rose into the sky, and as the day lengthened, my healing scar began to ache. Therma was right: the sweltering heat from the sun easily penetrated the break in my porcelain armor. By noon, I was blinded by the pain.

"Your grip is strong," Solís commented. "So why do I feel like you might let me fall?"

"I have a break in my armor," I said, understanding for the first time the true purpose of my outward perfection.

"I thought so," he confessed, his disappointment immense.

"I am not immune to your fire."

"I cannot help you." Solís was remorseful. "I cannot lessen the burn."

"I know. I will carry you to the end of day. I will make sure you're safe."

Through sheer stubbornness, I delivered Solís to the Lunar Spire, collapsing to my knees after letting him go.

As the sun set into the Southern Abyss, my discomfort lessened, and I began to feel like myself again.

The Face of Night arrived to mock my success. He hovered over where I knelt and brushed my long hair away from the back of my neck.

"And so it begins," he criticized upon catching sight of my wound, but he took off with the moon before I could ask what he meant.

I wanted to disappear.

The portal to the Solar Citadel awaited, but I did not wish to go home. Instead, I made the precarious trek down the spire staircase.

The sunstone given to me by the Solards sat heavily in my pocket. I flipped it through my fingers, silently cursing my lack of freedom. They said they had to play along. Night spoke like we were old friends. Therma trembled as if she knew my temper well—everyone seemed to know who I was except me.

Taunted by the unknown girl living inside of me, obsessed with the elusive secrets she kept, I realized I could not let this go until I knew the truth.

What did she know?

What weren't they telling me?

The only way to find out was to dig a little deeper. I thought of my aching head wound—it was the only way to reach the past.

I had a choice to make: live ignorantly without pain, or suffer to learn the truth.

I wanted to see my memories again. I wanted to know the girl I used to be.

The decision was simple: I chose pain. I chose truth.

I raced through the rows of Bitlings and Jiffies toward the Tower of Time. Did he know me, too? Did the glass soldier know my story? At the structure's base, I paused—there were no doors or windows, no way to enter. I glanced up and saw the boy staring out from behind the glass clockface. He looked sadder than usual. I stepped back and waved my arms, hoping to catch his attention. He glanced down at me and shook his head.

Another mystery to solve.

I left the Face of Time where he stood in his glass tower. One day, I'd reach him. One day, he would see that he did not need to be alone. For now, I had to focus on myself. I had to fix myself before I could fix anyone else, and in order to mend, I had to break.

I crossed the Solards at the Solar Citadel's entrance gate. They gave me a nod, which I returned with a glare—the searing sunstone in my pocket was a constant reminder that these guards were not my friends. Past the gathered Lumineers, who were too focused on feeding the sun to notice me run by, and up the stairs to my tower. Within the hollow sun sculpture sat my vacant throne—Therma was nowhere to be seen.

Excellent.

I needed privacy.

My hand delicately caressed the tender scar on the back of my neck; it was time to meet the girl trapped inside. Though it seemed easiest to reopen an existing wound, I worried I might hinder its ability to heal. My hands and arms were unwise options, as their proximity to the sun during the day was too close and the pain would be too great. I turned my attention to my ankle—it was the safest choice.

Each ray of the ornamental copper sun adorning my throne was sharpened to a point. I unscrewed a single metal ray from the bottom of the sun, then walked onto my balcony, firmly holding my daggered key to the truth.

The Face of Night soared with the moon toward the top of the Northern Unknown, which meant I had a little over six hours to seek the truth and seal the break before sunrise. I sat on the floor, barricaded and hidden behind the golden bars of the railing. I lifted the copper ray, took a deep breath, and plunged its point into my ankle—a scratching snap echoed into the night as I cracked my porcelain casing.

The pain stripped my vision and sent my nerves into a state of shock. Heart racing, I clenched my teeth and tried to regain my senses. It took a few minutes for my body to adjust, but when it did, my sight returned and I saw what I had done.

The break was much bigger than I intended. I retrieved my broken piece off the ground and hid it in my pocket. Then I placed my finger on the fresh wound and my mind was taken elsewhere.

My awareness fell through a bottomless black hole. I could not see where I came from and I could not see where I was going. My screams came out as whispers—there was no one here to save me. Where was the girl I saw last time? A terrifying alarm rang through my head. Was this the end?

As my fears grew too large to contain, my cognizance hit an imaginary floor. The landing was hard, but the freefall ended. I looked up to see the girl I used to be standing before me. She stood tall, enveloped in a beam of light. I could not see her face.

"I found you," I cried.

"You shouldn't have called me here," she stated, no emotion in her voice.

"I didn't call you—if anything, you called me!" I was perplexed. "You've been here all along."

"I belong in the graveyard," she continued, ignoring my objections. "You need to let me go."

"I am you, and you are me."

She shook her head. "I was buried so that you could start over. You need to do better."

"How can I do better if I don't know what I did wrong?"

Her light flickered. "You chose to forget."

"I didn't choose anything. I was born like this."

"The past is a burden," she sympathized. "The decision he gives us is impossible. We lose either way."

She reached her arm out of the light—it was mutilated with unhealing scars. She was so broken that the light she hid within shone through her breaks.

"What happened?"

"The sun swallowed me."

I was stunned. "Have I always been the Face of Day?"

"Always."

"Why don't I remember?"

"Because you chose to forget," she repeated.

"Explain," I begged.

Her light dimmed as she declined. "I have to honor your choice."

"I can still feel you, and every other version of me, clawing at my insides. You're all disturbed and unsettled. I can hear your cries in my sleep."

"I'm sorry."

"Knowing the past will help me do better in the future."

She sighed, concealed by her beam of light. "It never has before."

"Solís warned me that the sun might try to consume me. I didn't realize he spoke from experience."

"Our destruction leaves the poor boy heartbroken every time. We are the only friend he is allowed to have here."

"I need to do better for him," I stated.

"Just beware: I was swallowed by the past long before I was swallowed by the sun. The pain is addicting. You will end up like me if you don't let me go."

"I am you, and you are me," I insisted, refusing to forsake my troubled self. "If you get better, I'll be better."

"Saving me will break you." She pointed her disfigured finger at my fragmented ankle. "Those cuts and cracks are the only way to get to me, and they will be your undoing."

"I will find a way to fix you."

"Look at you," she said, defeat in her voice. "We never change."

"I think you're wrong."

Frustration boiled within my heart.

I commanded my body to remove my finger from my ankle wound, and my awareness returned to reality. I was no longer deep within the chasms of my mind; I was back on the balcony of the Solar Citadel, staring at my self-inflicted wound.

"Did you find what you were looking for?"

I turned my head to find Therma standing in the shadows.

"How long have you been there?"

"Since I felt the searing pain of your new break."

"You can feel my pain?"

"I am bonded to you—it's how Father Time designed us this time."

A heavy sigh escaped my lips. "To prevent me from suffering the same fate."

Therma nodded.

I asked, "Did you know me in my previous Face?"

"I am forbidden to tell you."

"They still suffer. I can feel their ancient agony in my bones. I want them to heal so I can heal, too."

Therma's expression twisted with guilt, her resolution torn. She sat beside me on the floor. "If I tell you what I know, do you promise not to break yourself anymore?"

"I promise."

"Father Time created me after your first break. Since then, I've learned that your first break happened shortly after the Face of Chaos took over the sandclock. You let him wear your Face."

Horrified, I demanded, "Tell me more."

"From what I've gathered, all your struggles stem from love."

"Love?"

"So it seems."

"Love isn't destructive," I argued.

"Sometimes it's the *most* destructive."

I sat with this thought, then asked, "What kind of love did I know?"

"I do not know. I never met your first Face, but I've met every version of you since. At first, you were timid and wary to trust me. Then, you became secretive and elusive. I often found you writhing in pain from all the cuts and lesions you gave yourself. Sometimes, I arrived too late, and it ruined the start of day. Sometimes, the cuts got so bad, I could not mend you in time, and you were inevitably consumed by the sun." She shook her head, ashamed. "You never cared. You dug into yourself anyway."

"Why would I let Chaos wear my Face?"

"I cannot answer that, for I do not know."

Tears filled my eyes. "Why wouldn't Father Time want me to learn from the past?"

"He didn't make the choice to forget—you did." Therma sensed my crippling confusion, so she explained, "Before Father Time gives you a new Face, he also gives you a choice: remember or forget. You choose differently every time, but it doesn't seem to matter. The result is always the same."

"Why?"

"When you remember, your guilt for past mistakes consumes you. You dig into yourself and live there. When you forget, you develop an obsession with your mysterious past and dissect yourself to learn the truth." She paused, recalling what I had said earlier. "The only reason I'm breaking the rules and telling you any of this is because you said you want to heal."

"I do. I want to heal the past versions of myself so they stop torturing me."

"You're going about it wrong. Heal yourself, and they will heal, too."

"How can I heal if I don't know what I'm healing from?"

Therma's tone was grave. "You promised to stop digging."

"But I am not whole without my memories."

"You cannot be trusted with your memories," Therma warned.

"Maybe I am different now."

Therma glanced at my ankle and a look of doubtful compassion crossed her face. "So far, you are very much the same. It always starts this way."

My gaze locked with Therma's.

"Thank you," I expressed, genuinely grateful.

"Please don't make me regret breaking my promise to Father Time."

"I won't. I will be smarter than those who came before me."

"I've heard that before."

"I am different."

Therma smiled for the first time since I met her. "Let me mend that break—the sun will be here soon."

I looked over the balcony to learn that she was right; I had spent far too much time in the recesses of my mind. I took my broken piece out of my pocket and handed it to Therma. Her expression relaxed.

"This will make it much easier." She fit the piece into the gaping hole and began slabbing porcelain putty into the creases. Therma blew on the wet clay, hoping to help it dry, all while frantically monitoring the steady progression of time below.

"Will it work?" I asked.

"It won't dry in time."

"I need an additional shield," I realized. "Is there anything I can wrap around my ankle?"

"I have no bandages that can withstand the heat of the sun."

I examined my throne, which was made of sun-resistant copper—the sun rose through it every morning—then down at the copper sunray I used to pierce my ankle. The metal was pliable. I could bend and wrap it around my ankle until it securely covered my mended wound.

"We're already doing better than last time," I declared, though Therma looked unconvinced.

"This is a dangerous path," she advised. "You cannot wear a copper bandage forever."

"I won't have to once I figure out how to heal the Faces of my past."

The setting shadow of night consumed the throne room, and the tiny sun emerged from the throne's seat, obliterating the darkness with its light. No sign of Night in the crossing seconds of day and night, as usual—he never lingered in the Solar Citadel.

I grabbed the sun without fear.

I was immune to its heat, except in my broken bits. While my healing neck wound seared, my ankle merely suffered an uncomfortable tickle.

The copper armor worked.

We lifted into the sky and began the day.

Solís remained silent within his fiery chamber. Though I wished to interrogate him and ask why he spoke in riddles instead of speaking the truth, I decided to let him maintain his silence. He was sworn to secrecy like all the others. I could not fault him for that. I'd find the answers myself and prove that I could use the past to become better.

I landed in the Lunar Spire feeling stronger than ever and let Solís dip into the other side of day. The Face of Night must have been waiting on the roof because he transcended into the night sky without saying hello.

I slammed my hand against the sun sketch on the wall and flew through the portal. Back in the Solar Citadel, I had twelve hours to discover more of the past. I felt a pang of guilt; I had to break my promise to Therma and Solís. It was the only way to break the cycle of my ill-fated life.

The copper sunray worked well, both as a key to the past and as a heat-resistant bandage, but the trip from my ankle to my head wasted too much time, so I pressed the sunray's tip into my inner bicep instead. I made a small incision, only carving out a tiny piece of porcelain, hoping it would be easier to mend. I placed it in my pocket and touched the open wound.

A quick freefall and I landed in a dark corner of my mind. My former self waited for me there, cloaked in a shroud of light. If I wanted to fix her, I had to understand her first.

"I want to know you," I expressed cautiously.

"I told you to stay away," she said without turning to face me.

"I have secrets to uncover."

"How badly did it hurt to carry the sun with that fresh break in your porcelain armor?"

"I found a new way to survive the pain."

She turned to look at me—I still couldn't see her face, but I felt her envy as she saw the copper bandage wrapped around my ankle.

"It worked?" she asked.

"Well enough."

She turned back around with a huff. "It won't work forever."

"Maybe not, but it should work long enough to retrieve the answers I seek."

"Our past is not that interesting," she scoffed.

"But we knew love," I countered.

My revelation halted my past self's cynicism. Her light dimmed and she slowly faced me.

"We knew loss," she corrected me. "How did you find out?"

"Therma told me."

She spat. "Rotten traitor. I died trying to learn that truth, and she openly told you."

"I suspect to save me from a fate similar to yours."

"Yet you came back here anyway. Seems we're destined to burn."

"Tell me what you know," I insisted.

"Love weakens strong hearts." Her light began to dim.

"Who did this to us? Did you see a face?"

She nodded, stepping closer. The light concealing her was almost gone.

"Who did this to us?" I repeated.

She pressed her mutilated finger against my forehead. "You."

The shield of light vanished, revealing a marred face that looked a lot like mine.

I slapped her hand away. "No."

"We are to blame."

The disfigured scars on her scorched face remained eternally raw.

I cringed. "We did this to ourselves?"

"Yes. We always cope the same way."

I thought of Therma's recollection—I thought of the Face of Chaos.

"Why did I allow the Face of Chaos to wear my Face and overtake the sandclock?"

"Heartbreak. We were so devastated we allowed the Face of Chaos to assume our responsibilities, and he masqueraded as the Face of Day. It took too long for the Face of Night to realize an impostor wore our Face while we wallowed on the Lunar Spire's floor. Father Time was so disappointed."

My stomach plunged with horror.

She added, "Ever since, Therma has been our caretaker to ensure a takeover like that never happens again."

"We were weak," I said.

"We still are—you are proof of that."

I still believed I could change. "I want to be better."

"Then stop living in the past."

"It's hard to let go when you're screaming inside my head."

"I'm sorry. The terrors grip so tightly sometimes," she confessed—no one understood my struggle better than she. "I still hear cries from the past, too."

"How many of us are there?"

"I've lost count."

How many times did I repeat old mistakes? How many Faces would I need to fix?

I had to try. I released my grip on the fresh wound and ricocheted out of my mind. It was still night—the moon hadn't reached the axis of the Northern Unknown yet.

Therma sat quietly on the floor next to my throne.

"Welcome back," Therma said, a sad smile on her face. She held up an armband made of sun-resistant copper.

My secret was safe with her.

"I'm sorry I broke my promise." I gave her my broken piece.

"It's okay. I expected it." She fixed me as best she could. The putty remained wet beneath the copper band, but it would be safe from the sun.

Days came and went, and I could not stay away from the past. I played it safe—only digging to the first layer, but my collection of breaks grew larger each day.

"You have to stop coming here," my former self begged.

"If you keep screaming, I will keep coming."

She sighed. "I will be your undoing."

"Stop punishing yourself for things you cannot change," I pled. "I forgive you."

Tears filled her scorched eyes as a look of perplexed realization crossed her face.

"You forgive me?"

"Of course, I do."

Tears fell from her eyes.

I continued, "I will do better."

A smile crossed her face. "Thank you."

Her screams ceased—my forgiveness worked—but distant cries from the others continued. They wept like a far-off symphony of ghosts in my head. Still, I only went as deep as the first layer. She had become my greatest friend.

Therma did her best to keep up with my injuries, gathering suture clay and sun-resistant copper while I carried the sun through the sky each day. Ten months into my new Face and I was wrapped completely in a suit of copper armor.

"You're too heavy," Solís complained, speaking for the first time in weeks.

"That's rude."

"It's all the copper. It's weighing us down."

"It's keeping me safe."

"*I'm* keeping you safe," Solís corrected, "and I am tired. The sun has been tracking your scent for months."

I hadn't realized. "I'm sorry. I thought the copper was working."

"It won't work forever."

"How do I fix it?"

"Heal."

A request much easier said than done.

We finished the day, and as I walked toward the portal, Night stepped in my way. He carried a little version of Luna—it was the first time I'd seen him in months and his expression was sour.

"What have you done to yourself?" he spat, his glare piercing through me.

I glanced at the copper bandages around my arms and legs, then back up at Night.

I scowled. "I'll never be perfect."

"You were supposed to be *better*."

"I will be."

"You're already broken." He shook his head. "You didn't even last a year."

"I'm still here."

"Until you're not," he chastised. "The sun will consume you like it always does."

I showed no sign of fear or surprise, and Night laughed. "You've already dug up your past," he scolded. "You know what will become of you, and you're still doing it anyway."

"I'm smarter now."

"Copper armor won't shield you from the sun forever."

"I know." My voice was defiant, but meek. "I'm working on it."

"It's a pity." His condescending tone sparked an anger I'd not felt before. "Such a pretty Face wasted. You'll be gone soon, and your next Face will be spoiled, too. I feel bad for the mortal Host we reside in—they'll never know what a good day feels like."

"Go away," I demanded. "You know nothing about the day."

His pompous expression twisted with disappointment and guilt. For a moment, it looked like he held some compassion toward me, but then his harsh demeanor resumed and he ascended into the sky with the moon.

I was alone again—I was my only friend. Perhaps that was why it was so hard to let go of the past; she understood me unlike anyone else could. I thought making friends with the past would set me free, but it only bound me tighter.

Forgiving the Face that came directly before me wasn't enough—I had to forgive every Face I ever wore. I had to dig deeper so I could forgive them all. Once I understood who I was and accepted those parts of myself, maybe my obsession with the past would subside.

A dangerous quest—the past was buried deep. I worried I might not succeed.

I told Therma of my plan.

"No!" she objected. "It will kill you."

"If I fail, you can tell the next Face of Day all that I learned so she doesn't need to dig it up for herself."

"I tried that with you," she argued. "And you still went digging."

"I need to forgive the lost parts of me."

"You just want to know the whole story."

"Don't you?"

"No. We would be safe here if you just did your job without asking questions. You're making the same mistake as all the others."

"They didn't have a sun-resistant shield of armor."

Therma shook her head, her expression spent. "I've watched you burn too many times."

"Father Time always replaces me."

My comment hit a nerve and Therma's enervation shifted to outrage.

"It's a nightmare to watch the sun swallow you in flames! A nightmare to clean up your scorched and disfigured pieces! Do you think of anyone other than yourself?"

I paused. "I thought I was just another new Face to you."

"You may not remember me each time you come and go, but I remember you. I know you well, even when you wear a new Face. It's still you in there."

"Aren't I getting better?"

Therma's depletion came out as a sigh. "The armor idea is new," she confessed. "But it's just a bandage, not an evolution of your spirit. Underneath that copper armor, you are the same."

I uncurled the copper wrapped around my forearm. The wound underneath had not yet healed.

"The more breaks you have, the longer they'll take to heal," Therma warned. "This is how it happens every time, right before I lose you again."

"Maybe I need to die so the next Face can really live."

Therma's eyes filled with tears.

I continued, "You told me what you knew of my past, and it helped. I heard it, and though I wanted to know

334

more, I also wanted to do better. The Face I visited in my memories told me even more, and instead of wallowing with her in sorrow, I decided to forgive. Doing so healed her. Imagine if I could heal them all. Imagine if I could learn the full truth as well. I could relay it to you, you could tell the next Face of Day, and we can end this cycle."

"I don't want to lose you again."

"If it ends that way, it will be a sacrifice for the greater good."

She shook her head. "It's unnecessary."

"I can feel their anger and remorse. It lives deep inside me, even if I don't fully understand the cause. They are broken and I need to fix them. Healing them heals me, too—they are my only friends."

Therma's energy turned cold.

"I am here to serve you," she surrendered, her tone disappointed. "And I will honor your choices."

"I'm sorry," I confessed.

"You don't need to fix me, too."

Therma turned and left for the remainder of the night.

Remorse surged through me—I always let her down.

I had to move onward. I took off my copper armor to let my wounds breathe. Skin barred to the night sky, my scars became too many to count, and the recent breaks throbbed with pain. Tonight was not the night to begin my dangerous new mission; I let my body rest instead.

Each night of healing strengthened my porcelain-coated skin, but also weakened my weary mind. Cries from the past sang me to sleep, and their screams often woke me up. I could not escape them.

The more I let the past fester, the louder it became.

Solís went quiet again, letting us navigate the day in contemplative silence.

A week passed without a visit to the past. The edges of my breaks sealed and I felt stronger than ever.

"You look good," Therma noted as I returned to the Solar Citadel after a day with the sun. Skeptical hope lined her voice.

"Solís told me the sun sensed my weakness; it smelled my breaks. I had to become whole again to prevent a catastrophe."

"That was wise," Therma noted. "Will you stay this way?"

"I cannot. I still hear the Faces of my past. They will not let me go."

"What if your forgiveness does not heal them?"

"I have to try."

I resumed my dig.

Days turned into weeks—my forgiveness was the cure. I came and went each night, healing as many of my old Faces as I could before returning to execute another day. Every so often, I'd take a few nights off to heal my fresh breaks—I did not want to burn alive like the past versions of myself—but I always returned to my destructive quest as soon as my wounds healed.

On the eve of our twenty-fifth year, I dug deeper than ever before. The space was painted black and I could see nothing.

"You shouldn't be here."

I blinked my eyes, but they would not adjust.

"All the crying and screaming; you left me no other choice."

"I did not summon you," she objected. "You summoned me. You dug me up from my grave and dragged me here."

"When the first Face told me that, I believed her, but I've come to realize that you all taunt me from afar. You might be buried elsewhere, but I feel every ounce of anger, sorrow, and resentment you cling to. It claws at me and keeps me bound to our destructive past."

"If I'm so rotten, just let me go."

"I can't when you refuse to leave me alone."

"I break everything I try to fix," she brooded.

"I forgive you."

She shook her head. "You can't fix me."

"I just want you to be at peace."

"Impossible. I caused this mess."

I had reached the final layer—I was at the root of my woes.

"How?"

"I let Chaos wear my Face."

"You were heartbroken," I said to console her.

"I was." A dim light in the room turned on and my ancient Face sat in its shadows. Next to her sat a black kitten with black marble eyes. Its stare was unrelenting—I was not welcome here.

My old Face cradled her knees to her chest and sat with her back to me. Black sludge from the fire she had endured streaked her golden hair, and her ribcage was half-exposed where her breaks had let in the sun.

"Who broke your heart?" I asked, hoping to finally find the missing piece to the puzzle.

"I broke my own heart. I sabotaged everything I loved."

"Why?"

She lifted the kitten with marble eyes and stroked its back.

"I knew no other way to cope." Her frail body trembled. "I am sick. I am a monster."

I finally understood why my forgiveness did not work with her—she needed to forgive herself.

"You don't need to beat yourself up," I offered. "A lot of time has passed, and I am okay. We are okay. The past is over, but the hurtful memories that you still nurture remain."

"They define me."

"Let them go."

"What would I be without them?"

"Free."

"You don't understand how quickly it all unraveled. I lost everything all at once. It was the only way I could feel some sense of control."

The black-eyed kitten purred.

"Set yourself free."

She took a moment to consider this. "You feel okay in the Face you wear out there?"

"Yes. And you're right—I cannot fix you. You need to fix yourself."

"How?"

"Forgiveness."

"My choices almost caused the destruction of everything."

"The choice to hang on to your guilt does the same—why do you think the sun burns us alive every time? Because we stopped evolving after you. You keep us rooted here in this vicious cycle."

Her voice quivered. "So, I am to blame for our wicked past and all of our failed futures."

"Stop feeling sorry for yourself and make a change! Things can still get better."

Another light flicked on, revealing more of her.

Her melted eyes sat halfway down her face. My stomach flipped as she stared at me, contemplatively blinking her bloody eyelashes.

"You look unsure." She stood from the floor and sauntered toward me. "Do I scare you?"

"No," I lied.

"Then why do you recoil at the sight of me?"

"I now see the horror of where I've been. You live here in the darkness, festering in self-pity and guilt."

My honesty halted her in her tracks.

"And you still think I ought to forgive myself?"

"Yes. You have the power to save our future."

Her neck tilted in consideration, cracking and showering the floor with ash. She dropped the kitten, who landed gracefully and hissed in my direction.

I continued, "Do you realize how many expired Faces I had to sift through to find this pit where you wallow? You thought your choice to let Chaos wear your face almost destroyed everything—what do you think replacing the Face of Day constantly does to this mortal mind? You are the reason we all failed. Fix it!"

"You are strong," she sneered. "If I am the cause of each successor's demise, perhaps I am also the reason you evolved."

"I might not survive the morning."

"Why?"

"Because I am here, trying to make you see reason."

"You want me to forgive myself?" she asked, extending her arms to showcase her monstrous and deformed figure.

"Yes," I repeated, aware this visit was no longer going as planned.

"No," she snarled, recoiling into herself and retreating into the shadows.

"Then you've doomed us to repeat this cycle forever."

"We deserve it!"

She lifted the kitten off the floor and cradled it in her arms. It stared at me with its black marble eyes and wore a triumphant smile.

Tears fell down my face.

My failure doomed us all.

I returned to reality, choking on the fresh air as I reemerged from my mind.

"What happened?" Therma asked, combing my luminescent hair with her fingers in an attempt to comfort me.

"Do you remember anything about a kitten with black marble eyes?"

"No," Therma answered.

I shook my head. The kitten did not matter; what mattered was the fiend that gave it shelter.

"I am a monster."

"No, you're not." Therma helped me sit upright so she could mend my latest fracture. She grabbed my wrist and examined the wound. "I need more putty. I'll be right back."

"We are forever cursed while that creature takes shelter in my mind," I explained, wallowing in my rediscovered misery as Therma left the room.

"Love her anyway," a voice I did not recognize advised.

I turned and found the fox-eared Face of Worthiness sitting on my throne. She lounged casually, combing her long, bushy tail with her pointed fingernails. Her kind, mossy gaze bore into me.

"Why are you here?" I asked.

"To be your friend."

"I don't need any more friends."

"I promise I can help if you let me."

"How?"

"Show love to your past self."

"You did not see her. She is unlovable."

"She is you, and you are her."

"She wouldn't forgive herself."

"It's because she cannot love herself, so maybe she needs you to send a little love her way."

The words Worthiness shared were kind and insightful. Then panic set in.

"Have I been given this advice in my previous lives?"

She shook her head. "I was missing during your previous lives. Malsana infected me, too. But I am back now, and together, we can overcome the monster's lingering hold of us."

"Who is Malsana?" I asked.

"She is the black marble sickness that took root in this mind."

I gasped. "The kitten … it is a sickness?"

"Yes, but we are on the mend. The warden has already awoken and confined Malsana to a new prison. Now, we just need to heal our remaining wounds with love."

"I thought forgiveness would be enough."

"Sometimes it is. But I think that extra-complicated face of yours might need a little more love than forgiveness."

"Will that monster always live inside me?"

"I believe so." Her expression softened with empathy. "Love yourself anyway."

I took a deep breath, ready to entertain this idea. "I can try to love my broken bits."

The moonlight grew brighter and I realized it was almost time to face the day.

The Face of Worthiness vanished, disappearing in a neon flash as Therma returned to the room. She packed extra putty into my deep cracks, finished her patchwork, and wrapped three sheets of copper around my wrist.

"This is the last time you'll need to fix me," I assured her.

"You promise?"

I nodded. "I won't dig into myself anymore. I can love my most broken Face from afar."

Solís arrived, dark flames intertwined with the brighter ones.

"You look different," I observed.

"I feel the same."

I eyed the burning star Solís sat within.

"Are you ready to start the day?" he asked.

"I suppose so." I turned to look at Therma. "Thank you."

"Tomorrow will be a better day," she expressed.

I ascended into the sky with Solís, who returned to his normal silence the moment we exited the Solar Citadel.

The sun's flares latched to my wrists, searing through the copper bandage.

"It's burning through my armor," I expressed to Solís.

"I warned you."

The fire melted the first layer of copper.

"You're going to let it consume me?"

"I cannot hold it back any longer."

The sun burned through the second layer of copper.

"One more day," I begged. "Help me this last time. I won't let myself break ever again."

"I wish I believed you."

"I found a way to change."

"Then I hope you choose to remember when Father Time gives you a new face."

All the copper melted, leaving me exposed. Tendrils of fire coiled around my arms and snaked into my wounds. As the heat entered my broken bits, I howled in agony. It was the same pain I had suffered so many times before. The flares entered my body, consuming my existence bit by bit. As the fire ate me alive, a full recollection of every life I had lived before crossed through my mind. Every memory returned as the familiar suffering stripped me of life.

I once had wings that set me free, but I traded those in the day I let Chaos win.

Long before I lost my wings, Malsana arrived. The marble-eyed monster—she marked the beginning of my end. She infected me long ago, and when I could not rid myself of her, I had to learn how to live *with* her.

Instead of battling her, I adopted her as a friend. In the midst of chaos, her love had been the only constant, the only solid thing left to hold. She had offered me a sense of control while the world around me fell apart.

I surrendered all of me to her.

My ability to love and be loved—I sabotaged, for her.

Those who tried to love me anyway—I shunned, for her.

I paused as the most harrowing realization came to light: through it all, I had stopped loving myself.

Between Malsana manipulating me and my decision to let Chaos wear my face—it all transpired due to my lack of self-love.

It was a horrible memory.

I understood now why I kept it buried.

I understood now why the reemergence of Worthiness was so pivotal in my healing.

Still, I struggled to believe that love could vanquish the monster inside me. With the marble-eyed kitten nestled in the depths of my mind, how could I ever truly heal? Malsana kept the root of my sickness alive. She had to be removed so that I could heal.

As flames covered me, my resolution weakened.

I was burning alive.

This newfound truth would die with me.

Despite all my efforts to do better, I became another Face in need of forgiveness.

Would I be strong enough to do better next time?

The sun's flames licked up the last of me.

The monstrous face of the ruined girl I used to be flashed before me one last time, and I thought to myself, *I will love you most.*

Darkness covered me.

The Face of Worthiness

When: The 25th Cycle
Where: Jane's mind — The Ring of Thrones
Who: The Face of Worthiness, a.k.a. the Fox

She burned alive anyway.

I cursed under my breath, aggravated that my intervention had not been enough.

Was I too late? What would it take to stop this suffering?

At the foot of my throne grew a solitary rustleweed. Its prickly leaves scratched my ankle as it sprouted.

"That's new," the Face of Trust, whose throne sat beside mine, noted.

I knelt beside the spiked weed and touched its tallest thorn.

"A gift from Father Time." A droplet of blood pooled on my fingertip. I licked it clean. "This weed knows all of my secrets."

"What use is that?"

I wasn't sure.

Why would Father Time send me a rustleweed when I needed a way to turn back time? I needed to save the Face of Day. I needed to show her how to love herself anyway, no matter the circumstance.

Trust continued, "You have a lot of work to do if you hope to fix the destruction caused in your absence."

I glanced before me — she was right. Though Chaos was contained, he still smothered the Pocket of Time, and the black marbles Malsana had left behind were scattered all over this mind.

"She's everywhere, isn't she?"

The Face of Trust nodded. "She left her mark on everything."

This revelation was damning.

"The scars she left are everlasting," I said. "I won't be able to rid each pocket of her completely."

"To do so would be an impossible feat," the Face of Trust agreed.

"Still, there is love left to give."

"Love?"

"To ourselves, to the Host. We are worthy. We are enough, even the tainted parts touched by darkness. We must love every little broken bit."

The rustleweed hummed a familiar melody, and suddenly, I knew what I had to do.

I glanced at the trembling sun, which was now carrying its own weight across the sky as Day burned in its wake. Soon, she would fall, but not before I delivered the final piece of her healing.

I knelt beside the rustleweed and snapped off a branch. Eyes closed, intention ablaze, I tossed it into the ether and watched as it fluttered into the Southern Abyss.

This was my gift.

This was the love I had to give.

The Face of Awareness

When: The 25th Cycle
Where: Jane's mind — The Graveyard, Southern Abyss
Who: The Face of Awareness, a.k.a. the Gravedigger

What once held plots with buried mementos was now a meadow of newly planted evergreens—my graveyard was unrecognizable.

Dropped from the whirlwind grip of Father Time, I landed in the freshly sowed field.

I remembered the girl I saw in the mirror through the warden's recollection.

My obligation belonged to Jane.

Father Time vanished from the sky. His departure rained ash over my redesigned home. Like snow, it covered the pine needles and left me feeling cold.

Luna wept as she traveled through the Southern Abyss.

I turned my attention toward the Northern Unknown to see the sun and the Face of Day traveling precariously across the sky—Day trembled beneath her suit of copper armor.

Along the Ring of Thrones sat a chair I had not seen in years—a throne covered in foxglove and honey blossoms, and upon it sat a glowing fox girl. The Face of Worthiness was back where she belonged.

As Luna crossed the southern axis, a familiar heat singed my skin. I looked toward the sun in horror.

The Face of Day was burning alive.

"Not again," I lamented.

Luna had retreated back into the center of the moon, disinterested in witnessing my retrieval of Day's newly fallen pieces.

Shards of porcelain rained down on me.

I had forgotten what it was like to pick up the discarded pieces with clear vision. In the shadows of my blindness, I always immediately buried everything I found. There was no autopsy before banishing the memories to their graves. In my haste, I had missed an entire step.

Amid the shards of porcelain fell a rustleweed branch.

It flipped and twirled as it made its way toward me. When it landed in my palm, I understood where it came from. A gift from the fox—a token of self-worth.

It came with no note or explanation, but its importance knew no bounds. This was the key to survival. This was the piece we'd been missing all along.

Self-love.

The Face of Day limped toward me, hopelessly cracked and charred. She wasn't a pile of broken porcelain—she was a functioning memory.

"Have you always arrived here with your consciousness intact?" I asked.

"Yes, and you always buried me before I got the chance to speak."

"I'm sorry for that. I had lost my way."

She nodded, knocking her tiny porcelain nose off her face.

I continued, "Why have you fallen out of the sky again?"

"I am stronger than before, I swear. It's just this pesky final piece I need to solve."

"What piece is that?"

"Malsana—she still lives in the deepest recess of my mind. If I could just remove her, I could heal."

"You already know the way to heal," I reminded her.

"I do?"

"Love yourself anyway."

"Even with the marble-eyed sickness lingering inside me?"

"She might live there forever—her roots are planted deep. You need to accept her, practice forgiveness, and love yourself enough to stay strong despite her presence."

"I don't know if I can."

The thorned branch in my grip rustled.

My heart skipped a beat.

"We have to work together," I said, a revelation as much to me as it was to the Face of Day. "You, me, and Worthiness—together, we will find the strength to heal."

I handed her the rustleweed branch, which she accepted hesitantly. Upon holding it in her hands, her eyes brimmed with tears.

Sometimes, words weren't enough; sometimes, understanding had to be felt.

A surge of confidence filled her mind, overtaking her senses and carrying her sorrow away on the tides of yesterday. She saw herself for who she was—brave, intelligent, and worthy.

When she opened her eyes, the tears fell.

"I am enough," she said, her voice strong and soft.

I nodded. "You are you, no matter the darkness you carry. Cover it in light. Shape it into strength."

"I am better today than I was yesterday," she realized.

I smiled. "We all are."

The Face of Day tucked the rustleweed next to her exposed heart. It settled there, where it could take root and blossom.

"Let me go," she advised.

I grabbed her hand and we walked to the edge of the forest.

There was nothing left to cling to, nothing left to hold.

"You won't be seeing me again," she said.

"I think that's for the best." I squeezed her hand gently.

A smile crossed her fractured face as she took a step over the edge. She never fell, she merely dissipated into nothing.

Gone was the girl of many broken faces.

No wonder I always struggled to let her go—she was me, and I was her.

We were better now, no longer destined to break beneath our heavy past. Our strength came from all we had lost. And in the space left by our losses, we gained wisdom.

We thought we were broken, but we had love left to give.

The Face of Day

When: 25ᵗʰ *Cycle*
Where: Jane's mind — Solar Citadel, Northern Unknown
Who: The Face of Day

When the light returned, I was back in the Solar Citadel. My porcelain armor was gone, and I writhed on the floor — flesh raw and burned.

"Why does it always end this way?" I sobbed.

"You know why," Father Time chastised.

"I was doing better this time."

"Stand," he commanded.

I forced my aching body to my feet.

Father Time stepped closer and hovered his hands next to my face.

"Which do you choose: to remember or to forget?"

"I want to remember," I declared without hesitation.

Father Time's shoulders relaxed ever so slightly as he nodded.

He stripped my face off my skull and replaced it with a new one. Cool, malleable porcelain oozed down my disfigured flesh, coating it with a soothing layer of protection. The sting of the burns subsided and my heart's pace returned to normal. I was healing. I was whole.

I remembered everything and suddenly understood why remembering was worse.

For the first time since he gave me life, Father Time's cavernous eyes showed compassion.

"Remembering is never easy, but it will make you stronger," he offered.

"I agree." A tear fell down my perfect porcelain cheek.

He continued my rebirth, sending thousands of flames carrying a sun-resistant glaze across my body. They tore up my newly crafted porcelain, leaving broken trails of blackened cracks. The transformation hurt, but it did not compare to the wrath of the sun.

I gritted my teeth and let Father Time prepare me for the days ahead.

When he finished, I lifted my hand and examined my new cracks.

"I will fix them," he assured.

"No," I objected. "They are perfect."

"They need to be sealed so the sun cannot enter through them."

"I don't want another bandage to hide my truth."

A smile stretched across Father Time's wrinkled face. "I think I have a solution."

I trusted him and let him cover me once more in flames. Immune to the heat, I did not feel the scorching tingle as the dancing flames filled my wounds with gold.

He explained, "Golden scars to remind you how far you've come."

"Thank you. I feel more like myself this way."

His face brightened slightly, revealing his mournful gray stare. "I used to think that letting you forget was best. I thought that maybe, if you didn't remember, you'd stop punishing yourself for who you used to be." He paused in thought, his affection directed at me. "But inevitably, whenever you forgot, you'd kill yourself trying to dig up the past. So, I let you have the choice: remember or forget. It never mattered which one you picked, though. It always ended the same."

I held great respect for him—he only ever tried to help, and my incessant failure broke his heart, too.

He continued, "But I sense something has changed."

"*I* have changed."

"I believe you," he professed. "Turn around."

I did as he instructed.

He placed his ice-cold hands onto my shoulder blades and wings sprouted from my back. Enormous and white, they stretched wide with splendor.

"Thank you!"

"I stopped giving you wings after you let Chaos wear your face, but I think it's time to trust you again."

"I won't let you down," I promised, then thought of what I had learned when my memories surged. "I have a question."

"Yes?"

"Why did he jump?"

"The Soldier of Time?" Father Time's gray eyes lowered. "He thought he was saving everyone from Malsana. He did not understand how the monster worked. He only killed a small part of her, a tiny fragment of her delivered to him by Chaos. Chaos thought he could wear his face, too, but I intervened."

"The same Chaos that wore my face?"

"It was a potent strain of chaos this mortal vessel inherited."

I took a deep breath. "So, it wasn't my fault that he jumped?"

"Is that what you thought all this time?"

I nodded.

"He loved you, and Chaos used that love against him. Seems he used it against you, too. You did nothing wrong."

The weight in my chest lessened. "Thank you."

Father Time had minimal capacity for emotion, but in this moment, he smiled empathetically. It only lasted a second before he disappeared in a burst of dust.

Empowered by the past, I was ready to forgive. And above all else, my love would burn brightest within my broken bits.

A final note from the Fox

I told you it would be dark.
I warned you it would be heavy.
But we made it through.
Though the monster would always live inside us, it held no
power once we decided to love ourself anyway.
I wish I had been there for Jane through it all, but sometimes,
learning the hard way provides a much deeper lesson. We
survived, thankfully, and our arduous efforts allowed us to
blossom.
With hard-earned wisdom rooted in our heart, our
compassion, empathy, and ability to love and forgive flourished.
On the other side of destruction, we found new purpose: a
reason to fight, to live, to hope, to grow—we would no longer
choose ruin over love.

Thank you for reading *Into the Foxhole*—I hope you enjoyed the story! If you have a moment, please consider leaving a review on Amazon. All feedback is very helpful and greatly appreciated!

Amazon Author Account:

www.amazon.com/author/nicolineevans

Instagram:

@nicolinenovels

Facebook:

www.facebook.com/nicolinenovels

YouTube:

@nicolinenovels

Want to learn more about Solís and Luna?
You can see where they come from and how they got into Jane's mind by reading *The Gears Duology*.

The Gears Duology:

Book 1: Gears of the Sun
Book 2: Rise of the Moon
(Both books can be purchased on my website or Amazon)

To learn more about my other novels, please visit my official author website:

www.nicolineevans.com